Harry Dickson

THE AMERICAN SHERLOCK HOLMES

IN THE SAME SERIES

THE AMERICAN SHERLOCK HOLMES

Harry Dickson vs. Mysteras
The Tribunal of Terror
The Path of the Gods
The Devil's Bed

From The Secret Files of The King of Detectives
Translated from the French by
Stuart Gelzer

A Black Coat Press Book

Acknowledgements: We are indebted to A. Verbrugghen, Johnny Bekaert, Jean-Luc Rivera, Richard D. Nolane and Jean-Michel Nicollet for their assistance in gathering the documents and information that made this book possible.

Original publication:
Mystéras: *Harry Dickson* No. 103 (1933)
La Cour d'Épouvante (*The Tribunal of Terror*): *Harry Dickson* No. 104 (1933)
Le Chemin des Dieux (*The Path of the Gods*) *Harry Dickson* No. 106 (1934)
Le Lit du Diable (*The Devil's Bed*) *Harry Dickson* No. 147 (1935)

Visit our website at www.blackcoatpress.com

ISBN 978-1-64932-086-5. First Printing. September 2021. Published by Black Coat Press, an imprint of Hollywood Comics.com, LLC, P.O. Box 17270, Encino, CA 91416. All rights reserved. Except for review purposes, no part of this book may be reproduced or transmitted in any form or by any means, electronic or mechanical, including photocopying, recording, or by any information storage and retrieval system, without permission in writing from the publisher. The stories and characters depicted in this book are entirely fictional. Printed in the United States of America.

TABLE OF CONTENTS

Introduction

The origins of Harry Dickson are detailed at some length in our first volume, *The Heir of Dracula*, which also includes a profile of the character and a timeline. Suffice it to say here that the original series of pulp magazines which eventually became *Harry Dickson* began in Germany in January 1907. It ran for 230 weekly issues, ending in March 1911, with covers by the renowned Berlin Academy artist Alfred Roloff.

Sixteen issues of the original German series were adapted into French, in 1907-08, but it was only when the Dutch-Flemish publisher Roman-Boek-en-Kunsthandel re-launched the series in December 1927 with Dutch translations of the original German magazine, coining the names "Harry Dickson" and "Tom Wills" for the first time, that *Harry Dickson* truly took off.

The following year, Belgian publisher Hippolyte Janssens decided to translate the Dutch series into French, entrusting its editorship to Belgian author Jean Ray, starting with its 20th issue. The French series began in January 1929 and lasted 178 issues, until April 1938. The Roloff covers, which had been purchased in bulk from the German publisher, greatly contributed to its success.

Today, Harry Dickson's popularity in France continues to rival that of Sherlock Holmes, Arsène Lupin and Fantômas. There have been a dozen reprints of his adventures, as well as new stories written by Gérard Dôle and Brice Tarvel, and two competing comic-book adaptations.

The four original stories presented here were translated from the original 1933-34 magazines, and feature Mysteras, one of the very few recurring villains in the series. (Georgette Cuvelier, a.k.a. The Spider, was another one.)

Jean-Marc Lofficier

Harry Dickson

Le Sherlock Holmes
AMERICAIN

No 103   ? ? Mystéras ? ?   Prix fr. 1.50

Soudain l'avion mystérieux tournoya, et son pilote tomba dans les flots.

HARRY DICKSON VS. MYSTERAS

1. The Death Chamber

Miss Delphina Cruikshank may not have been the most talented novelist in Britain—not by a long shot—but she was certainly the most eccentric.

Old Cruikshank, her father, had done all right in India, where the piratical rascal had made a stupendous fortune, which he left to his daughter on his death; she was soon besieged by dowry hunters. She wasn't good-looking, but—though lacking talent, as we've already mentioned—she had plenty of common sense. Her suitors were sent packing. She announced publicly that from now on she would live for the arts, and especially for literature. Matching her actions to her words, she began to write; a few months later her first novel was published in Paternoster Row. Surprisingly, the book wasn't bad, and people of taste began to consider Miss Cruikshank in the light of her talents rather than her wealth. Other novels followed the first, and led to a career: fame found this woman of letters.

She'd reached the age of forty when her writing took an esoteric turn much appreciated in England. That change seemed to apply as much to her life as to her writing: demanding total isolation, she withdrew forever into her ivory tower—in this case not a figure of speech, because Miss Cruikshank built a dwelling that resembled a lighthouse on a lonely shore: a cylindrical tower almost a hundred feet high, whose only windows were those at the bottom for the staff quarters, and those at the top for Miss Cruikshank's rooms.

We linger over the architecture because it'll be important later. Picture the structure like this: the bottom twenty feet or so had windows and doors; then came sixty feet of smooth, uninterrupted wall; then came the arched windows that let daylight into the writer's rooms. An elevator led from the ground floor up to that aerial apartment, but it too had its peculiarity: only Miss Cruikshank could operate it. If her servants wanted to come up, or to let up a rare visitor, they had to telephone first, and Miss Cruikshank would decide whether or not she wanted to see anyone. There was no other way to reach the quarters of this modern Muse—not even a staircase or a fire escape.

"What if you hurt yourself someday?" she was asked. "No one will be able to reach you to help you."

To which Miss Cruikshank replied that anyone trying to reach her level should simply do what she'd done, and start at the top—a feeble enough witticism, but one that made the rounds of literary London.[1]

Miss Cruikshank's peculiar house stood in a quiet part of Wood Lane, on the former grounds of the Franco-British Exhibition of 1908. It was surrounded by vast overgrown gardens within a high encircling wall topped by iron palings and broken glass.

The tower was capped not by a platform, but by a steeply curved cupola. Under that half-glass dome Miss Cruikshank had installed a kind of astronomical observatory. She spent a few hours at a time there occasionally, but it wasn't to study the stars.

A few hundred yards from her tower stood dismal Hammersmith Prison, adjoining Wormwood Scrubs. Using a powerful telescope, the lady novelist could observe the interior of the prison as easily as if she'd been sitting on its ominous outer walls. That gave her gripping material for her stories, and was responsible for the success of one of her most recent books, *The Great Jailbreaker*.

---

[1] In the original French, her joke involves ladders, and turns on a particular sense in French of the expression, "to pull the ladder up after oneself"—meaning in this case, "after me they broke the mold, I'm unique."

On the evening this story begins, Miss Cruikshank was comfortably settled in that observatory with her eye pressed to the viewfinder of her telescope. For several days she'd been watching some very odd goings-on in the prison. She'd noticed that the light in a small garret under the roof of the second wing of cells had stayed on all night. Normally it was used as a storeroom for old metal bed frames—something Miss Cruikshank had learned easily enough, thanks to her telescope. But for the past few days she'd been watching workmen up there: electricians were carrying out the instructions of an old man in a frock coat that made him look like a Victorian professor. They ran wires and installed switches, and a heavy marble table covered with indicator lights filled one wall.

The previous day the professor—that's how Miss Cruikshank thought of him—had personally installed a number of devices, none of which she recognized. She did her best to figure out what they were for, but in vain—though she was by no means deficient in scientific learning. What intrigued her above all was a kind of tall glass cage holding a large metal solenoid. Without knowing quite why, Miss Cruikshank found all this laboratory apparatus a little ominous—and she'd resolved to keep a careful eye on that strange room in Hammersmith Prison.

A few hours after the equipment had been installed, a number of officials came to see it, and Miss Cruikshank thought she recognized members of the Ministry of Justice, including several well-known persons.

"I wonder what they're plotting," she grumbled with her usual ill humor. "Everything seems to be ready: all the copper shines, all the nickel glows like a full moon, and the professor's there, rubbing his hands together like a proud child."

The lights-out alert echoed around the prison. At once, all the dimly lit cell windows went completely dark; only the window in the room full of mysterious equipment remained lit—with a harsh white light cast by the powerful lamps that had just been switched on inside.

Two cars drove up quickly and vanished under the prison entrance porch. Anticipating that something extraordinary, something awful was about to happen, the lady novelist couldn't help shuddering with dread. But curiosity won out, and she changed her telescope viewfinder to a greater magnification that brought the room even closer.

Then she started—the room was full of people, of whom she recognized several: the eminent anatomist Weiler; Burley, dean of the medical school; the private secretary to the justice minister; a few prison officials; and lastly the little professor. He was going from one device to the next, giving voluble explanations. At the end he opened a small frosted-glass door in the cage and beckoned to his listeners. Miss Cruikshank could easily see the aversion on their faces and their gestures of polite refusal.

Finally the little professor glanced at his watch and made a sign; one of the prison officials went away, while all the rest stood waiting, contemplating the mysterious apparatus in silence.

Then the scene changed: the audience parted to make way for two uniformed guards leading a main in chains; preceding them all was a clergyman carrying a Bible.

"Ah!" murmured Miss Cruikshank in horror. "Now I understand. There's a capital punishment coming up, and they're going to try a new method, a new system of execution—death by electrocution! That explains the mystery; it's awful, yet still fascinating."

The clergyman stepped to one side, and the man in chains came fully into the light. He was tall and thin, and his gaunt face gave him the look of some bird of prey. He was dressed not in convict's garb, but in elegant black street clothes, and the whiteness of his linen was impeccable.

"I've seen that face in the illustrated papers," thought Miss Cruikshank. "That's Baltimore Harmon, who murdered the banker Probst in Park Lane. He was sentenced to death, and—since he's a bold bandit who puts on the airs of a gentleman—he must've volunteered to trade the sordid hangman's noose for the electric chair!"

In the death chamber they'd brought out an ordinary chair, and one of the guards made as if to strap the condemned man to it. But Harmon waved him off, and they simply put the chair inside the glass cage without further ceremony. Then one of the officials stepped forward and spoke to the clergyman, who offered the Bible to the condemned man to kiss. After that Harmon walked straight to the chair and sat down—but then he seemed to change his mind, and asked the little professor for something. The latter agreed, and took a cigarette from a pocket case. Someone held out a lighter, and a moment later Baltimore Harmon took a drag and exhaled a cloud of blue smoke.

A series of lights on the control panel glowed dark red. The little professor set his hand on a lever of hard rubber; the visitors instinctively drew back against the rear wall.

All the floodlights overlooking the prison courtyards began to flicker.

"The lights are dancing! The lights are jumping!" murmured Miss Cruikshank—echoing the tragic refrain of convicts in American prisons, who know by that flickering when the current is being drained to supply the execution chamber where a man is dying.

"So this is the end!" said the lady novelist.

Far away, Baltimore Harmon had slumped down slightly in his chair. The little professor opened the cage door and motioned to the guards. They took hold of the motionless dead body...

"The end! The end!" Miss Cruikshank said over and over. "How fragile is a human life!"

In the death chamber, the visitors chatted together, nodding in approval. Harmon's body had been taken away. The little professor paused a moment to consider his apparatus; then, almost regretfully, he followed the visitors as they exited.

The room went dark, as dark as the whole prison.

13

2. Sensational News

"Here's London, looming up out of its fog," murmured Harry Dickson with regret, watching the dark houses of Poplar draw near as the train slowly followed the wide curve of the embankment. The famous detective and his assistant Tom Wills were returning from a holiday: after a series of difficult cases and exhausting investigations, they'd treated themselves to a week of fishing in the lochs and trout streams of Scotland.

"A week without a newspaper, Guv! The good life!" said Tom happily. "I suppose we'll have to measure our mail by the pound."

In Baker Street their housekeeper, Mrs. Crown, greeted them with her usual slightly bad-tempered smile. "Well! What I had to invent not to give away where my employers were!" she said as soon as they were settled in the parlor. "It seems there's news in London, and the experts at the Yard are all to seek, of course.

"First there's the lady who lived in an inaccessible tower, and she's disappeared. I said right away it was an airplane—you don't have to be Harry Dickson to figure that out. What good would an airplane be if you couldn't use one to escape from a tower? Then there's the condemned man who's also escaped—but that's a different matter, and harder to solve, because he was already quite dead. And since things always come in threes, there's the doctor, the one who zapped the dead man, as they call it—zapped him with electrickery, like in America—and who's been murdered. That's just revenge by the dead man's pals, that's what I told Goodfield when he came here looking for your help. Can't disturb the master for that, says I—I've solved the mystery for you, and you don't bother Harry Dickson for such poppycock."

The good woman stood there, arms akimbo, waiting for the praise that, in her opinion, seemed a little slow in coming.

Dickson smiled, while Tom, hugely entertained, made faces behind the honest housekeeper's back. "Read all about it in the *Herald*, the *Times*, the *Daily*!" cried Tom. "Latest investigations by Mrs. Crown, famous lady detective, lead to arrests of over a dozen international criminal bands!"

"That's right, go ahead and laugh, young idler! After all, it's not my job," she grumbled. "I'll go see what's for dinner. As for all those human interest stories, see if I ever waste my breath again serving 'em up to you tied up neatly in a bundle! You can just find out for yourselves by reading the newspapers!"

And, like an offended queen, Mrs. Crown went off to her kitchen to see to her stove and her saucepans.

Harry Dickson had immediately plunged back into the daily grind and was already sorting the mail—luckily less bulky and less urgent than Tom had feared—and when he was done he picked up the newspapers. With a certain astonishment he read about the sensational events Mrs. Crown had given them a preview of—though in print the facts she'd lined up and presented in her own way were laid out a little differently.

The murderer Baltimore Harmon had been executed at the beginning of the week. He was a crook, originally from America, who'd been convicted of a number of murders with robbery as their motive. But, with the consent of the crown and of the minister of justice, Dr. Brownless had been permitted to test his new electrocution device on him. The condemned man himself had agreed, because Dr. Brownless had promised him a quick and painless death.

The execution had been carried out in total secrecy, not at Newgate but at the less prominent Hammersmith Prison. The test had been considered a complete success. Baltimore Harmon had been struck dead in an instant. But then things got complicated.

Old Professor Brownless had been authorized to remove the body to his own laboratory for an autopsy, once six court medical examiners had certified the death. The execution took place at midnight; at three in the morning the nursing attendants at the workhouse next door had brought to body to Dr.

Brownless at his laboratory in the shabby Harlesden Green neighborhood, not far away.

According to the doctor's servants, he'd napped only briefly, and by four o'clock they could hear activity in the laboratory. At eight in the morning, when Dr. Brownless didn't show up for breakfast—though he was a man of punctual habits—his valet knocked on the laboratory door, but got no answer. The door was locked from the inside, and the valet couldn't open it.

When there was still no sign of the doctor by nine o'clock, the valet decided to force open the laboratory door. He gathered the staff and broke the lock. The first thing they saw was Dr. Brownless, slumped against his dissection table. He was dead. But what was even more frightening, the table on which the body of Baltimore Harmon should've been stretched out was empty!

There were bloodstained scalpels on a glass-shelved cart next to the table, which itself was splotched with blood. Imaginative souls declared right away that Harmon hadn't been dead, and that he'd woken from his coma under the doctor's knife, and had killed him and fled. The police soon put an end to that theory—because Dr. Brownless had been killed by a bullet in the back of his neck! Someone had therefore shot him from behind with a revolver... someone who then made off with the body of Baltimore Harmon. That's what the newspapers reported—with major or minor embroidery that added nothing to the facts but idle, fantastical speculation.

The other sensational news item Dickson found in the papers concerned the mysterious disappearance of the writer Delphina Cruikshank, whom the reporters called England's richest and most eccentric woman. The fact that Delphina Cruikshank had vanished the same night as the murder of Dr. Brownless didn't mean that the two cases were connected. But here the enigma was complete.

How could she have disappeared? We would refer readers back to the description of the lady novelist's tower home. The elevator that only she could control hadn't operated the entire night. The staff's doors and windows on the ground floor were closed and locked: no one could've left the tower that way. But the windows of the writer's aerie at the top of the tower were also locked. When the morning stretched on with no call from their mistress, the servants themselves had rung her apartment, and gotten no answer. They went out into garden and shouted up to her in unison, but the high-up windows remained stubbornly shut.

Fearing some mishap, the butler telephoned the fire department, and they came immediately and raised their tallest counter-weighted ladders. A fireman went up, broke a windowpane, opened the latch, and climbed in. A few moments later he called down to his crew that the apartment was empty. He sent down the elevator, and the servants came up. But they found not a single trace of Miss Cruikshank.

The police arrived, and Scotland Yard sent Superintendent Goodfield. The latter, boasting that he was a friend of Harry Dickson's, tried to apply what he thought were the great detective's methods. He could find only one logical solution: Miss Cruikshank had used a long rope to climb down. But a descent from such a height can't be done without leaving marks, and none were found.

"Perhaps a parachute?" wondered the good superintendent. But the closed windows, and the lack of any outside platform on the tower, any balcony or terrace, negated that theory.

"Besides, why would she have done it?" murmured the voice of reason in the superintendent's ear. "She'd have to have gone stark raving mad, and that's a desperate solution of last resort... Anyway," thought Goodfield, "an escape like that would've left traces, signs, but there's nothing, no more than in the palm of my hand... Ah, if only I knew where to find that damned Harry Dickson," he grumbled in conclusion. "But every time I'm stumped by a case he's fled without leaving an address."

At least that's what Dickson, after he finished the newspapers, could read between the lines of the splendidly reproachful letter Goodfield had sent him while he was away.

Running off without leaving an address is a low trick to play on a friend! complained Goodfield in his letter.

"We'll have to go apologize to dear old Goodfield, my boy," said Dickson to his assistant with a laugh. "I won't be sorry to get back in touch with real life, and especially with… a mystery."

They'd just arrived in front of the cold, dismal headquarters of the Yard, when Superintendent Goodfield came bounding like a young man down the steps to the street and leaped into a car.

"Hullo, superintendent!" Dickson called out. "Might there be enough room for some friends?"

"Dickson! Mr. Dickson!" cried Goodfield. "Here you are at last! Climb in! You've shown up like fish on Friday— which is to say you're most welcome. I'm running off—well, rolling off—to Cruikshank Tower, as they call that madhouse. I don't need to ask if you've seen the papers, since otherwise you wouldn't be here," he added a little mockingly, glancing sidelong at his famous friend.

"And what do you expect to find at that tower that you haven't already?" asked Dickson. "I imagine it's given up its secrets by now."

"Well, no, that's the problem! If you can believe it, the guards on patrol in the no man's land around Wormwood Scrubs claim they saw lights in the tower last night. I got the news by telephone, and I sent a constable over directly. The doors to the apartment at the top of the tower had been left sealed, and the seals weren't broken. On the other hand, three of the guards all tell the same story; so I'm off to see what's up."

It took a while to reach Latimer Road, but the time wasn't wasted: Goodfield expanded on what he called the mystery of the book tower—though without telling his listeners anything they hadn't already learned from the newspapers.

The murder of Dr. Brownless, while just as puzzling, struck Goodfield as less mysterious than the disappearance of Miss Cruikshank. "The light last night at the top of that look-

18

out tower," he grumbled, "that'll keep all the reporters in London entertained for a week!"

They were driving along Wood Lane, an endless empty road with only a few scattered houses, brand new yet already peeling—and then in the distance they caught sight of the tower rising above a clump of trees.

A respectable-looking servant came out to meet them as they entered the gates, and as soon as he heard who they were he began a litany of complaints. "I'm delighted you're here, gentlemen. I was planning to gather up my bag and baggage and be off, like all the rest of the staff. They say this strange house is haunted, and I'm ready to believe it. As long as Miss Delphina was here we put up with the ghosts, because we were well paid to do it, but now that she's gone there's no reason for us to go on living in a place as dangerous as this. If you want my opinion, it's the spirits—the ones who sing in the tower some nights—who carried off poor Miss Delphina for her sins."

"What's all this about singing ghosts?" exclaimed Goodfield. "I'd like to hear more about this, Mr. Saunders."

The head servant shrugged. "Unfortunately I can't tell you much. Every now and then in the middle of the night we could hear strange noises in the tower. Sometimes it began as a high, distant, piercing sound and ended as a low rumbling; sometimes it was the opposite; but each time the tower seemed to shake with fear. I can't describe how dismal a sound it was. When we mentioned it to Miss Delphina, she'd laugh or get angry, depending on her mood, so we decided it was best not to speak of it again. Last night the tower sang again several times, and then—ah, gentlemen, I lack the courage to tell you more."

"Oh, come on, try!" said Goodfield. "If the singing ghost decides to come down, I'll put him under arrest, and he won't get off with less than six months on the treadmill, or my name isn't Goodfield!"

Saunders just shook his head unhappily. "You oughtn't to joke about such things, superintendent, because if you'd seen what I've seen!... I have to confess something—oh, don't look so serious, it's not a criminal matter, to my mind—but I must tell you that I'm engaged to be married. Her name is Miss Leadston, and she's the head housekeeper here. She likes to read, and you might say she's a wee bit fanciful; such that in the evenings, rather than sit and talk with me in the parlor, she'd drag me out into the brambles and wild oats of that damned garden.

"Last night, not long before midnight, we were strolling along that avenue of Lombardy poplars you can see from here, when suddenly she cried out and said, 'Oh, James, through the trees I saw lights on in the tower!' I looked up, but the foliage screened my view. Still, I have to say that I also thought I saw a brightness that went dark in a moment. We came quickly back, making sure to keep to the shadows of the trees. When we reached the great lawn we stopped, hardly daring to cross that open space.

"The moon was bright enough that we could see as clear as day. There were no lights on in the tower except the one in the little parlor next to the entrance hall, where Mary, the cook, sits every night reading the newspaper—a room that yokel has no right to be in, and that she has the nerve to call her boudoir, what do you think of that?...

"Well, my fiancée pinched my arm and murmured in an odd voice, 'James, look up and tell me if I'm dreaming: because I don't dare say what I'm seeing.' And what did I see, gentlemen? Leaning out of her high window, looking off into the distance—Miss Delphina herself! The tower is very tall, and yet I recognized her easily. I should say that at that moment I felt no fear. 'Well,' I said, 'she's come back.'

"My fiancée pulled me back under cover of the trees and began talking nonsense. 'And how would she have got in? Answer me that, James, and make it quick, or I'll think you've been drinking, in which case you may consider our engagement to be off, for I won't have a drinker for a husband. So, tell me, how would she have got in? The doors to her apartment have been sealed, and the power to the elevator has been cut off by order of the police. The entrance gate is locked, and you can see Mary's silhouette where she's sitting calmly in the parlor. No, I tell you it's her ghost—poor Miss was a victim of the spirits who sing in the tower!'

"Miss Leadston was right, gentlemen. When we went back out onto the lawn, the window was closed and there was no sign of Miss Delphina. We almost ran back to the house. Irma, the scullery maid, told us the tower had sung again. And later that night it happened once more."

Saunders fell silent and looked very serious. "My fiancée left this morning, gentlemen, and my duty is to follow her. However, I'll gladly go with you, one last time, to our poor mistress's apartment. And anyway, only you have the authority to restore power to the elevator and to break the seals on the doors."

Without further ado Goodfield and his friends, along with the butler, rode the elevator to the upper level. As the constable had said, the seals were intact, and Goodfield had to break them.

They entered the empty apartment. Dickson let his glance wander around. "I'm sorry I wasn't here for the first investigation. But since you were, Goodfield, you can tell me if you think anything's been moved."

The superintendent turned full circle like a squirrel in a cage. "Nothing seems to me to have moved. But let's have a look around all the same."

They did so, and finished, by way of a narrow cast-iron staircase, up in the observatory dome. Here as well, everything was in its place, and Goodfield said that in his opinion not a speck of dust had been disturbed.

Now it was Harry Dickson who turned full circle; he stopped, facing the powerful telescope on its tripod, its tip protruding just slightly from a window. He put his eye to the viewfinder and gave a chuckle of surprise.

"What is it?" asked Goodfield.

"Have a look for yourself, Goodfield," came the answer, "and tell me what you see through that fine instrument."

The superintendent hastened to do so, and he saw a strange room appear in the circular frame of the viewfinder. "Good lord!" he muttered. "That's the new execution chamber they set up a few days ago at Hammersmith Prison! An odd coincidence, wouldn't you say, Mr. Dickson?"

"Oh, certainly," replied the detective carelessly, "a very odd coincidence."

He said no more, but Tom Wills, who could read his employer's face better than anyone, noticed an unusual light in his eyes. Still, Dickson added not a word, and his assistant understood that this wasn't the time for questions.

As they were returning to the great semicircular parlor that comprised half the area of the apartment, Dickson suddenly asked, "What bank did Miss Cruikshank use?"

It was the head servant, Saunders, who replied. "It's thought she didn't have one, because she hated them all. Miss Cruikshank's fortune was mostly invested in real estate: farms, land, and rental properties that brought her a steady income. But people say most of her wealth was in cash, which she kept in the great strongbox you see here. I'm told she kept over five million pounds in good Bank of England bills in there, plus her jewels, which were magnificent, though she never wore them. I believe it, because I once saw this safe standing open, and it was crammed full of bundles of high-denomination bills stacked up like old books!"

"We'll have to request authorization to open that thing," muttered Goodfield, gazing with respect at the enormous black steel strongbox that extended from floor to ceiling.

Tom had come closer to have a look, and he whistled softly. "No need for authorization, superintendent—this strongbox is open!"

"My word, it's true!" said Dickson.

The door to the strongbox had been left slightly ajar, so carefully that a casual eye wouldn't notice. Dickson seized the heavy nickel handle and pulled: the steel door with its multiple locks swung open.

A cry rang out from all four men. "Empty!"

The massive strongbox gaped open before them like an enormous silent black laugh. Not a scrap of paper, not a speck of dust, lay on the shiny steel shelves. A small inner safe, no doubt meant for storing jewels, opened just as easily as the strongbox, and was just as empty.

"Should we try taking fingerprints?" suggested Goodfield.

Dickson shrugged. "I don't know whether a crime has been committed, but if one has, we're dealing with criminals out of the ordinary, people who don't leave their prints any more than their signatures. But feel free to waste your time."

Goodfield stubbornly wasted his time, while Dickson went on searching the apartment. Several hours had passed before they decided to leave. Goodfield seemed almost unreasonably disappointed; Dickson, as he often was at the start of a challenging case, looked anxious and withdrawn.

"No prints," grumbled the superintendent.

"Solid walls of pure granite," said Tom, who'd spent a couple of hours tapping on the walls—which had made Goodfield laugh, since he wasn't much of a believer in secret passages. Only Dickson seemed to have found something: a few sheets of blue-tinted paper covered with small, crabbed handwriting.

"Evidence?" asked the superintendent.

Dickson smiled and shrugged. "Oh, I doubt it. Just the beginning of Miss Cruikshank's new novel."

"Really? What's it called?" asked Goodfield, his mind elsewhere.

"Just *Mysteras*."

"A stupid title," said the superintendent. "It doesn't mean anything."

"That's right, it doesn't mean anything."

Saunders—not wishing to remain alone in that accursed tower—said he'd catch a ride back to town with them. They resealed the apartment doors, shut off the elevator, triple-locked the outside door, and left the tower uninhabited.

3. Mysteras

The old Earl of Warchester, after a quarter century as a staple of the scandal sheets, had lived to see his obsessions forgotten by his peers. A new day brings new ways; puritanical Old England had gradually grown more tolerant, and people were ready to call Lord Warchester a madman rather than a servant of Satan.

The fact is that Warchester had spent the best years of his life poring over spell books, studying ancient tomes on sorcery, trying to procure a hanged man's pickled Hand of Glory—in short, striving to become a master of the occult sciences.

He lived in a dark manor house perched on a tall cliff in Cornwall, a place that provided the perfect setting for its owner's diabolical doings. But Warchester was rich, and of royal blood; the Prince of Wales condescended to visit him once a year during shooting season, to go out on his eccentric host's abundant bird-hunting grounds and fire off a few rounds. Warchester played a worthy host to his eminent guest. The old manor house held countless artistic masterpieces and splendid antiques, and it shone for those days of pomp. It was during one of those times of banqueting and festivity that this tale begins.

Though it was only early September, the weather had turned overcast and chilly. Large flocks of sheldrakes were heading south. Those fine birds usually landed around the old manor and spent a few days at the large ponds nearby. Being a hunter, even the heir apparent to the throne of England made sure not to miss his chance to shoot sheldrake and bustard. The prince had therefore let his cousin know that he'd be pleased to come spend a few days at Warchester Hall.

The usual commotion began right away: the rooms for guests of honor were prepared, the kitchens made their ovens roar night and day, the gamekeepers tripled their rounds, and set up bird blinds and reed huts to shelter the hunters.

Though the exalted visit would break into his routine and tear him away from his beloved studies, old Warchester couldn't hide the pride he felt each time the occasion came around.

"Chase," said he to his personal manservant a few days after the prince's arrival, "you'll hear my royal cousin ask me, as he does every year, the perennial question he likes to ask to make fun of me a little: 'Well, Warchester, have you managed to make a deal with the bleak and awful Prince of Darkness?'"

Chase shook his white-haired head. "And your lordship will reply, as you do every year, 'Your Highness, time is on my side. I haven't yet succeeded, but the day is coming.'"

Lord Warchester smiled enigmatically. "You're wrong there, Chase! That's not what I'll tell His Highness—not at all!"

Chase bowed respectfully and waited patiently for his master to elaborate. But the old gentleman didn't mean to: he only smiled and gently shook his silvery mane.

"Chase," he went on, changing the subject, "this will be the tenth time His Highness has condescended to come hunt on the Warchester grounds, and this time I mean to make him a gift of something incomparable, something my royal cousin has coveted since he was a boy! Can you guess, Chase?"

"Nothing could be too good for His Highness," the old manservant said skillfully.

"I'm going to give him the shotgun of the Earls of Warchester."

Chase's mouth fell open in surprise. The Warchester shotgun! A one-of-a-kind treasure! A hundred years ago it had belonged to the Maharajah of mysterious Nepal, who gave it to the grandfather of the present earl for having saved his life during a tiger hunt. It was a weapon considered at that time to be without peer, and had been crafted by the greatest armorers of England and Spain. The Hindu ruler had had it inlaid with precious gemstones, among which were fifteen priceless rubies.

The shotgun was now displayed in a case made of unbreakable glass, in a special room at the manor, with bricked-up windows and a steel door armed with an array of locks worthy of the latest bank vault. It was a rare privilege indeed to be allowed to view the Warchester shotgun. Sometimes the old earl withdrew into the room, triple-locked the door, and spent long hours contemplating his treasure. No one was invited to join him then in his admiration. Sometimes with his own hands he lit a fire in the hearth—whose opening had been barred with a special grate to keep thieves from getting in that way—and he lingered in the presence of his treasure.

"Chase," the earl said now, "it's not just to mark the tenth time he's come hunting here that I'm giving His Highness the gun, but also to celebrate the successful conclusion of my labors! Yes, Chase, the spirits of fire have finally deigned to answer my repeated appeals."

Chase bowed again, no doubt to hide the concern that furrowed his brow.

"You may withdraw, Chase," said his master. "I'll spend the rest of the evening in the gun room, and no one will be allowed to disturb me. Since it's a little cold, I'll light the fire myself, as usual."

That said, the old earl rose and went slowly into the gun room. Chase accompanied him to the door and wished him goodnight. He heard the squeak of the locks turning, then the repeated click of an old lighter the earl was trying to get to spark…

Poor ventilation made the room feel oppressive. A fire built of big logs soon warmed the dark blank walls. Two seven-branched candelabras with tall candles spread a gentle light. The earl pondered the thick bars across the hearth, as if he wanted to imprison the flames; then he settled into the only chair, a curule seat facing the glass case.

The Warchester shotgun shone, as splendid as a constellation stolen out of a perfect summer sky. The rubies threw out flames of color, and the fire from the diamonds and emeralds ran together into a peaceful fairy-tale glow the whole length of the ebony and pink-ivory stock and the barrel plated in pure gold.

Suddenly a voice emerged from the shadows. "Warchester!"

The old gentleman started, and looked into the fire—and yet his expression betrayed none of the terror one would expect after hearing such a mysterious call. "Spirit of fire, I attend!" he said.

"Why do you wish to give the prince, your cousin, the weapon that belongs by right to the spirits of fire?"

Warchester didn't answer, and his hands tightened on the arms of his chair.

"The Maharajah of Nepal was born of fire," went on the voice, "and the gifts he gave to mortals must someday return to the great inheritance of fire. I command you to throw that weapon through the bars of the fireplace, and thus render it to the flames from whence it came."

Warchester sighed and shook his head. "No, I can't do it."

The voice broke into sardonic laughter. "Beware, Warchester! The gods of fire cannot be refused!"

Full of his learning, the old earl replied energetically, "Spirit of fire, I spent many long years calling you, and finally you came. If you did so, it was my art that forced you to. You're trying once again to escape from my power. But you know that the scriptures and the spells have given me mastery over you. You cannot command me—rather it is I whom you must obey. In the name of the great King Solomon, in the name of the seventh door, seven times holy and dreadful, in the name of the Book of Spells and the Key of Solomon, I command you to tell me your name, unclean spirit of night and flame."

"My name is Systarmès!"

The Earl of Warchester's hands shook. "Spirit of fire, you know that possessing your name gives me the power and the right to summon you to appear!"

"I know it," the mysterious voice replied softly.

"Systarmès, I summon you to appear!" cried the earl fiercely.

There was a moment of terrible silence.

"Here I am," said a calm voice.

At that awful moment Warchester dearly wished he could flee, and he was afraid to turn toward the fire, where the voice came from. Finally he resolved to do it.

Its dark hands gripping the high bars of the grating across the hearth, a tall black shape stood erect. Warchester had trouble making it out, because it seemed to be draped in an enormous dark and shiny cloak.

"Systarmès!" stammered the earl, filled with a terrible fear at the sight of the Satanic creature who'd finally answered his call.

The creature's only reply was to push aside the bars, which bent like reeds, and step silently into the room.

"Systarmès! I command you to come no closer!" cried the summoner of evil spirits.

But the demon seemed untroubled by his order, and advanced until he stood two feet from the terrified, petrified earl.

"Systarmès… I command you…"

The evil one began to laugh, and stretched out two long claws toward the reckless wizard's neck.

"Systarmès…"

"Idiot!"

It was said coldly and dryly, with entirely human scorn; but Warchester could no longer hear. His head was tossed from side to side like a broken puppet's in the mysterious intruder's hands.

"These things break so easily," snickered the man in black. Then, without another thought for the man he'd just strangled, he turned to the gun case and tested the glass. "Unbreakable glass!… Ha!"

With a simian gesture he struck the glass, which shattered in spite of its claims. The man carefully removed a few shards, reached inside, and took hold of the Warchester shotgun.

At that moment, from the back of the glass case, a strange arm of steel burst forth and struck the profaning hand, while a hundred alarms began to ring madly through all the corridors and guardrooms of Warchester Hall.

Harry Dickson put down the manuscript—because that was merely the opening of Miss Cruikshank's new novel in progress, which chance had put into the famous detective's hands.

"A fairly routine start to a crime novel," he mused. "That spirit of fire... Systarmès will probably turn out to be some thief of genius who'll have the whole world's police up in arms and get away with countless brilliant heists and slip through the cleverest nets of justice. It's a plot as old as the hills... Huh, Systarmès is an anagram of Mysteras, the title—of a novel that'll probably never amount to more than these opening pages... It doesn't get us very far, and yet..."

Dickson tossed the pages into a desk drawer without finishing his thought aloud.

Mrs. Crown brought in tea and the morning papers, still smelling of fresh printer's ink. Like many people in her station, she considered it her duty to glance at the papers before handing them over to her employer, so as to serve them up wrapped in her own commentary, which she now provided.

"I gave these papers no more than a glance, sir," she said scornfully, "because it's all lies. Imagine, the Prince of Wales won't go hunting because his gun's been stolen—as if the likes of him can't find another gun. I wasn't born yesterday, and your newspapers are good for nothing but wrapping up cabbage and asparagus."

She carried herself away with dignity; but her employer sat frozen for a moment as if struck by lightning, then unfolded the scorned newspaper. His heart stopped as he read the banner headline:

SHOTGUN OF THE DUKES OF HUNNINGHAM STOLEN!
Night Before Prince of Wales's Visit!

29

Duke of Hunningham Found Strangled by Empty Case!
Heartrending Details!...

Dickson groaned and held his head in his hands: the further he read in the *Daily News*, the more he found himself rereading more or less the opening chapter of the novel he'd almost tossed in the trash basket. All he had to do was swap the Earl of Warchester for the Duke of Hunningham and leave out the odd meeting between the earl and Systarmès, the spirit of fire. But the manor in Cornwall, the old gentleman's dabbling in the dark arts, the marvelous shotgun of the rulers of Nepal, the annual visit by the Prince of Wales, the unfortunate duke dead in front of the smashed glass case—it was all there.

"But if it's all true," he murmured, "did the booby trap work?" He thought it over and gave a bitter laugh. "The chapter was written well before this happened. So if I admit a correlation between these pages and the crime—and how could I not?—I'm forced to conclude that the thief in real life wouldn't get caught like the one in the story did, because he'd know about the trap in advance... Let's see what Scotland Yard has to say."

"Mr. Dickson!" cried Superintendent Goodfield over the telephone. "We were just about to ask you to go to Hunningham Hall without losing a moment, and trust me, this is at the insistence of persons in high places."

"Do you know anything beyond what's in the morning papers?" asked Dickson.

"Indeed. I have to tell you that the glass case..."

"Was armed with a booby trap, I know," interrupted Dickson. "Well, what was in it?"

"Say, how about that! You already knew! You're a devilish customer!" said Goodfield admiringly. "Well, then, Mr. Dickson, there was a calling card caught in the steel jaws of the trap, and the name on it was one that I have a vague feeling I've seen before. Wait a moment... Ah, yes—Mysteras, that's what it was."

4. Fear Hall

Whipped on by the storm, the ragged wall of the Atlantic swell hurled itself against the land. Foam-crested waves struck the ocher Cornish coast like so many medieval battering rams. Hunningham Hall towered over the chaos from the heights of the great cliff on which it stood. Apart from a handful of brave servants, this ancient seat of English peers had been abandoned. Young Lord Baysland, heir to that line of stern noblemen, showed little interest in spending the best years his life in the owl's nest—his irreverent name for the tragic manor.

Two gentlemen from London were nevertheless staying at that sad spot: Harry Dickson and Tom Wills. What were they doing in these charmless surroundings? Was it the investigation? Dickson had managed it with his usual care. He'd concluded that the thief—Mysteras, as he called himself—must've been bold beyond measure to get into the house. And Dickson still didn't know how it had been done: the tall grating across the fireplace remained perfectly intact, its bars anchored in the solid stone walls.

One thought continued to nag at him: how had Delphina Cruikshank managed to describe the crime—down to its most unusual details—more than three months before it was carried out? For an analysis of the ink had shown that the handwriting was already at least three months old when Dickson found the manuscript in Cruikshank Tower.

Interviews with the staff had shed no light on the case. At this point the detective had no objection to dropping the case and leaving. Chase, the head servant, had done everything in his power to help him, and had racked his brains for any useful detail that might advance the investigation. The detective had made careful note of the good man's statement. A transcript of some of Dickson's questions and Chase's answers appears below:

Question: Did any strangers visit here in, say, the last six months?

31

Answer: No one. During hunting season last fall, His Highness and a few of his close friends did us the honor of choosing to spend five days at the manor. Since then not a single outsider has been admitted to the house, and no one has even asked for permission to do so.

Q: Has there been any turnover in the staff?

A: No, but we did lose one servant to an unsolved accident that some people claimed was a crime. He wasn't replaced.

Q: Can you tell me about that accident or crime?

A: Of course. Miller was a quiet, dedicated young man, though a little laconic. He'd been in service here more than fifteen years. His only recreations were fishing and rabbit hunting, because his lordship had given him permission to shoot the rabbits that infest the countryside and decimate the meager crops in the area. At the end of February of last year, on a fine night, he'd gone out to hide in a copse of trees overlooking the plains to the west. He wasn't back in the morning. Suspecting an accident, I had the area searched in all directions. My fears were warranted: they found poor Miller—but in such a state!

He was lying at the foot of small rocky hill, his head beaten to a pulp, one arm torn off, his gun lying ten yards away, completely smashed. How could a fall from the top of that hill have done such damage? That's what the coroner asked at the inquest, and to this day no one's been able to give an answer. The jury rejected a murder verdict only because Miller's wallet was found untouched in his pocket, and he was in the habit of carrying all his money with him.

Q: Did they find any fingerprints or footprints or any other clues around Miller's body?

A: None. But around then something strange happened at the manor, and I had quite a job calming down the staff. Phantom bagpipes were heard in the house, and even in the countryside nearby. It was a queer and terrible sound that came from everywhere and nowhere—you'd have said it was a giant incompetent piper. It hurt your ears to hear it, it followed you down the furthest corridors, sometimes even into your sleep. His lordship, who heard it just as we did, couldn't hide his satisfaction. I'm sure you know his interest in the dark arts, and he claimed it was the spirits of air or fire that he'd been summoning for many years, now trying to communicate with mere mortals.

Several times, servants who were up late saw a squat shape running through the corridors of the manor. And one night Bellows, the scullery maid, and her fiancé, Chomett, the night watchman, got a better look at it. They'd stayed outside on the terrace that looks over the sea, admiring the moonlight on the water, when suddenly the phantom piper began his hellish music. Bellows and Chomett were frightened, and they came inside right away and spent the rest of the evening around the kitchen fire. Since the terrible noise had stopped long since, they decided to go up to their rooms, but Bellows made her fiancé go along with her up to the floor for the women servants.

To get there they had to cross the whole length of the second-floor hall, which is really more like a broad mezzanine. Bright moonlight shone through the arched windows. When they reached that mezzanine they thought they heard a noise, and they hid behind the statues lining that hall. That's when they saw a shape standing still by the reinforced door to the room where the shotgun of the Dukes of Hunningham was kept. At first they could only see an unmoving black silhouette, but just then a ray of moonlight struck the glass over a painting and reflected onto that door. Imagine their shock and their horror when they saw that the thing that came by night was some sort of monstrous insect, like an enormous beetle. Bellows and Chomett didn't dare go up to their rooms; they went silently back to the kitchen and spent the night there.

When they told the duke the next day, he seemed delighted. "The spirits of fire sometimes assume strange forms," he said. "I've got an interesting book here that mentions a fire god taking the form of a broadsword and even a hardwood chair!" I myself have thought it over many times since then, and I think those two witnesses weren't far wrong, since the phantom piper's music sounded at least as much like a beetle's buzzing as like bagpipes.

Q: Has that noise been heard often since then?

A: Oh no, it's been months since we last heard it.

Q: Try to recall—did you hear it again shortly before the crime at Hunningham Hall?

A: Yes, I remember, two or three days before. And since his lordship told me the night of his death that he'd just made an important discovery that he was going to share first with His Royal Highness, I thought it must be connected to the return of the ghostly music.

Harry Dickson had thanked the honest devoted servant, and sunk back into his thoughts. "It's the novel come to life once again," he murmured, "and the most extraordinary thing is that the head servant's name in the manuscript, Chase, remains Chase in real life!"

That was all he'd learned in his investigation. For many detectives it would've amounted to no more than gossip and nonsense; but for Dickson it must all have meant something, because he'd made careful note of Chase's replies, and in an expansive moment he confided to his utterly bored assistant, "Tom, my boy, that ray of moonlight that exposed the giant beetle might be the thing that illuminates this entire case."

"What!" cried Tom. "You're not going to rely on balderdash like that to solve this terrible case, are you, Guv?"

"Balderdash? Damn, Tom, is that what you call the first and possibly the best links we have in the great chain of proof?"

The conversation had ended there, because Dickson had put on his raincoat and hurried out of the house with long strides, to roam the desolate countryside around the ancestral home of the Hunninghams.

Tom Wills went back to the gloomy parlor that had been provided for the London detectives. Addressing the stern family portraits, he grumbled at the fate that kept them idling in this rattrap. "And why in fact are we still hanging around here?" he wondered.

That day was like all the others the guests at the manor had spent there. Dickson went wandering around the fields and moors; Tom smoked endless cigarettes in that dark parlor with its stiff, uncomfortable furniture. And once again he repeated his perennial question: "Why in fact are we still hanging around here?"

He was reaching for the ashtray to stub out—in the already impressive pile of blackened butts—the cigarette he'd just finished, when in the middle of the table he noticed a sheet of white paper, folded in half, that he didn't remember having seen before. Anything to pass the time: he picked up the paper and unfolded it.

He shuddered all over, and it seemed to him as if the furniture around him had shifted and rotated slowly. He recognized the small, crabbed handwriting that covered the page: it belonged to the vanished lady novelist!

"Maybe it's a page that fell out of the chapter the Guv has," he said, trying to reassure himself.

But from the very first lines he read, he had to admit it wasn't so. The page seemed to have been extracted from a chapter, and to be missing both the beginning and the end. Tom read eagerly:

"... But the forefather of the Warchesters showed himself to be unworthy of the friendship of the Maharajah of Nepal. The wonderful gun, worth a fortune in Europe, only kindled in his breast a desire for greater wealth. A loyal retainer from the mountains had prepared a caravan of seven elephants loaded with treasures destined for the Nepalese prince. Great celebrations were underway in the prince's palace to welcome the caravan. Warchester was among the guests. Cursed a thousandfold is the guest who repays a prince's hospitality with criminal ingratitude!

"When the caravan was six days away from the prince's capital, Warchester gave some excuse or other to take his leave. The Maharajah was sorry to see him go, but the wishes

35

of his guests were his command, and he let him depart, laden with magnificent gifts as well as the splendid shotgun. But Warchester turned aside from his route and went to intercept the caravan. What exactly happened? Will it ever be known? The jungle keeps its secrets. The caravan never reached Nepal, and the prince never again saw his friend Warchester."

Thus spoke the nameless person, to whom Mysteras listened with fear and respect.

"Mysteras!" the person said. *"The treasures stolen from the Maharajah of Nepal have crossed the black water and now sleep in the same castle as the gun given in friendship to a thief. Mysteras! Destiny wishes you to return to that accursed house. The awful Goddess of Vengeance will walk by your side. Mysteras! You were born from death, and no human power can destroy you. Go! A formidable man will stand in your way. The goddess will inspire your words and your actions! Clear the obstacles from your path, be they human or not, and take back the treasures stolen from the great prince of Nepal by his perjured and triply treacherous friend..."*

Trembling, Tom tucked the page in his pocket and looked around in fear, as if Mysteras were about to leap out of the shadows. But he saw nothing but family portraits.

The sound of voices drew him from his anxious thoughts. Chase, the head servant, came bustling in. "Mr. Wills, here's some company for you. The heir of the Hunninghams and our new master, Lord Baysland, has arrived. I imagine Mr. Dickson will be happy to meet him. In any case, his lordship says he's delighted to know you're here, and he wishes to see your employer immediately. Excuse me, I must go see that everything's in order to receive his lordship properly."

"Damn!" mused Tom. "I'd have given a lot to have the Guv here now. First, I have to give him this sheet of paper, which is bound to interest him. Sure enough, all you have to do is swap the name Warchester for Hunningham. And if Miss Cruikshank, when she was writing this page, had the advantage of the same power of prediction as in her first chapter, I'd say it amounts to a visit here from the terrible Mysteras!"

He went back to his room to spruce himself up in a manner worthy of the nobleman whose guest he was today.

Dusk was falling, and in the great halls a profusion of lamps and candlesticks were already lit when Tom came down to the dining room. The table was splendidly set with an extraordinary abundance of flatware, silver, and crystal. A constellation of candles lit the somewhat medieval decor. Three places had been set on the damask tablecloth.

Chase was just giving the arrangements one last quick look, and belaboring the attentive staff with countless instructions.

"Has Mr. Dickson already come back?" asked Tom.

Chase looked at him in surprise. "I would assume so, Mr. Wills. Your employer went off toward the shore as soon as lunch was over. I met him going down the steps, and he said he expected to be back by four."

"But it's seven now!" cried Tom.

Chase was about to reply when the door opened, and a tall figure appeared on the threshold. The head servant bowed deeply.

"His lordship, Lord Baysland-Hunningham," he announced.

The new arrival glanced around the room, spotted Tom, and came straight to him with his hand out. "Mr. Wills," he said, his voice a little raspy but pleasant, "I'm delighted to find you here at my place. I hope your distinguished employer won't keep me waiting too long—I've been eager to meet him for as long as I've been reading about his achievements in newspapers all over the world."

Tom bowed. "He should've been back by now. I'll admit, I'm a little worried about him: he's always so punctual, and here he is, three hours late!"

"Really?" cried Lord Baysland. "Ah, such are the burdens of your difficult trade. Never mind, Mr. Wills, we'll have a cocktail while we wait for Mr. Dickson's return."

The heir of the Dukes of Hunningham was a sparkling conversationalist. One cocktail followed another. Tom, flattered and a little stimulated, had lost track of time. Chase came in and murmured briefly in his new master's ear.

"Nine o'clock!" cried Lord Baysland. "How time flies in your company, Mr. Wills! And I'm told Mr. Dickson is still not back from his walk. Shall I have dinner served?"

Tom sobered up in a flash. "Nine o'clock! But I don't know what to think, my lord! My employer should be here! I'm sure something must've happened to him."

"Come now, Mr. Wills," said Lord Baysland reassuringly, "Harry Dickson isn't a child, to get lost like Little Red Riding Hood! We'll dine at our convenience, and if you like, I'll send out men with lanterns to have a look around."

Tom sat back down with a sigh. He felt like he was choking, and he thought he wouldn't be able to do justice to the dinner.

A servant had just set down a splendid mushroom pie—which in other circumstances would've made Tom cross-eyed with anticipation—when Chase hurried in. "A fisherman from Land's End has just brought a message for Mr. Wills," he said, handing the young man a crude, crumpled envelope, damp from the night fog.

Tom opened it feverishly and withdrew a scrap of paper; on it were a few words in Harry Dickson's handwriting: *Don't wait for me, Tom. I'll be away all night and perhaps part of the morning.*

"Good news, I assume?" his host asked politely.

"In any case, enough to calm my fears," said Tom, with a sigh of relief. "I beg your pardon, my lord—I thought for a while I might not be able to do justice to this excellent dinner. Give me a chance to catch up!"

Lord Baysland burst out laughing, and they went on to spend a delightful evening together over dishes both subtle and abundant, and bottles of noble vintage wines—perhaps more of the latter than would do to maintain Tom's wits at an even keel.

He went to bed a little groggy, and fell straight into a dreamless sleep.

Dreamless? Not quite…

Suddenly Tom thought an enormous blowfly was buzzing around his room. The sound bored into his head like a drill. He tossed and turned in bed.

"No fly could make a noise like that," he mumbled, still asleep. "It's more like a big beetle at the window…"

—"Beetle!" Even in his sleep the word struck him, and he awoke. He sat up, his mind still spinning. A distant, stubborn, nagging sound was fading away, as if the walls, the very air, were vibrating like the inside of a great conch. It was a dark night, and only a faint milky light came through the high arched window, darkened by ancient stained glass. Soon the sound had faded to a murmur, lost in the sound of the surf against the cliff.

Tom was wide awake now, and his heart beat a wild tattoo. He was afraid! Why? He couldn't have said exactly, but all of his earlier anxiety had returned. He felt the need for reassurance, but his noble host wasn't there to chase away his morbid thoughts with a laugh or a quip.

"Let's reread the Guv's note. That'll help a little."

By feel, he found the scrap of paper in his coat pocket, as well as his electric flashlight, which he switched on. *Don't wait for me, Tom…* he read again.

But the first time he'd been reading by flickering candle-light, whereas now the round bright beam of his flashlight followed the words across the page.

"Oh!" The paper trembled in his hands. At first sight it looked like Harry Dickson's handwriting—but the hard clear light of the electric flashlight revealed alterations and retouching.

"This is a forgery!" Tom had almost shouted that cry of horror aloud. The note was fake, and that suggested the worst. In a flash he was up and dressed. What to do? Wake Lord

Baysland, rouse the servants? He decide to do neither, and to handle matters himself.

He quietly opened his door and looked out at the darkness of the great hall. A single lamp at the far end threw light on a statue of Prometheus in chains fighting with a vulture. The lamplight stretched out the shadows, and the marble shapes looked so threateningly alive that Tom was prompted to reach for his revolver. But there was nothing but shadow and silence—barely the melancholy sound of the surf on the shore, barely the soft cry of a kestrel heading out into the night to hunt.

He advanced on tiptoe, unsure which way to go. He was a few feet from the sinister statue, which looked more frightening than ever. Maybe out of bravado, maybe out of a need for reassurance, he walked right up to the statue and touched the marble.

Suddenly his hand was seized, and another terribly icy hand was clamped over his mouth. Tom struggled fiercely to break free, but he managed no more than to slide to the floor and bang his head against the tile.

"Will you hold still, little fool!"

Ah, never did a sweeter sound reach Tom's ears than that insult, spat quietly by an angry voice—his employer's!

"Mr. Dickson!" stammered Tom as he got up, bruised but elated.

"Quiet! Our lives are at stake. He'd kill us without a moment's hesitation. Ah, it gave me such a fright when I saw you come out of your room. Fright, and yet my heart was also filled with joy," murmured Dickson, pressing his assistant close. "What luck, my boy, that you slept soundly and slept until now—otherwise you'd have been done for as well."

"As well?" asked Tom, for whom the words suggested some further vague menace.

"Alas, my boy, I want to spare you for now the sight of a truly awful scene. You and I are the only ones left alive in this house—unless that Satanic creature is still lurking somewhere, as is likely."

"The servants?" asked Tom.

"The kitchen, Tom... it's horrifying—a slaughterhouse. They must've been put to sleep by some sedative in their drink. And then a monster fell on them. I wonder what saved you."

Dickson pulled his assistant behind the statue of Prometheus.

"I heard the phantom bagpipes, Guv, or rather a giant beetle."

The detective took his arm. "Ah, I think that explains why you're still alive, my boy."

"Is the bagpiper some kind of guardian angel, Guv?"

"Not in the least, my boy. But once it heard the bagpipes, the monster had something more important to do than to finish you off. It'll all become clear later."

"But what are we doing waiting here, Guv?"

"We're hiding, Tom, that's all," Dickson said somberly. "I don't yet know the strength of the beast, so I don't dare risk showing myself. Still, I think I've learned enough to lead it promptly to its doom."

"So we can talk a little, in a whisper?" asked Tom.

"It'll pass the time, since we might be here a while," replied Dickson. "Here's my report—as short as it is terrible. It was almost four, and I was getting ready to come back to the manor, when I heard a car. From where I was at the top of the cliff, I could see a magnificent roadster heading to the Hall, driven by a gentleman in sporting dress."

"Lord Baysland," murmured Tom.

"Really? In that case he must've been resurrected, because a half hour earlier I'd found the body of that poor man in a hollow in the dunes near here."

"But I had dinner with him," protested Tom with great feeling.

"Or with whoever was posing as him," said Dickson. "Anyway, I followed the car with my eyes until it went behind the dunes and out of sight, and the sound of the engine was muted. I was waiting for it come out around the next bend, and

I was beginning to wonder why it was taking so long—when I was hit violently over the head with a truncheon and pushed off the cliff into the sea. Ah, Tom, if it weren't for this marvelous little soft helmet I wear under my hat when I'm on the warpath, it would've been time to write the late Harry Dickson's obituary!

"But it was a man in full command of his wits and his muscles who fell into the sea. I had only to swim underwater for a while, till I reached a nearby cove, to persuade my mysterious attacker that I'd met my end. I didn't get back to the manor till well into the night—alas, too late to prevent the butchery of the staff. I ran to the nearest village and went to work with telephone and telegraph: I hope not in vain. Your turn to report, my boy."

Tom told him quickly about the forged note, and then remembered the sheet of manuscript he'd found in the parlor. He knew what it said almost by heart, and he repeated it to his employer.

Dickson remained silent a long while when Tom had finished. "Everything follows, my boy," he murmured. "It's all logical, as usual, even in this hodgepodge of mysteries and apparently unmotivated crimes. If that page had fallen into my hands, there's a chance I could've altered the tragic course of the night's events, but fate decided otherwise. Now I'm sure only of vengeance."

Suddenly a piercing sound began, grew, and quickly faded away.

"The phantom piper!" cried Tom.

Dickson pulled out his watch, which had a luminous dial. "Half past midnight... We have almost four hours ahead of us in which to work—barely enough. Come, my boy!"

"But what about the danger you spoke of before, Guv?"

"That's over. Come on," said Dickson in a loud voice, as if he felt certain no one could hear them.

They went downstairs to the ground floor. Tom hesitated by the kitchen door, which stood ajar. Dickson motioned for him to stop. "No need to fill your eyes with that sight, my boy," he said sadly. "They were struck down like beasts at the slaughter, but vengeance is nigh, I promise you."

They left the house at a brisk pace and crossed the flagstone courtyard, then passed through the gate that opened onto the barren countryside. The moon had risen and the night was reasonably bright. Dickson strode toward a definite goal, leading Tom along with him.

Behind the dunes the detective stopped and looked around at the landscape. "Do you notice anything, Tom?" he asked.

"Hmm… not much. Yet it seems to me this spot is smoother, not as broken up as the ground everywhere else around here."

"Well done, my boy," his employer said laconically.

Out of a package he drew from his pocket, Dickson extracted long dark sticks, which he began to plant in the ground, leaving only a wick above the sand.

"It looks like you're planting mines, Guv!"

"Of course I am. Here you go, help me by putting some there, and over there, and then over there."

Without waiting for an explanation, Tom followed his instructions. An hour went by in near silence, until all the dynamite had been buried.

As Tom was planting his last mine, he noticed objects glittering on the sand, and picked them up. Then he ran to his employer, pale with emotion. "Look what I just found, Guv!"

He held out magnificent emeralds and a large diamond of the first water.

"The second chapter of the novel explains everything, my boy, incomplete as it is," said Dickson as he examined the stones. This is in fact an insignificant part of the treasures of the Maharajah of Nepal, stolen a hundred years ago by a Hunningham. Now look out, it's time for the Bickford safety fuse!"

Dickson struck his lighter and lit a long black cord, which began to burn gently. A tiny glowing dot ran across the sand.

"Shake a leg, Tom. We've only got ten minutes."

They'd taken shelter behind a high dune before suddenly the earth shook and a clap of thunder rang out, followed immediately by a second and a third. When they came out from hiding, the detectives could see smoke rising in the distance where they'd planted their mines. The breeze from offshore soon cleared the smoke, and the ground was revealed—torn apart as if by an earthquake.

"That's good enough for now, my boy," chuckled Dickson. "We still have almost an hour. Rather than undertake any new investigations, we'll get a little rest at a place on the cliff where even the seagulls' sharp eyes won't find us."

"An hour, Guv?… Why an hour? What'll happen then?"

"Well, my boy," said the detective mischievously, "then someone we know will come hurrying to the manor to find out how his friend Tom Wills spent the night."

"Who, Guv?" cried Tom.

"Why, your charming host from last evening, Tom: good old Mysteras!"

Far away, toward the Channel, the sea glowed yellow. Dickson shook Tom, who'd fallen asleep with his head on the hard granite that served as his pillow.

"Time to get up, my boy. We don't want to miss the show." The detective held his watch in his hand, and worry creased his brow. "I hope they'll be there," he murmured.

"Who's THEY, Guv?"

"The two rival parties, my boy!"

Dickson's eyes roamed across the empty sea. "Hell," he muttered, "what if it doesn't come off? If not, I'd have done better to light my fuse at a later time—but I want to catch the perpetrators alive, and not reduced to a jelly."

Tom was about to ask for those mysterious words to be explained, when suddenly Dickson took his arm.

"Listen! Listen hard!"

"Good God! The phantom piper is playing his bagpipes in the countryside now, and no longer inside the manor!"

The sound that reached them was muted by distance and by the thin fog that filled the air.

"Now look at the place we dynamited, my boy."

Tom did so, and rubbed his eyes. "I don't see a thing, Guv!"

"Then look up!"

Tom raised his eyes: a silhouette rapidly crossed the sky. "An airplane!"

"Yes, my boy, with a super-fast engine that's also super-silent—or rather, one whose hum doesn't sound like the rumble of a normal airplane engine. It's a dashed remarkable innovation, and one that does credit to the inventor who conceived it for particular uses."

"Crikey, Guv! It seems they've noticed the condition of the place they meant to land! Look how they're hesitating!"

Indeed, the airplane was circling, staying cautiously above the ground.

"To land there now would be suicidal, my boy, and they must know it. As for landing elsewhere, that's no good—I doubt there's another decent landing spot for forty miles around."

"They're looking, Guv. They're heading out to sea now."

"Ah!" murmured Dickson. "Will it all come to nothing?"

He turned toward the open sea—and gave a shout of joy. Far off, on the surface of the water, a black line had just appeared, and then another. They were moving rapidly on a course parallel to the shore.

"Submarines that just surfaced, Guv!" cried Tom.

One of the submarines had drawn nearer to shore, and now men emerged from the hatch and began to run along the curving deck of wave-dashed steel.

"I see! They're preparing an anti-aircraft gun!" cried Tom, thrilled by the speed of the maneuver.

The airplane overflew the sea at low altitude, apparently unconcerned by the submarines. Suddenly a white sphere, like a cotton ball, appeared in the sky to starboard of the plane, followed by a crisp bang. The airplane pitched violently and gained altitude. But now the second submarine joined the action, and within a few seconds white balls bracketed the airplane. A series of crisp, angry bangs followed.

"Shrapnel!" said Dickson. "Too bad for whoever's in that cockpit!"

Now surrounded by explosions, the airplane swerved wildly, trying to escape the fatal cross-hairs. Suddenly a white ball formed just above it, and the airplane tipped to one side as if it were starting its final fall.

Both detectives cried out, and other cries echoed theirs from the men on the submarines. A human body had just fallen from the airplane and was dropping like a stone toward the sea. With a great splash it hit the surface and vanished. The submarines steered for the spot it had struck. Sailors heaves out ropes and grappling irons.

"Damn it!" cried Dickson. "The job's only half done!"

Indeed, far above them the airplane regained altitude and then disappeared into the clouds...

"Do you recognize him, Mr. Dickson?" asked the submarine commander some time later, after he'd welcomed the two detectives aboard.

They were looking at a body that the sailors were about to cover with a tarp. The dead man was tall, with an aquiline, expressive face. Harry Dickson studied the body in silence.

"He was hit at least a dozen times by shrapnel," said the commander. "But our orders were explicit."

"You did the right thing," said Dickson. "Though all you did was kill a man who was already dead—at least officially."

"What are you saying?" asked the commander, dumbfounded.

"This man is none other than the murderer Baltimore Harmon, who was executed a few months ago at Hammersmith Prison."

"If it were anyone but you saying so, Mr. Dickson," murmured the commander, "I'd think I was talking to a madman."

Harry Dickson slowly shook his head. "Still, I must ask once more that you keep this completely secret, commander. My job isn't done yet."

"But, Guv, after all—you got Mysteras!" cried Tom Wills.

"Mysteras, and not Mysteras," replied Dickson, staring up at the clouds into which the unknown airplane had vanished.

5. The Enigma of the Tower

Harry Dickson and Tom Wills returned to London that same day, after having the police seal off Hunningham Hall, and requesting that the army keep watch over the manor. They came home to Baker Street with the same joy they felt anew each time they reached safe haven after trouble.

"Guv!" said Tom as if he'd just remembered something. "I say, Guv, do you recall how at Cruikshank Tower there was also some kind of mysterious singing. Still, I don't think that one was an airplane."

Dickson slapped his assistant affectionately on the back. "As it happens, I've been thinking about that most of the way home—as something that could be very useful to us. And here's the proof." He handed Tom a letter.

The brief message was divided into two columns, headed *The tower sang on this date... at this hour...* followed by a list of dates and times.

Dickson couldn't contain a cry of delight. "We're making giant strides toward solving this enigma, my boy!" he said, rubbing his hands with glee.

"I didn't know you'd put a watchman at the tower, Guv."

"A watchman only in a manner of speaking, my boy. In fact, it's a sensitive microphone concealed in the entrance hall of the tower, with a wire hidden in the high grass of the garden and running to an army post in the no man's land around Wormwood Scrubs, where I'm paying a man to listen in."

"Are we going out there, Guv?" asked Tom.

"This very evening, my boy, and we'll spend the whole night if we have to," said his employer. "I predict our vigil won't be in vain."

Twilight found them before the lady novelist's peculiar tower, now quite unoccupied. The melancholy autumn evening made it look black and menacing, with its stone walls stained by rain and hail, and its windows discolored by mold.

"It's ominous, Guv," said Tom. "A good match for Hunningham Hall."

Dickson checked the seals on the front door, found them intact, and broke them with a shrug. "Useless, all these layers of sealing wax," he said. "They'll be just like this wherever they were put."

A damp, icy air struck their faces as they entered the strange house. They would've had to call the electric company to get the power turned back on—without which they couldn't use the elevator to get to Miss Cruikshank's apartment. Tom had wanted to do it, but his employer had talked him out of it.

"Don't even think of it, my boy: that would be enough to keep away the person we're waiting for. I believe he's so shy he wouldn't show so much as the tip of his nose if he suspected we were within thirty miles of him. If he feels safe up there, it's precisely because when the elevator's out of commission there's no other way up."

"Neither for him, nor for us," objected Tom.

"Remains to be seen, as they say in Normandy," chuckled Dickson.

Now the young man looked up at the high smooth walls of the tower with a certain concern, and shook his head doubtfully. "There are alpinists who'd balk at that, Guv," he grumbled.

"I have no intention of climbing that mirror-smooth surface lie a housefly, my boy! Have you forgotten that if we don't have the elevator, we still have its cable?"

For men skilled at every sport—as were the two detectives—to climb a hundred feet of cable was no great matter; but the axle grease that coated it presented a challenge. Luckily Dickson had thought of everything: the rough cloth overpants and sharkskin gloves he pulled out of a small bag came in very handy.

Five minutes later Tom joined Dickson on the top floor landing, facing the only door into the empty apartment.

"Everybody's been trying to figure out how someone could leave this floor without a parachute or rope ladder," said Tom, "and you solved it in no time flat, Guv!"

"This rough and ready method might work once or twice, my boy, but not regularly—not with the servants present downstairs."

"Then what other way could there be, Guv? We've looked everywhere!" said Tom almost indignantly.

"We've looked everywhere without seeing anything, it's true; but you don't always have to see to solve something. I've thought it over a lot in the past few days, my boy, working from the idea that *there had to have been* a way out!"

"And so you've found a way to the top of the tower that no one can see, Guv?" Tom was more incredulous than ever.

"Of course I found it, my boy, because *it was impossible that it not be where it had to be!*"

While he spoke, Dickson had opened the door to the large semicircular parlor. A little daylight lingered, coming from the last beautiful bands of sunset gold and scarlet in the west.

"We'll look around to see that nothing's been moved, and check for prints," said Tom—but his employer called him over and pushed him into a chair.

"Take it easy, my boy. What good would prints do us, since we're about to meet the man who left them?"

"The man or the woman," said Tom sullenly. "I have a theory that Miss Cruikshank is behind all this, and if anyone shows up in a while, it can only be that damned scribbling female!"

"You seem as certain as you are spiteful!"

"Guv!" cried Tom. "You've gotten into the bad habit of leaving me in the dark all the time, but here I feel I've hit on the truth: only Miss Cruikshank could come back here!"

"Very well, my boy. Now you're talking like Goodfield and all the other bigwigs at Scotland Yard. All right! I'll say only that you're wrong—that's enough for now."

The detective sat down as well, though he shifted the position of his chair. Shadows gathered fast, the first stars appeared in the sky, and soon the darkness of an autumn night had fallen.

"Will we have long to wait, Guv?" asked Tom.

"There's no reason to think so. Anyway, we'll be warned in time."

"Really? By whom?"

"Why, by the singing ghost in the tower. Who else, my boy?" Dickson laughed. "But keep your revolver ready in your lap, as well as your flashlight."

"Do you know where the mystery man will come from, Guv?" asked Tom.

"Of course, my boy, to within an inch," replied the detective very seriously.

"Unless it's a woman," griped Tom.

"If you insist…"

Silence fell in the room. Dickson breathed heavily, as if he'd fallen asleep.

From time to time a gust of wind filled the tower with a mournful sound that made Tom jump. "Is that the singing ghost?" he asked anxiously.

"Not at all, my boy. I assume the servants, who were used to it, would recognize the sound of the wind," replied Dickson. Then he asked his assistant to please keep quiet. "Your patience won't be tested much longer," he promised.

Tom started, and drew his employer's attention to a strange sound that seemed to originate from the floor. At first it was like a long muffled cry, then it grew more and more piercing and seemed to be coming closer, rising toward the top floor; meanwhile the whole tower seemed to vibrate like a string instrument played by a giant bow.

"Look out!" said Dickson in a hard voice. "This is it, my boy. The tower has sung to announce the visitor, the great mysterious one. Raise your revolver!"

The noise had stopped, and was followed by a long metallic grinding, and then Tom saw a thin line of light appear before him. Stunned beyond measure, he realized that the line traced the edge of the door to the strongbox, which suddenly began to open.

"Don't move!" shouted Dickson, and both detectives switched on their flashlights.

A small man dressed in an aviator's leather clothes and helmet stood before them, silent and obviously confused.

"Kindly have a seat," said Dickson politely. "I've been waiting for you to show up in that splendid little secret elevator, running on power stolen from the electric company. Tom, my boy, please close the blinds—we don't want anyone to interrupt us from outside. Then use the telephone to call the electric company and ask them to turn the power back on: I'd like to be able to see while we talk."

The visitor hadn't said a word, and had dropped into a chair facing Dickson, who was still playing idly with his revolver.

A few minutes later, bright lights came on all over the room. Dickson leaned politely toward the intruder. "Would you be so kind as to remove your driving goggles, if only to please my assistant, Tom Wills?"

The visitor shrugged, and in one quick move pulled off the goggles and tossed them aside.

Tom whooped with delight. "Miss Delphina Cruikshank! What did I tell you, Guv?"

Dickson didn't reply, but continued speaking. "We're going to talk a bit, since that's why I came. This is not an interrogation; I myself will tell the story of a mystery."

The intruder moved slightly, but the detective preempted her gesture. "Put the handcuffs on her, Tom!"

"Oh, Guv!" protested Tom, remembering the lady novelist whose books had given him so much pleasure in the past.

"Quick, my boy!" scolded his employer, and Tom obeyed, shaking his head. The visitor didn't move as the humiliating cuffs went on, but her eyes shone with anger.

"Miss Delphina Cruikshank," began the detective, "was a writer of greater talent than she was generally credited with. She especially enjoyed doing her own research, and doing it secretly. At night she mingled in the seedy crowds in the city's worst neighborhoods, without anyone recognizing her, because she had a wide variety of disguises. To come and go as she pleased, when she built this tower she had a little hidden elevator installed—one that went unnoticed until today. How? Because it was concealed in the simplest possible way: it shared the same shaft as the main elevator! When it reached this level its rear was flush with this wall, and its door opened into... the strongbox.

"Who would've looked for a secret door within the smooth walls of the elevator shaft, hanging over a yawning hundred-foot drop? So much for the secret passage. And there's no crime in it—every man is lord in his own castle, and can build it as he pleases. Since Miss Cruikshank was careful to send the architects and builders abroad, handsomely paid, no one gave away her little arrangement. The ghostly singing in the tower was nothing but the hum of the little secret elevator.

"Now, let's take a short detour into Miss Cruikshank's past. As we know, her father made his fortune in India—specifically at the court of the Maharajah of Nepal. There he was given the mission of avenging an ancient wrong done to the deceased rulers of that mysterious kingdom. He gave his oath to recover the Hunningham shotgun and the treasures stolen from the long-ago rajah. But Cruikshank returned to England and forgot his oath. Still, when he sensed his end was near, he felt guilty, and he passed on his mission to his only daughter.

"Well, Miss Cruikshank was a writer above all, and she carried out her mission… in her imagination—that is to say, in the form of a novel. In that work of pure fiction, she created a formidable character, a man endowed with spectacular powers who obeyed her blindly. She'd done her research on the Hunninghams, which is why the fictional details in her book so neatly match reality.

"That's when fate intervened. From up in her observatory she witnessed an electrocution at Hammersmith Prison. But Miss Cruikshank had a genuine grounding in science, and she could tell that the professor who was carrying out the experiment was faking it! She knew the body taken to Dr. Brownless's laboratory after the execution was not a cadaver.

"Miss Cruikshank was gifted with a certain knack for bold, decisive action. A strange and almost monstrous plan sprang instantly into her mind. She'd recognized the condemned man as a murderer by the name of Baltimore Harmon—a daring, intelligent criminal. If she could recruit him, and persuade him by hypnosis that death had no power over him, she would have something close to a criminal superman at her command. Her 'Mysteras' had become flesh before her eyes. With her writer's imagination she could visualize him following her orders and carrying out old Cruikshank's sacred mission!

"She didn't hesitate. She left the tower and tailed the sinister convoy to Dr. Brownless's laboratory. I can picture her slipping into the room while the professor was trying to reanimate the executed man. A parenthesis: You might ask why the scientist was doing it. My answer would be, Brownless may have been an eminent man of science, but he was devoid of feeling or scruple. His dream had always been to carry out a vivisection—on a strong, healthy, intelligent man! And he'd now managed things so as to get the resurrected Harmon into his powerful clutches!

"Miss Cruikshank must've concluded the same thing, and she arrived ready to confront Brownless with threats. But now it was time to strike a deal. In spite of his scientific cruelty, she still thought the professor was a gentleman; she revealed her whole plan to him, and promised him a fortune. Brownless hesitated: he was aware of the wealth of the Cruikshanks, and knew that the price she offered was spectacular. He began to dream of bigger things.

"'And what about the treasures of Nepal?' he asked.

"'They'll be restored to the present rajah,' she replied firmly.

"What passed through the scientist's mind? Will we ever know? Visions of enormous wealth rose up in him. He agreed, and turned his attention to Harmon's body, and brought him back to life. The birth of Mysteras, you say? Not so fast..."

Harry Dickson fell silent, and looked at the sullen, mute figure, who seemed to be almost asleep in her chair.

"And then," went on the detective, "*Brownless killed Delphina Cruikshank!*"

Tom Wills cried out and stared at his employer as if he thought he'd gone mad. "But, Guv, Miss Cruikshank is right here in front of us!"

Miss Cruikshank eyed them calmly. "You're a remarkable man, Mr. Dickson. Would you ask your assistant to remove my handcuffs for a minute?"

Dickson hesitated briefly. "All right," he said finally.

Tom, not knowing what to think, obeyed mechanically.

Once her hands were free, Miss Cruikshank took off her aviator's helmet—and her wig came off too. One rub with her thumb changed the shape of her nose, and another wiped away a few lines of makeup.

"Dr. Brownless," said Dickson, "I hope you'll be a good sport, and accept defeat with dignity—when you were so close to victory."

"Dickson," said the professor after a painful moment of silence, "I have little to add to what you've already said. Still, one detail is missing, and I don't mind telling you about it. Miss Cruikshank indeed withheld nothing from me, about her wealth or about her life. She told me the secret of this tower, that is to say the secret elevator, and the underground passage that leads outside the estate, passing under the abandoned earthworks of the prison no man's land. She mentioned the fortune in cash hidden in this strongbox. And as she spoke I felt rising in me an awful resentment—that I'd been unable to form such an ingenious plan myself.

"Mysteras could become a source of prodigious power, especially for whoever pulled that criminal puppet's strings. As Miss Cruikshank talked, winning me over more and more to her plans, I saw her face reflected in a mirror, and was struck by a certain resemblance between us. At that moment she made the admission that doomed her. 'I owe you the truth, professor,' she said, 'since from now on our fates will be connected. I'll tell you the great secret of my existence…'"

Brownless stopped, and looked at the detective ironically. "Well, Dickson, I'll give you three guesses."

Dickson squinted, but through his almost closed lids his eyes sparkled. "Really? Well, professor, I'll take that challenge. Miss Cruikshank told you a secret—one that cost her her life. There's only one thing that could've done that, one secret that would've allowed you to kill her with impunity."

"And that is…" interrupted Tom, shivering with anticipation.

"The one that made it possible for you to leave behind her body, disguised as Dr. Brownless. For that to succeed, Miss Cruikshank had to have been a man!"

"You're a devil of a fellow!" cried the scientist. "You've got it! In fact, old Cruikshank had a son and not a daughter—or rather, to be perfectly precise, he had no child at all! The boy he adopted was none other than the son of the Maharajah of Nepal, who meant to kill him at birth because his astrologers had seen in the stars that the boy would grow up to murder his father. Cruikshank stole the child and, to allay all suspicion, he passed it off as a girl.

"When Delphina Cruikshank learned the secret of her (or rather his) birth, he had only one desire: to punish the treacherous enemies of his race—the Hunninghams!

"I'll go back now to the final scene, in the laboratory. I stepped behind Miss Cruikshank and dropped her dead with two pistol shots. With some acids and corrosive gases, I bleached her hair, which she kept short under her wig. I used hot iron to transform her face—and I make claim to be one of the finest surgeons in England. I managed to give her a certain resemblance to me. You should know that I live very much withdrawn, and few people see me ordinarily. I have no family. The subterfuge worked perfectly: they barely examined the body, the autopsy focused on the ballistics report, and no one wasted a moment worrying about the victim's face.

"Anyway, that done, I took care of Baltimore Harmon, who was alive but still only semiconscious. I left the house with him and went to Cruikshank Tower, where I took possession of the fortune hidden in the strongbox. I also ran across the manuscript of Miss Cruikshank's novel, of which you found a fragment, Dickson. Following a strange impulse, I decided to match my actions to those of the story. Ah, Dickson, if you hadn't intervened, and if I'd been able to live out that novel to the last page—what a wave of terror I would've unleashed on the entire world!

"In the story Mysteras turns out to be a consummate villain, but not quite the evil genius I'd hoped for. Basically he just dreams of murder: he loves killing people. On one of my nocturnal visits to Hunningham Hall, I had the bad luck to lose a large part of Delphina Cruikshank's manuscript, and that loss disconcerted me strangely, as if I'd lost my leader or an adviser."

"I found one page of it," murmured Tom.

Brownless fell silent.

"And then what?" asked Dickson.

"I think you know the rest as well as I do!"

"And the treasure of Nepal?"

"You'll find the famous shotgun in the underground passage beneath this tower. As for the rest of it, it didn't amount to as much as people thought. I imagine the Hunninghams must've depleted the hoard considerably. What we did find in the cellars of the manor—and it was certainly still a fine haul, of magnificent stones—we loaded onto the airplane. We flew to London, where we intended to hide the treasure along with the shotgun.

"But luck was against us. When we flew over the place in the suburbs we'd chosen as our landing strip, we could see a company of soldiers camped out on it. We had no time to lose—we had to get back to the house in Cornwall, and the night was far advanced."

"You had to finish off Tom Wills," interrupted Dickson, "because in his fever for riches your Mysteras had forgotten about Tom."

Brownless nodded with resignation. "What can you do? Crime is an endless awful spiral—one thing leads to another. The airplane I'd bought was a powerful machine to which I'd made a few improvements of my own. We flew back at top speed, without ever having landed. I especially enjoyed the welcome you put on for us over the Channel when we returned," the professor concluded with a wry smile.

"And the treasure?" repeated Dickson.

"The firing from the submarines had mortally injured my airplane. I crashed into the sea within sight of the French coast. The treasure is still inside my plane, a hundred and fifty fathoms down. I was picked up by a motorboat, which took me to Cherbourg, where I had the luck to catch a flight leaving for Croydon. Luck or rather bad luck, because I think that for me, Harry Dickson, you represent bad luck."

"And the Cruikshank fortune?" asked Tom.

"Come, I'll put it straight into your own hands," said the professor solemnly.

He went to the strongbox, followed by Tom.

"Stop!" cried Dickson.

Too late! With a quicker and stronger swing than would've seemed possible for such an old man, the scientist had sent Tom sprawling across the floor, and before Dickson could grab it the door of the strongbox slammed shut.

"Hoodwinked!" cried the detective.

The tower sang...

Two hours had passed before they located the underground passage. They found neither the Nepalese shotgun, nor the Cruikshank fortune, nor Dr. Brownless—the true Mysteras.

Would he ever be seen again?

Harry Dickson wouldn't say what he thought, but more than ever before he made ready for a great struggle. And for now the question was open only to speculation...

Harry Dickson

LE SHERLOCK HOLMES
AMERICAIN

No. 104 ■ ■   La Cour d'Epouvante.   ■ ■ Prix fr. 1.50

Tout à coup quelque chose changea à la cour d'épouvante ; Harry Dickson entrait en scène.

THE TRIBUNAL OF TERROR

1. Mr. Hamilton's Dreams

"My dear sir, your case calls for a doctor, or even a neurologist—but it's hardly worth the attention of a member of Scotland Yard. You should know that!"

The pompous tone, the grating high-pitched voice: Superintendent Goodfield, who could hear it from his office, groaned unhappily as he pushed away the file he'd just been looking through. "That's Baskett, preaching logic once again to some unlucky plaintiff. Dickson, you can't conceive the sheer stupidity of Baskett."

The great detective was paying a call on his friend Goodfield at Scotland Yard; he seemed well acquainted with Baskett's powers, and he began to laugh quietly.

Across the hall an unsatisfied voice said, "Very well, if that's how the official English police treat English citizens, I'll just have to apply to some private detective."

"Private! Private!" Baskett's harsh voice replied. "That's right, go this instant and consult the famous Harry Dickson, and maybe he'll interpret your dream, Mr. Hamilton. I hope he can—but members of the official police are not *fortunetellers*!"

A door slammed.

"This is how I drum up business," said Dickson, rising. "I'd like to have a word with that poor man who's just been shown the door."

"No need to trouble yourself, Dickson," Goodfield hastened to say. "I'll have the duty officer bring him here. I'm curious myself to hear what this Mr. Hamilton could've said to Baskett, who's really too high-handed."

A few moments later his office door opened and Hamilton was shown in. He was a lively, pleasant-looking old man; his rosy, healthy face was framed by a fine white beard. He might easily be taken for a retired professor with a good pension, living a life free of worry or care.

But as soon as he saw him the superintendent rose with a deferential manner. "I beg your pardon, Mr. Hamilton. Your name is shared by many gentlemen in the City, but I had no idea it was Mr. Frederick Hamilton of Rose Grange who was wrestling with the impossible Baskett. I owe you an apology, but I can offer you compensation."

Hamilton smiled and said he felt no resentment toward Baskett. Having come to the great metropolis in work boots, as they say, he'd risen—thanks to steady labor and a quick mind—to a great height. The Frederick Hamilton Iron and Steel Works were known around the world. Now in command of great wealth, which he devoted almost entirely to charity, Hamilton enjoyed the esteem of all London, and the love of the poor in particular.

"That compensation, sir," went on Goodfield, "is the introduction that it's my honor to make immediately: this is Mr. Harry Dickson."

Hamilton cut short his explanations with a wave, and turned eagerly toward the detective, who smiled at him.

"I've heard lots about you, Mr. Hamilton," said Dickson. "You're a gentleman who does credit to his country, and I'm very honored to meet you."

The old man shook his hand warmly and sat down in the chair the superintendent offered him. "I'm happy to meet you likewise, Mr. Dickson," he said in a clear, pleasant voice. "But I'll tell you straightaway that this encounter greatly serves my interests. May I tell you what brought me to Scotland Yard and led to my interview with that somewhat less than amiable fellow whose name I believe is Baskett?"

"I was about to ask you to do so, Mr. Hamilton, since that worthy official was so good as to refer you to my services," said Dickson.

"The walls have ears, at Scotland Yard even more than elsewhere," said Hamilton. "So kindly give me your attention, gentlemen, and perhaps you won't be so hard on me as that worthy Baskett."

"A plague take him!" muttered Goodfield.

"I've had a terrible dream!"

Goodfield started, and eyed Hamilton a little doubtfully, while Dickson remained impassive and looked off into the distance.

"I'd been brought before an assize court and charged with an extraordinary crime."

"Dreams are often crazier than that!" burst out Goodfield. "Why, just last night I was the guest—in a dream, of course—of an African king in the heart of the equatorial jungle!"

Hamilton shook his head gently. "If I may, it's not the same. As with anything else, I should begin at the beginning. A few days ago, let's say ten days to be exact, I had this bizarre dream for the very first time—note well, I say *for the very first time*. I found myself in an enormous white room, with a slightly vaulted ceiling, very much like a courtroom at the Old Bailey. I was being arraigned before a tribunal of eleven judges. Oddly, the chief magistrate and the ten associate judges of that strange court were dressed in black robes, but on their heads they wore white hoods of ermine fur.

"The chief magistrate was standing, and I could see his eyes shining under his white hood. 'Hamilton,' he said in a hollow voice, 'do you know before whom you appear today— or rather tonight?'

"I was more surprised than frightened, and I was mostly talking to myself when I answered, 'Since I went to bed at ten as usual, I assume that I'll wake up as usual in my bed, and that right now I'm having an odd dream, thanks to indigestion.'

"'Go ahead and assume you're dreaming,' replied the judge in that same cavernous voice, which was quite unpleasant to hear. 'But you stand now before the Tribunal of Terror, which rules by special exception over the actions of certain mortals. Do you know what you're accused of?'

"'How could I know?' I cried. 'I've never harmed anyone!'

"'Your whole life you've been exploiting pitiful, helpless humanity. Think it over!'

"Suddenly I was surrounded by darkness and silence… I woke in my bed in the morning, quite pleased that it had all been no more than a dream."

Goodfield was about to offer his thoughts, but Dickson forestalled him. "Let's hear your second dream, Mr. Hamilton."

The old man nodded firmly in agreement. "It happened three days later, Mr. Dickson, and took place in the same location. The judge asked if I'd thought it over.

"'Why would a dream make me think things over—and think about what?' I asked.

"Will you return the wealth of which you've unjustly despoiled the suffering world?'

"I shrugged. 'Only in dreams do you hear questions as stupid as that,' I said.

"'Think it over,' said the judge again, 'for you must appear before us again.'

"The scene vanished, and I awoke as I had the first time… but I felt a little tired, and in spite of myself I was thoughtful and afraid. I suspected it was some stubborn delusion caused by age and fatigue—because, though I'm retired, I still work hard. I decided to consult my physician. Dr. Dorgin is no great scientist, but since he's been treating me for years I trust his diagnoses. He didn't seem very alarmed by it all, and he prescribed a sedative."

"Which didn't keep you from having the third dream," said Dickson.

"Another one?" cried Goodfield.

"This time," said the old man with a shudder, "I appeared suddenly before the Tribunal of Terror, but I was no longer free: I was seated in a great chair of dark wood, with my hands locked in steel cuffs.

"'Have you thought it over, defendant Hamilton?' asked the judge.

"'Balderdash!' I cried. 'I don't believe in you, you're shadows, smoke, not even proper ghosts!'

"Then I noticed, up on the judge's bench, something white that looked like a stuffed ermine. The strange judge had followed my glance, and he petted the creature. 'This is Tulushka,' he said. 'She's going to bite you a little, to encourage you to think better thoughts.' As he said that, he gently squeezed the animal. At that same moment I felt my whole body shaking terribly.

"'Today Tulushka will be merciful, and will be satisfied with just two caresses like that,' said the judge, and a second blow, even more painful than the first, shook me.

"'Soon Tulushka will make her wishes known through my mouth,' the terrible hooded man went on. 'Here's her handshake goodbye.'

"I gave a long cry of agony, because the pain was unbearable, and all my limbs were still aching when I awoke in my bed. That horrible beast kept her word: the next night I awoke before the unmoving tribunal, bolted to my chair. The judge said not a thing, but just urged the beast at me. For a long while I twisted and turned on my torture chair, in the throes of the most awful agonies."

Harry Dickson raised his hand. "How does the judge want you to restore your wealth to the poor?"

Goodfield was astonished. "It sounds like you're talking about real people, not just phantom nobodies in a dream!"

"Superintendent, you make a good point," said Hamilton, "but I wouldn't be at Scotland Yard if I thought they were just phantoms. To answer your question, Mr. Dickson: the judge gave me rather curious instructions about it. I'm to convert three quarters of all my assets into dollars and pounds sterling, to put it all into a sack, to go to the seaside on the night of the new moon, and at midnight to throw the whole thing into the surf. He calls it returning to chance what I won by chance—which is a little different from what he said at first."

"Or else?" asked the detective.

"If I don't obey, I'll be condemned to death and executed the following night before the Tribunal of Terror gathered in high council."

"What does Dr. Dorgin think about all this?" asked Dickson.

"First he began asking me questions that would come more naturally from a policeman than from a doctor. He wanted to know if my bedroom door was locked or bolted; if nothing had been disturbed in my room; if I had retained any tangible marks from those strange nights. I almost got angry."

"And you'd have been wrong to," said the detective soberly. "His questions were in fact very sensible, and I find myself obliged to ask you the same questions again."

"Of course, Mr. Dickson. My bedroom is both locked and bolted. Nothing in my room has changed when I awake. I don't understand what's meant by tangible marks—it's genuinely a dream—but even so, crime can't be ruled out."

"Is that your opinion?"

Hamilton smiled and shook his head. "That's the opinion of an expert. When I gave Dr. Dorgin the answers I've just given you, he almost lost his head and said the case was beyond his competence. He referred me to the greatest neurologist in London, Professor Garfield-Borinsky, whom I saw as soon as I could. The specialist heard me out patiently, then took me into his laboratory and gave me his firm opinion: 'Hypnotic suggestion, more than likely with criminal intent. Have your intimates watched.' Upon which he dismissed me, because he's not a sociable man."

"If I'm not mistaken, sir," broke in Dickson, "you live year-round at your beautiful estate called Rose Grange, north of Harwich, set back from a very fine beach that's still quite private."

"The East Downs, indeed, Mr. Dickson."

The detective turned to Goodfield. "Didn't you tell me, my friend, that you were looking forward to a couple of weeks of rest in some quiet, charming spot?"

"Certainly. I was sorting my files when you came in, and tomorrow I plan to take the train to Folkestone."

"The East Downs are a better beach than that."

"What do you mean?"

"I was going to suggest to Mr. Hamilton that he invite us for a couple of days, you and me, to Rose Grange," said Dickson.

The old man clapped his hands like a delighted child. "Really? It's more than I dared hope for! Yes, if in fact some mysterious hypnotist is involved, you'd be the one to find it out, Mr. Dickson—especially if this excellent Mr. Goodfield is there to assist you," he added graciously.

"Done!" said the detective, and they shook hands all around.

2. The First Night at Rose Grange

Rose Grange was the most charming of estates. Built in the somewhat antiquated style affected by Englishmen of the old school, the house of gray stone stood amid lush greenery. Rose Grange wasn't a modern reproduction; it had its own history. Toward the end of the eighteenth century it had belonged to the gentry of these parts, the Dedlocks—aristocrats, but with a bad reputation.

It had been abandoned around 1830, and stood in ruins for almost a hundred years, when it became the property of a doctor from the village. It was from him that Mr. Hamilton had bought the place; and Hamilton had then carried out significant improvements to make the house what it was now: a quasi-princely home, though on a restrained scale.

We rejoin Harry Dickson, Superintendent Goodfield, and Mr. Hamilton just as they were wishing each other goodnight, after a splendid dinner, whose menu Goodfield, something of a gourmet, promised to remember.

The night was warm, and an odorous mist rose from the tired earth. Fields baked all day by the sun gave off an intense smell of vegetation, while a fresher tang of salt and damp seaweed blew in from the sea, whose slight phosphorescence was visible on the horizon.

Dickson felt not the least ready to sleep; drawn by the sweetness of the summery night, he lingered at his window. He could hear the last sounds of the servants in the house: dishes being stacked, doors being locked, tired footsteps. One by one the amber lights in the windows went out, leaving the gray mansion façade to blend into the surrounding night. From the next room he heard bedsprings squeak, followed by gentle snoring: Goodfield had already gone away to dreamland.

In the distance the crescent moon rose over a hedgerow, and silvery light struck a fine straight white road leading due north to the horizon. "It's like an invitation to go for a stroll," Dickson said to himself. He didn't hesitate for long before giving in to the night's temptation.

His window was the height of a man above the ground, and Dickson was perfectly willing to use the schoolboy's exit: he let himself drop quietly onto the soft earth of the garden. Scorning the gate—locked anyway—he crossed a low hedge in a single bound and found himself standing on that lovely white road.

With a light heart he began walking toward the horizon, against which he could see silhouetted the foliage of some woods or parkland. At that moment he wasn't thinking about being at the start of a case: he seemed to have forgotten he was a detective—as if he was on holiday without a care in the world. For a walker like Dickson, a mile in a straight line was quickly done, and the second mile took scarcely longer. "I'll turn back at the next mile marker," he said.

But man proposes...

He could already see the squat shape of the granite mile marker in the distance when he spotted a light shining slightly to his left, at the edge of the woods he'd noticed before. He considered it with a thoughtful eye. "It's a window," he concluded. "I didn't know we had neighbors this direction. Didn't Hamilton say that the countryside is fairly empty to the north, and that you have to go through the woods before you reach the first farms? The village Rose Grange officially belongs to lies to the south. Let's find out what kind of neighbors these are."

After shining for a few minutes, the light went out and didn't come back on. But Dickson had noted its direction and went toward it without hesitating. He had to angle off the road to the left and make a diagonal across a large fallow field, where he struggled through nettles and tall weeds to reach the edge of the woods.

There all was quiet and dark; the branches of the trees murmured gently in the breeze off the sea. Only a couple a glow worms shone in the thickets. "Well, it wasn't them producing a light that bright," he chuckled. Then, still keeping to the right course, he pushed straight on through the underbrush.

After scratching his hands considerably on brambles and wild rose thorns, he reached a kind of path that, for lack of better, could be called a trail. He followed it, and soon came to a small hillock of soft earth. "I see," he murmured. "To be visible from the road, the light must've shone from the top of this hillock, otherwise the dense underbrush would've masked it as effectively as a wall. Let's have a look."

Under the arching boughs of ancient oaks and copper beeches it was quite dark; not one ray of the crescent moon on the horizon found its way in. As he climbed the hill Dickson kept tripping over rubble and masonry, as if there were ruins nearby. Indeed there were: above the crumbling walls of a chapel rose the remains of a small bell tower.

Using his pocket flashlight, the detective found a door hanging off its hinges that swung open at the first push and led to a small nave ending in a kind of altar dominated by a single crucifix. The damp air inside this abandoned sanctuary smelled of mildew. A frightened moth flew down from the rafters and circled the electric light.

A rusty iron hoop hung in front of the altar, with the stub of a candle stuck into it. Dickson touched the candle wax: still warm and soft, and a few drips had stuck to the stone floor tiles. Someone had been here, without a doubt.

"Some lingering worshiper," he thought, "or some nocturnal pilgrim fulfilling a vow... Ah! How about that!" he exclaimed out loud.

Against the front of the altar was propped a sign made of white cardboard, on which a few lines were hastily scrawled in charcoal: *Forget that crook Hamilton—go protect Tom Wills!*

Tom Wills! What was his beloved assistant's name doing here?

The threat wasn't even veiled: either Harry Dickson would drop the Hamilton case, or some unknown criminal would lash out at Tom Wills. The detective was filled with intense anxiety. He'd left Tom in London, though he'd meant to bring him along; but Tom had been ill, and the night before his employer left he'd taken a turn for the worse. Not that he was in danger: his doctor had diagnosed a mild case of flu— but one that could become serious if it went untreated. So Tom was in London, far from his employer's protection, and sick, and therefore shorn of his usual means of defense.

What to do? Around that lonely chapel lay the forest and the night. Dickson would've lost precious time searching the impenetrable thickets. He resolved to go straight back and confer with Goodfield. Without losing a moment he retraced his route, plunging through the underbrush with the thrashing movements of a swimmer.

When he reached the road he saw lights—lights shining at Rose Grange, from three windows, while a powerful acetylene lamp glowed at the gate. He began to run. As he approached Hamilton's mansion he could see that the acetylene lamp belonged to a bicycle leaning against the gate. Shadows moved around the garden.

His footsteps must've been heard, because Goodfield's loud voice came booming out of the night. "Ho there, Dickson! Is that you?"

"Present!"

"Come quick. There's a telegram from London addressed to you."

As if they had wings, Dickson's feet barely touched the tarred road, so fast did he run. He sensed doom circling...

"Well, quick, let's have it!" he panted as he raced to join Goodfield, Hamilton in pajamas, and a telegraph courier.

"I opened the telegram, Dickson," began the superintendent. "It's from Mrs. Crown."

Barely letting him finish, Dickson tore the telegraph form from his hands and held it in the beam of the bicycle lamp. *"Tom's condition very serious. Come immediately. Edith Crown,"* he read in a low voice.

He put the telegram in his pocket and turned to Hamilton. "You have a telephone, I believe."

"Indeed, but after nine o'clock we have no service. The telephone office closes after the last train, and the telegraph office an hour later."

"May I used your car, Mr. Hamilton?"

"Of course! It's a brand-new Pontiac. Right now, with the roads empty, it'll get you to London in an hour."

Dickson said not another word during the few minutes it took to get the car ready at the gate. As he got behind the wheel he beckoned to Goodfield. "I'd like you not to go back to sleep, but to keep watch over Mr. Hamilton."

"What do you fear, Mr. Dickson?" asked the old industrialist.

"Everything and nothing! But I'd like Goodfield to keep watch, not in his room but in yours, sir! Play checkers—Goodfield can beat you like nobody's business!"

Dickson was already stepping on the accelerator with an impatient foot, and the powerful vehicle shot like a bullet down the white road.

The new road from Harwich to London didn't turn aside for any of the seaside resorts along the coast, but resolutely cut across the great sandy flats of Essex. Dickson would therefore only have lost precious time if he'd tried to reach a spot from which he could call London: he preferred to rely entirely on himself and the speed of his car—which served him well, because the speedometer showed that he was exceeding a hundred kilometers an hour... and then it reached a hundred and twenty! The road raced by under the wheels like a conveyor belt. Lights emerged out of the night and then vanished. Soon a reddish glow appeared due south: he was nearing London.

He met no delay getting through the shabby streets of the dockside districts. Along the great downtown avenues the tall arced streetlights seemed to rush forward to meet him: Hyde Park... silent Marylebone... Baker Street...

He raised anxious eyes to the well-known windows of his home: they were dark, all seemed quiet. He muttered a curse—because the idea of a trick had suddenly occurred to him.

"Well, Mrs. Crown, what's the meaning of your telegram?" he asked his worthy housekeeper when, in answer to the bell, she'd opened the door, her eyes full of sleep and her nightcap askew.

"A telegram! Sweet Jesus! I who don't even send postcards to me own family!" cried the good woman.

"Tricked!" muttered Dickson. "But let's see how Tom is."

He found the young man already awakened by the loud doorbell, looking bright-eyed and well rested.

"So, my boy, you're not doing too badly after all?" Dickson asked after he'd summed up the telegram trick for his assistant.

"The medicine the doctor gave me has put me back on my feet, Guv," replied Tom, "and I'm all ready to go with you."

"What do you mean, Tom?"

"It's simple, Guv. They've tried to get you away from Rose Grange, at least for a few hours, while some mysterious X got the elbow room he wanted at Mr. Hamilton's house. It's true that our friend Goodfield's there... but honestly, just between us, do you really think he'll be much help to the man you're trying to protect?"

Dickson pinched his assistant's ear. "Well said, my boy, and since I believe your fever's broken completely, I have nothing against your coming with me. Off we go!"

"If you come back again tonight, I won't open the door a second time!" cried Mrs. Crown, furious at seeing her employers staying out all night. "You can sleep at a hotel or under a bridge, for all I care!"

The Pontiac made a U-turn, and a half hour later was back on the white road along the coast.

"I'll have been gone about three hours," murmured Dickson. "Lots can happen in three hours!"

In the distance, the triple-blink beam of a lighthouse pierced the night with its fiery eye.

"We're almost there," said Dickson, stepping on the gas.

Bang! Bang! The car swerved—and only the driver's quick thinking saved them from a crash.

"Both front ties blew out!" roared Dickson. "Hell and damn, what are we driving on here?" He'd gotten out, and was sadly considering the broken bottles littering the road.

At that moment shadows burst out of the roadside brush, two sacks were skillfully flung over their heads, and both detectives were thrown to the ground. Quick hands used strong ropes of hemp and leather to render the two men helpless.

3. The Second Half of the Night at Rose Grange

"You're not paying attention, Mr. Hamilton. As a result, I'm taking your man… and now king me! If you're not careful I'll wipe the floor with you inside ten minutes!"

Goodfield was triumphant. He'd moved into Hamilton's room with everything he needed for a cozy vigil: a bottle of aged whisky, some new Holland pipes, and a large pouch of Belgian tobacco. "I don't like the English blend," he explained to his host. "But how about the phenomenal Semois tobacco grown by the great Martial Denis! Just smell that aroma!"

Hamilton nodded and smiled. He moved a piece on the checkerboard, which was tiled in black and white like a Flemish kitchen.

"I hope nothing serious has happened to young Tom Wills," went on the good Scotland Yard superintendent. "It deprives us of Dickson's company tonight—but at least I'm here!"

The old man nodded again.

"Just get a whiff of this tobacco," said Goodfield once more.

His host obeyed, and breathed in the aromatic cloud. "Excellent, indeed. That hint of lemon verbena is especially pleasant—I'd even call it surprising."

"Semois tobacco doesn't smell like lemon verbena," said the superintendent, almost offended. "I assume it's the cologne you use that's giving off that smell."

"I don't think so. Here, put your pipe down for a moment and smell for yourself."

Goodfield set down his long white clay pipe and breathed in. "But… you're right. Oh, Mr. Hamilton—what a bewitching odor!"

"It goes straight to your head, doesn't it?" Hamilton pressed his hands to his temples.

"I'll open a window," said Goodfield. "The air in this room seems oddly thick, and I wouldn't like to hear anyone blame good old Semois tobacco…"

He rose, but immediately had to sit back down and grip the arms of his chair. His pipe fell to the floor and snapped.

"This… isn't… natural…" stammered the superintendent. "My head… is… spinning… Ho there… Mr. Hamilton… we mustn't… allow…" His head dropped onto his chest.

Hamilton, meanwhile, was slumped motionless in his chair, his eyes fixed on the pink candles in their silver candlesticks; candles whose flames seemed to get smaller and smaller.

"Are you dreaming, Mr. Hamilton?"

"And you, Mr. Goodfield?"

"I believe so—but everything around us seems so real!"

"That's how I feel, and yet logic tells me we're dreaming. But I think I've got the answer."

"I wouldn't speak of it here."

"Why not, Mr. Hamilton? We're speaking in our dream. Soon we'll wake up and go on with our checkers game. But first I'm going to carry out a little investigation into the use of lemon verbena as a perfume!"

"What do you mean?"

"That someone has played at releasing some narcotic gas in your room, a gas which has the property of inducing certain dreams, and almost always the same dream."

"Say, that's more or less what Dr. Garfield-Borinsky told me."

"If Harry Dickson were here, he'd say it wasn't the first time he was the victim of a drug like that... Hullo there—you, say something!"

Goodfield was addressing one of the people dressed in dark robes with collars and hoods of ermine who faced them across a great high courtroom bench. But not one of them moved; only a terribly frightening light glowed behind the openings in the hoods.

"So this is the Tribunal of Terror before which you appear in your dream, sir," said Goodfield. "I'm awfully happy to have come here myself."

They were both seated in dark wood chairs, with their wrists and ankles bound in steel cuffs.

"I seem to remember those sweethearts as being more talkative," went on Goodfield.

"Up to now the chief magistrate has done all the talking—the one who's standing."

"Well, he's certainly quiet tonight. But, like the song says, 'Everything's allowed when we dream,'" chuckled the superintendent.[2]

"Yes," whispered Hamilton.

"Still, tomorrow I'll get my hands on whoever's playing at releasing smells like that in people's bedrooms, and ruining the odor of good Semois tobacco. It's a disgrace."

Only the flames of the candles attached to the rear wall gave any sign of life in this peculiar courtroom.

"I'd sure like to be able to move," went on Goodfield, "My legs are all pins and needles. Ah, whatever rascal has dared play this practical joke on an official of Scotland Yard, working in His Majesty's service, I'll make him sorry he did it! Hmm… Now they seem to be tapering off their damned perfume."

Hamilton's head bobbed.

The candle flames shrank till they were very small, and suddenly the Tribunal of Terror and its peculiar phantoms vanished into the darkness.

"You're not very well going to beat me at checkers if you're asleep, Mr. Hamilton!" said Goodfield sarcastically.

Hamilton sat up and rubbed his eyes. They were seated in his bedroom, facing the checkerboard and their half-empty glasses of whisky.

"But we… were… dreaming…" cried Hamilton.

Goodfield nodded happily. "That's what I was telling you a little while ago in front of that silent Tribunal."

"But I remember everything you said to me! How's that possible in a dream?" cried Hamilton.

The superintendent shrugged. "That's not my problem. We were both drugged, and it's up to the experts to figure out how these peculiar effects were produced. I expect this complicated joke will wind up with a proper rash of arrests tomor-

---

[2] "Tout est permis quand on rêve," with lyrics by Tino Rossi, from the film *Le chemin du paradis* (1930).

row, Mr. Hamilton. If you agree, we'll even make the rounds of the house ourselves, and if we need to we'll wake your excellent servants from their beauty sleep."

Hamilton shook his head doubtfully. "They're good people who've served me for years, as honest and down-to-earth and guileless as goats."

"Oh, come now," began Goodfield, looking around the room—but then his gaze stopped on certain objects. "Mr. Hamilton," he said, "you're more widely read than I am. Can you tell me how long a dream is thought to last?"

"I believe it's rarely longer than a minute, even if you've gone around the world in that time. The experts agree that our minds work remarkably fast when we dream."

"Well, then!" replied Goodfield. "For once, I can't agree with the experts."

"Why?"

But in answer the superintendent only shook his head. "That's Harry Dickson's domain. I believe I'll have something of the greatest importance to tell him when he gets back."

4. Waking from the Nightmare

Tom Wills could feel that the sack wasn't tight around his neck, and he began to turn his head slowly. The folds of the improvised hood loosened; then the cloth slipped, first slowly and then quickly; and then the young man poked his head out and breathed freely.

He was stretched out on the floor in a room filled with strange dark shapes. A lantern set on the floor burned smokily in one corner. Next to him lay a body he recognized.

"Guv! Guv!" murmured Tom.

A muffled mumble came in reply; the sack over Harry Dickson's head was much more securely tied. But Tom had been trained in many skills. Though he was still tightly bound, he began to move by rolling from side to side. Soon he bumped into his employer. In one quick move he seized the tip

76

of the hood in his teeth and began to pull. The cloth gave way, and a few minutes later Dickson's head was free.

The detective breathed gratefully. "If only we could get our hands free too, my boy," he murmured very quietly, "we could begin to take steps."

Tom looked all around—but then he gasped in fear. "Oh, Guv! It's horrible! Look what's around us!"

Dickson sat up a little, and shuddered in horror just like his assistant. A hideous figure stared at him out of the shadows with cruel eyes. A black mouth full of repulsive broken teeth gaped at him in a silent laugh.

The detective closed his eyes, thinking he was having a nightmare. He recognized that demonic face: it was Liverpool Bill, the killer of women—whom he himself had caught and seen die by the executioner's hand on the scaffold at Newgate.

"Guv," begged Tom, "where are we? Look to your right!"

Dickson promptly did so. A trunk stood there, one of those dark wood chests popular with chambermaids and valets. It was plastered with stickers of all colors, the mark of countless railway journeys. The lid hung open, its hinges torn loose: and projecting over the sticky edge of the trunk were unspeakable things: two bony legs covered in thick blood, a cadaverous hand with knotted veins, its flesh horribly hacked apart.

"God almighty!" moaned Dickson, making a desperate effort. Though the rope cut badly into his wrist, he ignored the pain and broke one of his bonds. Then he feverishly undid the rest of the ropes that held him. Free! Before even thinking of freeing Tom, he threw himself at the horrible sights—hoping they'd dissolve into smoke like visions in a nightmare.

But the visions persisted, and remained solid, and as Dickson reached out for them he felt a terrible chill. And yet he burst out laughing. "Good God, Tom! We're at some imitation Madame Tussaud's! We've been locked up in the chamber of horrors of some wax museum!"

"Before we tour the exhibits, Guv, could you get me out of these ridiculous ropes?" sighed Tom, feeling like an enormous weight had been lifted off his chest.

"Fair enough, my boy," said Dickson, promptly doing as he asked.

Tom stretched his aching limbs, while his employer picked up the lantern and raised it over his head to survey his surroundings. Other grotesque, hideous wax manikins grimaced in the dim lamplight, but neither Dickson nor Tom paid them any attention. They approached a gray wall partition that seemed to be moving slightly in the dark.

"As I suspected," murmured the detective, rubbing rough fabric between his fingers. "We're in a traveling circus. As prisons go, it's not the most secure."

"Hmm—have a look at that character, Guv." Tom pointed to a slumped figure dressed in rags, its dangling head resting on a pile of coiled rope. "I think that's the vilest specimen in the whole collection!"

Dickson glanced at it absently, but then he grabbed Tom by the hand and drew him back. "Look out, my boy! Vile he may be, but he's still more dangerous than the rest—because this one's still alive!"

Indeed, the man's chest rose and fell with the regular rhythm of deep sleep. He was old, and shabbily dressed. His enormous head seemed mismatched with his scrawny neck, like a pumpkin on a slender stem.

"Handcuffs?" asked Tom briefly.

"And gag!" said his employer.

By the time the sleeper opened his dull eyes he'd already been rendered harmless: the same ropes that had bound the two detectives now left him powerless to struggle. In fact he did nothing, and only moaned quietly behind the gag that covered his mouth.

"I have to say, the poor devil doesn't seem so wicked," observed Tom.

"He has rather the air of an idiot," agreed Dickson. "But wait, once we've figured out where we are we can come back to him."

A flap of the canvas shook in the night breeze; the detective raised it and found himself outdoors. In the distance he could see the few lights of a sleeping village. Turning, he examined the shabby tent that had served as their prison. It was a low structure, without a platform. A sign hung over the raised entrance flap: *The Manzoni Show*. Nearby, a single circus trailer stood silhouetted against the night, while an emaciated horse tethered to a stake tried to crop the sparse dry grass.

Dickson set the lantern down inside the tent; then, revolver in hand, he approached the wagon. All was quiet inside. even so, he moved carefully, and switched on his flashlight only at the moment he pushed open the dilapidated trailer door. The interior was shabby, wretched, and empty. As he stepped inside, something crunched under his foot: a big lump of charcoal. Nearby lay a piece of white cardboard.

"All right," he chuckled. "Here's the sign maker's shop where they wrote the message I found in the chapel."

He went back to find Tom. "What peculiar kidnappers, my boy," he observed, "who leave us our weapons and our money."

"My theory is, they were in too much of a hurry to take them," offered the young man. "They had more pressing business to attend to!"

"I think so too. Now we have to find out what their more urgent business was!"

"Speaking of THEM, we're talking as if we know them," said Tom, giving his employer a sidelong glance.

Dickson just smiled. Then he went quickly back into the tent where they'd left their prisoner.

"Remove his gag, Tom. There's no one around to hear him even if he cries for help. I assume his bosses thought of him as the most expendable of their people."

In spite of gag and handcuffs, the prisoner had gone back into a deep sleep, and they had to shake him hard to rouse him.

"Brandy!" was his first word when he'd recovered his wits.

"Sorry, but we're a little far from the cellar," joked Tom.

The man seemed to understand, and he nodded. "Shilling to buy brandy," he requested.

"Aha! Can we strike a bargain?" laughed Dickson. "The poor bugger doesn't seem dangerous. He's just a cretin, a simpleton... but we might still get something out of him."

He made a brand-new shilling coin shine in the lamp-light.

"Pretty shilling!" cried the idiot. "One, two... hundred tots of brandy for pretty shilling! Oho! Must give pretty shilling to Scrubby, Guv'nor!"

Dickson slowly shook his head no, which seemed to make the poor wretch desperate, and he begged even more. "Scrubby show Guv'nor very funny men. But nasty man come and steal handsome red man, and handsome men who all of a sudden get very big."

"He's talking about the wax manikins," said Tom.

Fearing he wouldn't get his shilling, Scrubby wrung his hands. "Not Scrubby's fault if nasty man gave Scrubby's master many shillings to steal handsome red man and men who get very big!"

Losing hope that he'd learn anything from the idiot, Dickson gave him the shilling.

Scrubby went into raptures of gratitude. "Show Guv'nor pretty picture of handsome red man and other handsome men."

He took the lantern from Dickson's hand and led him to the trunk of severed limbs. Disdainfully tossing aside the wax legs and the painted wooden skeletons, he came to a pile of random papers, from which he pulled out a faded lithograph reading: *Star Attraction of the Manzoni Show—The Secret Tribunal.*

Dickson had trouble stifling an exclamation: pictured on the poster were twelve judges in black robes and ermine hoods, seated at a high courtroom bench, while an executioner dressed all in red stood before a chopping block with his ax ready.

The detective's expression of intense interest made Scrubby cackle with glee. "One more pretty shilling, all new!" he begged.

"You'll get five, Scrubby, a whole handful, if you answer my questions properly. What's that?"

Scrubby took Dickson by the hand and showed him a piece of stage scenery: painted canvas that could look like a judge's bench.

"And the men?" asked Dickson, pointing to the hooded judges.

"Very little, very little, then all of a sudden—poof!—very big! But they gone with nasty man." Then he pointed to the executioner. "But this one big handsome man!"

Dickson was thinking, and he only smiled at Tom, who was grumbling that this was all gibberish.

"Ask him instead how we got here!" said Tom.

"That's of little importance," said his employer, "but I'll make you happy." He repeated the question.

"Eat! Drink!" came the answer. "With master and nasty man. Then they big hurry to go, tell me watch you, else very angry and lots of kicks for poor Scrubby."

Dickson gave the poor man a few more coins, and he crowed with delight.

"We're going to have to step on it, Tom," said the detective. "I think everything's coming to a head, and the case of the Tribunal of Terror is going to be solved a lot sooner than we expected. As it often is, my boy, the whole thing was quite simple—you just had to think of it."

"Simple?" cried Tom. "I've understood nothing, Guv—and that too is how it often is!" he added bitterly.

"Listen, my boy, I'll just say this: we're looking at a criminal scheme that was fairly crudely and hastily thrown together, but that could've worked. It leads me to think the author of the plan must be so arrogant that he assumes anything he tries will succeed. Our arrival on the scene at the last moment must've seemed like quite a stick in his spokes, but he got us out of the way by very traditional means, even too traditional. He didn't kill us, because he must've considered two murders unnecessary, and also because he's not afraid of us—another piece of sheer arrogance."

He was still speaking when Tom pinched his arm. "A police whistle!"

Dickson listened, and agreed. Three blasts of a whistle with a particular tone rang out far down the road.

"A London police whistle, Guv. What's that doing way out here?"

"Have you forgotten Goodfield, my boy?" asked Dickson, rushing out of the tent.

The whistle sounded again, closer this time.

"A bobby in uniform, Guv!" cried Tom, and he pointed to a figure striding rapidly away along the paved road that led to Rose Grange.

"Goodfield!"

"Thank God!" cried the superintendent, retracing his steps and hurrying to his two friends. "Make it quick—I've think I've got the culprit!"

"Bravo, Goodfield," replied Dickson. "But I have to tell you that I think I know who it is."

"Sure!" laughed Goodfield. "We'll see about that!... But let me tell you quickly what's happened to me, and meanwhile let's hurry, if we want to save poor Mr. Hamilton from appearing once more before that damned Tribunal of Terror."

In a few minutes the detectives had been brought up to date on Goodfield's nocturnal adventures. When he was done he added slyly, "And now I'll share an observation that may seem trivial on the surface, but that was enough to give me the clue: while we were supposedly being arraigned before the Tribunal of Terror, the candles in Mr. Hamilton's bedroom burned down an inch and a half!"

"Bravo!" cried Dickson, shaking his hand. "You've in fact discovered the same thing I found out from another angle—though the greater glory falls to you, Goodfield. You solved it by deduction, which is to say by means of intelligence, whereas I owe a great deal to luck. You've just kinged your man and I want to acknowledge it."

Goodfield swelled with pride. "And since I'm about to carry out an arrest, I thought I'd put on my dress uniform. As you know," he added, "I rarely go anywhere without it."

Dickson smiled at the good man's vanity, but even so he pushed the pace toward the mansion whose dark shape rose up in the distance.

5. A Peculiar "Secret Tribunal"

Harry Dickson carefully considered the façade of the sleeping house. "Where exactly is Hamilton's room?" he asked Goodfield.

"The three windows looking east."

"Perfect. There are no lights on. And what are those other rooms, whose windows we can see toward the left?"

"A little science museum, if I'm not mistaken, which Hamilton has neglected for years, because he's given up his natural history hobby. The last window is that of a photographic darkroom, also abandoned by the owner of Rose Grange."

"All right! The windows are of smoked glass, but over time it's worn off a little, so we can see there's a little light on in that room," said Dickson.

"Say, that's true!" exclaimed Tom and Goodfield. "What can it mean?"

"That the Tribunal of Terror has met for one last session—the one we're going to put a permanent stop to."

Dickson gave careful instructions: Tom would stay outside, with the task of stopping anyone trying to leave or approach the house. Goodfield and Dickson would go inside and head straight to the darkroom.

No sooner said than done. They climbed the grand oak stairs on tiptoe and stopped at the darkroom door. It wasn't completely closed, and a thread of light could be seen around the door frame. Someone was there…

Hamilton stretched his aching limbs and rubbed his eyes. The apparition was there, just like on other nights. The hooded judges watched him with their glittering fixed stare. The chief magistrate stood unmoving, with his hand raised, speaking in a dark, menacing voice.

"Look behind you, Hamilton!"

The old man turned.

The scene had changed, or rather grown: on a table sat an open coffin, and on the floor lay the lid, with the hammer and nails needed to seal it. Hamilton shuddered. Next to those sinister objects stood a terrible figure: a tall man, dressed all in red, with a scarlet mask over his face. His red-gloved hands rested on a large broadsword. Hamilton recognized him as the typical executioner, familiar from old pictures.

The judge's voice went on, "Your last hour has come. Your head will roll!"

"I don't believe in you!" cried Hamilton. "I'm dreaming!"

"In that case," cackled the judge, "tell us where you hide the key to your strongbox, and what the combination is."

"Never!" cried Hamilton. "This may be nothing but hypnotic suggestion, but it's still criminal, and I won't say a word!"

"Well, then…" began the judge. Then the voice stopped, and a great silence fell.

With more surprise than fear, Hamilton observed the unmoving figures. But now he could hear a noise in the distance, the muffled sound of a struggle, and then footsteps approaching. And then Hamilton—who was waiting to hear his death sentence—opened his eyes wide in astonishment.

Something new was happening at the Tribunal of Terror: Harry Dickson had made an entrance! In front of him he was pushing a man dressed in old-fashioned formalwear, shiny from use at the seams, like a typical street tout. Behind them followed Goodfield, triumphant in his policeman's uniform.

"The show's over!" cried Dickson. "We'll have a good laugh, Mr. Hamilton!"

"As for the rest of you, nobody move!" thundered Goodfield, drawing his revolver and leveling it at the judges. "The first one who moves is a dead man!"

Dickson burst out laughing. "Put away your pistol, Goodfield, and put the cuffs on Signor Manzoni here. I'll take care of the rest of them—a tiepin should do it."

Strange to say, neither the chief magistrate nor any of his associate judges had moved. Dickson pulled out his tiepin and handed it to Hamilton. "Prick that awful judge—he well deserves it!"

The old man obediently took the pin and pricked the chief magistrate's hood. Bang! A sigh... and then no more magistrate!

"Now the others!" cried the detective, laughing harder and harder.

Bang! Bang! Bang! Ten bangs—and the Tribunal of Terror was no more.

"Little men who suddenly grow big!" said Dickson. "Balloon men, right, Signor Manzoni? I'm awfully sorry to have ruined one of the top attractions of your show."

"Now prick that fellow in red," chuckled Goodfield. "He's lasted long enough."

"Hmm," said Dickson. "That one's a little more durable, I think, because he's made of pure wax."

"Let's have a look!" Goodfield laughed as he approached the figure.

But Manzoni shrank back in fear. "No, no, don't touch it!"

"Trickster!" Goodfield slapped the showman on the back. "Ah, my man, you wanted to put one over on the officers of Scotland Yard! But you're not clever enough! All Goodfield needed was to notice that the candles had burned down too far during the so-called nightmare, to know that it wasn't a dream but a completely real scene, staged with care. A soporific gas—and an excellent one, whose effects wore off when you wanted them to—did the rest. You just had to carry Mr. Hamilton into the next room, where in seconds you could set up a tribunal with inflated balloon men, while you provided their voices from the darkroom."

"It wasn't me," moaned the prisoner.

"So who was it, then—him?" laughed Goodfield, pointing to the motionless executioner. "We'll see!"

"Get down!" shouted Dickson, violently tackling Hamilton and Goodfield and pulling them to the floor.

There was a blinding flash of light and a peal of thunder. A blast of fiery air blew out the candles. Then they heard a long cry of agony.

"Mr. Hamilton? Goodfield?" cried the detective, half rising.

"Here!" replied both men together.

"Thank God—my flashlight's broken."

"Mine still works," said Goodfield, switching his on.

A scene of devastation met their eyes. The room was full of debris. Canvas frames gave off a terrible scorched smell as they burned. The man in red had vanished; but Manzoni lay on the floor, his skull smashed, dead…

"A hand grenade!" explained Dickson soberly. "And no doubt the chief architect of this criminal scheme has fled the scene by now."

"What about Tom?" asked Goodfield.

The frightened Rose Grange servants were already gathering, brandishing a variety of weapons. Tom could be heard shouting outside.

"Not so loud, my boy." His employer leaned out one of the windows broken by the explosion. "Did you see anyone go by after the blast?"

"Nobody, Guv!"

"All right, Goodfield, let's search the house," said Dickson. "The bandit might not have gone far."

An hour later, they'd been through the whole house and found nothing. Dickson growled angrily: in the ruins of the Tribunal of Terror he'd come upon the fragments of a black wood chair—*one he recognized.*

"Goodfield! Don't assume this case is closed, my friend, because this awful chair has just taught me otherwise. We have to find the man in red! We have to!"

"But he can't have left!" cried Tom. "Look, the sun's rising, you can see the whole valley, and this house has an uninterrupted view. Anyone who managed to get away would've been visible for quite a while, and I haven't left my post!"

Dickson turned to Hamilton. "I believe Rose Grange was built on the ruins of an old house with a bad reputation. Do you know of any secret passages, Mr. Hamilton?"

The old man considered. "Not really, but there were rumors, which is why I had the old cellars walled up."

"Let's go!" said Dickson urgently.

Hamilton led them down to a heavy wall of brick, stained with age. "You can see it's solid," he said.

"Really? You think?" chuckled the detective, and he threw his weight against it.

A few bricks fell out, revealing an opening big enough for a man to get through.

"What a cool customer!" he said with admiration. "He had the patience to put the bricks back in place from the other side!"

The tunnel was dry and easy to travel. It led straight north. After fifteen minutes' walk they felt a fresh breeze on the faces, and emerged into the open air in the middle of a dense clump of brambles and nettles.

"Hell, I recognize this place!" cried Dickson. "We were here last night!"

Before them, only a few yards away, stood the tent of the waxworks show.

"Scrubby!" called the detective.

No answer. In a few strides he reached the tent and opened the flap... To the many artificial horrors, another had been added: poor Scrubby, whose throat had been cut by a criminal hand!

"Now what?" said Goodfield, once they'd notified the village authorities and completed the usual formalities.

"London!" answered Dickson laconically.

"I had a feeling you recognized the perpetrator, no?" pressed Goodfield.

"Yes. When we caught Manzoni I thought we had him, but he was just an accessory, not especially wicked. Whereas the other man... I knew him by his damned electric chair—you know, the one that doesn't kill you! Details about the way it was built stuck in my mind, since it was a fairly recent case."

"But..." whispered Goodfield. "If I understand you right..."

"Yes, indeed, my friend, we've been dealing with Mysteras! None other! The monster is back among us!"

6. A Declaration of War

So Dr. Mysteras had returned. Harry Dickson admitted that, though he'd always expected this resurrection, he'd thought it would happen on the far side of the world—not at the threshold of London. Mysteras... Once more he was using peculiar methods, borrowed from some unhinged novel—the very kind to frustrate routine inquiries. Dickson couldn't let them influence him; he began his investigation with his usual methodical logic.

He studied Hamilton's circle of acquaintance, but found less than nothing: Hamilton had made no new connections, and his servants, who'd been with him for many years, were above suspicion. Dickson paused for a while over Dr. Dorgin, but that good man had practiced medicine in the same village for over thirty years, while Mysteras had burst onto the criminal scene barely a year before! As always, the bandit Dr. Mysteras had acted almost alone, with a minimum of accomplices, believing himself to be a criminal genius, with total faith in his lucky star.

A week hadn't gone by before Dickson received a letter. He wasn't surprised, and had almost been expecting it.

Mr. Dickson,

Once again you've cost me dearly. To think, I was so near to getting my hands on a large part of the millions of that old thief, Hamilton. I know your methods a little by now: if you can't stop your victims, you spoil their arrangements and thwart their plans. You make life literally impossible for them. It's not going to work with me.

I'll tell you what I've decided: before I begin a new project, I'm going to get you out of my way.

This is not an ultimatum. I'm not making any conditions. It's a declaration of war, to the death. The vast globe isn't big enough for the both of us. That was said in the past by two of your greatest victims: Dr. Flax and the beautiful Georgette Cuvelier. I say it again now—but the difference is that this time the loser in the struggle will be Harry Dickson and not Mysteras.

I have a tremendous advantage over you: I always know where to find you, whereas I'm harder for you to put your hands on than smoke.

Farewell, Harry Dickson. I don't yet know whether I'll strike secretly in the shadows or openly in bright daylight. It all depends on my creativity—without which I'd find life awfully dull.

—Mysteras.

The detective set the letter down thoughtfully. It was a critical time. He knew his adversary meant what he said.

Tom Wills read the letter in turn. "We need to think about defending ourselves, not going on the attack," he murmured.

Dickson gestured vaguely; he felt a little thrown off course. "Mysteras is a supremely skillful creature. He has this advantage over other major criminals: he works alone or nearly so—the accomplices he uses are nobodies, puppets he gets rid of whenever he pleases, as witness the poor devils in the Manzoni Show. Where is he? The proverbial needle in a haystack… But for us, things are different: we live in the open, we move around in broad daylight, while he can spy on us from the shadows. It's a doomed game in which we really have only one chance."

"Which is?"

"I'm going to stake my faith on his own words, my boy: his creativity! I want to believe that he'll listen to that seductive voice, which will always be working on our side, buying us time, putting us more than ever on our guard."

"Myself, Guv, I'd rather play the same trick as always, since it rarely fails. Let's leave town, or at least look like we're leaving."

His employer cut him off with a wave. "Pointless! Mysteras must know that gag. He must even be expecting it, and no doubt he's positioned his artillery accordingly. Of course, my boy, we'll use our wits—but we're going to draw on one of the greatest assets of the police in cases like this: luck…"

"So we just wait till Mysteras feels like striking, Guv?"

"That's the plan, my boy. However, we'll make sure he doesn't strike! Pass me a couple of new Holland pipes and a fresh pouch of tobacco: it's time to go to work."

For now, work consisted of filling pipe after pipe and making the air in the room almost unbreathable from tobacco smoke.

It was late, and the lights in the street were already going out, when the detective set down his last pipe, rubbed his hands, and announced that all was well.

"Really, Guv?" yawned Tom, who was falling asleep over an illustrated magazine.

"Tom, if I told you that Mysteras is going to leave us in peace for a while, let's say for several days, I imagine that would surprise you."

"Rather." The young man was now fully awake.

Dickson drummed slowly on his wooden desk. "Dr. Mysteras, our old acquaintance, has just sent us down a false trail—our own! The first thing he needs is to replenish his bank account. Mark my words, Tom, the Hamilton case isn't over. It *must* start again in another shape. It's too far along, and Mysteras isn't a man who'd fail to play the trump cards that are still in his hand."

"All the better, Guv. I see we're not just going to sit here, waiting to be caught like frightened rats in a hole."

"And yet, my boy, we're going to *look* as if we are. For that, I'm sorry to say, we're going to have to split up. You'll have to stay here…"

Tom made a long face.

"—But your job won't be to sit idle, on the contrary. Indeed it won't be easy: you'll have to play Harry Dickson while still remaining Tom Wills."

"I get it! I have to make it look from outside like you're home."

"Exactly, my boy. You'll have to imitate my voice on the telephone, and in the evening, by the street-side windows, you'll have to parade around the jointed manikin that throws such a faithful shadow of Harry Dickson onto the curtains."

"And you, Guv?"

"I'll be in position at Rose Grange, where *inevitably, certain events must take place*, though as yet I have no idea what form they'll take. Be careful of the phone; I'll use it only in case of dire need. And now, my boy, goodbye and good luck!"

"What do you mean, goodbye? It's almost midnight, Guv!" cried Tom.

"For fifteen minutes, at reasonable intervals, make my shadow cross and recross in front of the window of the smoking room."

"And if Mysteras fires?"

"He won't—far from it. He's a man who's clever enough at logical deduction. The shadow will look to him like a trick."

"But it is a trick, Guv!"

"Wait... It's not a trick of the kind that Mysteras will be expecting. He'll think it's a trap. He'll assume the police are waiting in ambush in the neighborhood, on watch for the slightest move, the slightest suspicious sound. If he's out there spying on us, which is possible, he'll leave us alone. Meanwhile I'll go out by way of the roof, and tomorrow I'll be at Rose Grange. Buck up, my boy, I think we're going to have loads of fun."

The next day, Colonel B. W. Dalton, commander of the infantry regiment at Rochester, then on maneuvers on the east coast, received a visitor, a civil servant from the War Office, with whom he conferred at length. Following that interview, the regiment's field of operations was shifted slightly to include the village to which Rose Grange belonged. As a result Mr. Hamilton was forced to billet at his house a few soldiers whose requisitions for lodging were perfectly in order.

There were three of them, sturdy fellows in the transport corps; they had lots of time on their hands, which they mostly spent loitering around the garden. The leader, Captain Treavy, was a tall, thin, red-bearded man with a slight limp in his left leg from a wound gloriously received at the Flanders front; he was quartered inside the house, while his men slept outside.

Captain Treavy was a silent, fussy man; the morning after he and his men arrived he complained of rheumatism in his game leg and got immediate clearance from the colonel to skip the maneuvers and recover. He stayed mostly in his room, occasionally went outside in the noonday sun for a smoke, and now and then met briefly with Hamilton, his host, who'd given orders that he be treated like a prince.

Three days passed. The maneuvers were to last three weeks, and proceeded according to the rules of traditional English strategy. The soldiers billeted at Rose Grange had it easy.

The third day, toward midnight, Captain Treavy got up suddenly. He thought he'd heard a noise in the house. Anyone observing him at that moment would've gotten a surprise: he didn't limp, but strode firmly to his bedroom door and opened it to look out into the dark corridor.

The noise was coming from the room next to Hamilton's bedroom: the little science museum—the room in which the Tribunal of Terror had been staged. Instead of going there, the captain went to the darkroom next door. He seemed quite familiar with the layout of the house, because he needed no light to find his way. When he opened the door, he seemed surprised to find the little darkroom quite empty. Still, he went in cautiously, and pressed his ear against the door to the bigger room adjoining.

A voice could be heard: it was Hamilton's. "Leave me alone," it begged. "I don't know why you won't let me sleep in peace. I'm weary and ill. I'll do everything you tell me to…"

No one answered him, but after a few minutes the old man spoke again, in greater and greater distress. "All right, yes, I pledge to say nothing, I pledge not to contact Harry Dickson, I pledge to do whatever you say."

Silence fell again, followed again by Hamilton's voice, now in agony. "I'm in pain, you're hurting me… Ah! That terrible chair!… Leave me be!… I agree to everything… There are twenty-five thousand pounds in the strongbox, in hundred-pound notes, in five bundles of fifty bills… The password is META." Hamilton gave a muffled moan and fell silent.

The captain gently opened the door. The large room was dark, but a moonbeam provided sufficient light. Besides Hamilton, slumped in a chair, there was no one. The old man seemed to be fast asleep.

Treavy was about to go to him, when a shot rang out in the garden, followed by a voice calling urgently. The captain leaped to the stairs and ran outside.

Two soldiers from the transport corps, one of them holding a revolver, stood by the fence; a third soldier was searching a nearby lilac hedge. "I swear I hit him! He rolled over like a rabbit!" he muttered. "See for yourself, captain!"

Treavy approached and searched the hedge in turn.

"Here's proof I hit him," went on the soldier, tearing off a branch. "Look, the leaves are still wet with blood!"

The captain looked all around. "You forgot the ditch," he said curtly. "I know you can barely see it through the nettles that cover it. But the man might've escaped that way."

As if to prove him right, from the distance came the sound of an engine.

"A motorcycle!" cried the men.

"Take the car and try to catch him," ordered the captain. "But I doubt you can—the fellow is fiendishly clever—and I don't think he's wounded badly enough to slow him down. Listen to that engine go!"

The three soldiers ran off, and a few moment later a car sped away across the countryside.

The captain went on searching, and suddenly his foot struck a small metallic object. "The solution to the mystery!" he muttered bitterly. "A microphone that faithfully picked up whatever poor Hamilton said. Here's the cable leading to the house—damnably well hidden. As for Hamilton, I think I understand how he heard, or seemed to hear, a voice."

He went back to the house, where he found the owner not in the museum room but fast asleep in his own bed.

"Hypnotic suggestion! Quite an accomplishment at a distance!" muttered the captain. "Seriously, what a demon he is!"

He strode out of the bedroom and went straight to the strongbox in Hamilton's office. With expert fingers he spun the dials until the heavy door of the safe swung open to reveal two leather briefcases stuffed with banknotes—which Captain Treavy seized without remorse.

He tore a page out his notebook and scrawled a few words:

Received on deposit: twenty-five thousand pounds.
—Harry Dickson.

We'll summarize the events that followed as briefly as possible, because things began to move quickly around Rose Grange.

The next day Colonel B. W. Dalton withdrew his troops from the village. That same night, three of his soldiers—who seemed to have been left behind—burst into Hamilton's office just as a burglar stood cursing softly before the empty safe.

He was identified as an old ex-con with a number of pending sentences to serve out. He confessed right away that he'd acted for a third party, whom he claimed not to know.

"Where were you to hand over the money?" asked the police officers who examined him.

The man scratched his ear. "It's a rum story. He never said. 'I'll find you wherever you are,' says he. I don't know how a man I never set eyes on could make me both trust him and fear him. He must've been in earnest, because he paid me fifty pounds in advance. That's good money, so I did it!"

The man seemed sincere. They had to settle for his meager confession.

Two days later, back in London, Harry Dickson received a second letter:

You got the better of me, scoundrel! You stole my twenty-five thousand pounds! That's the bounty on your life—because this time I'll take it!

—Mysteras.

"Good," said the detective simply. "He's getting angry. That's a sign that he's weakening. But now he's coming for me. Keep a good eye out!"

7. The Chariot of Juggernaut

Then Mysteras withdrew into silence.

At this juncture there burst forth in London one of those mysterious, bloodstained cases that monopolize the talk of the town, rivet the collective attention, and fill the newspapers. A sect of fanatical, murderous Hindus had just been discovered. Fourteen Hindus had carried out the ritual assassinations of

English women and children in the London suburbs; they were caught, condemned to death, and promptly hanged.

Though they were people of little means, their hideout was remarkable: it was an old castle in the Stoke Newington neighborhood, that had been rented from its owner for three years. Inside it was found an enormous hall that the fanatics had created by knocking down all the interior walls, and that had been made to look like a Burmese temple. A terrifying blood-drenched statue of the goddess Kali rose over an altar still littered with dreadful human remains.

Harry Dickson had been called in, and he'd certainly wrapped up the case neatly. It had taken him only a week to unravel the whole business, which in his opinion had been fairly crudely plotted. He'd found the secret temple and delivered the culprits to justice and the noose.

Still, the great detective wasn't satisfied, though he didn't say so to anyone but his assistant, Tom Wills. "This case bothers me and displeases me, my boy," he said. "It *lacks logic*. Everything about it is *too artificial*. The goddess Kali, or rather her statue, was made of stucco—cheap gimcrack. No self-respecting Hindu would sacrifice so much as a fly before that bogus piece of paint-daubed plaster. The temple and all of its decor and furnishings were hastily thrown together. None of it was real—it would barely do as a shabby operetta stage set.

"Yes, the Hindus weren't actors, they were genuine assassins. But what pathetic creatures! Wretched vagabonds, recruited in dockside dives—peanut vendors, peddlers of fake carpets—who spent the two weeks of their reign of terror stuffed full of native narcotics: opium, betel nut, and so forth. It was like a sinister, bloody piece of theater, whose purpose I don't understand.

"Who rented the castle? A genuine Burmese, or rather a Tamil, who showed up dressed like a lord. But the investigation revealed that he was a former merchant from Rangoon who washed up in London and lived here in dire poverty right up to the day he rented and moved into the castle. He was the only one of the gang with any culture, and he wasn't a fanatic in the slightest. Yet he died honorably, without talking."

"The case is over as of this morning, Guv. The temple's been emptied by order of the court, and the pieces that seem like they might be important are now cluttering up the private museum at Scotland Yard—where they're hard pressed to know what to do with all that bloodstained plaster work."

"It's not over as far as I'm concerned, my boy," protested the detective, "and I want to get to the bottom of it. What would you say to a little outing to Stoke Newington, after dark?"

"Why after dark? That's not exactly a cheering prospect!"

"Because I feel like there's still some presence behind all this, some power whose motives I don't know. Someone or something unknown who hasn't left the place or given up the game."

Night was falling when they beheld, across a patchy lawn, the dark walls and crumbling turrets of the sinister castle.

"The police seals are still on, Guv," observed Tom.

Dickson shrugged and led the way to a small postern door in the left wing of the castle. They had no trouble removing the large police seal of red wax, and their lock picks got them into a vestibule that led to the service stairs.

They had to break two more seals to reach the dreadful temple hall. It stretched out before them, empty and haunted, lit by the last rays of sunset coming through a line of high windows at the very top of the wall. They advanced through the shadows, silencing their footsteps—though with no reason to expect anyone to be here.

Then Tom grabbed his employer's arm nervously and made him stop. "Did you see, Guv? THAT wasn't there before! The police took everything away! There shouldn't be so much as a stool left here!"

Dickson had also seen it. With a serious, anxious eye he considered the strange shape that loomed out of the shadows and caught the last embers of daylight. It was an immense chariot mounted on tall wheels that shone with a sinister glow. The base of the cart was a perfect closed cube, but above it rose a kind of openwork minaret topped by a pepperpot turret. Horrifying figures decorated the four corners of the fantastical vehicle.

"The chariot of Juggernaut!" murmured the detective.

Tom shuddered with horror. He recalled what he'd read about that terrifying feature of Hindu festivals of the previous century: the dreadful chariot that advanced amid the cries and chanting of the fanatics, who threw themselves under its wheels and allowed themselves to be crushed by its monstrous slow-moving weight. He knew that the English had explicitly forbidden those murderous processions, had destroyed the chariots everywhere without exception, and had condemned their drivers to death.

Yet here, a few miles from the heart of London, in the midst of modern civilization, before their eyes stood one of those incredible killing machines,

But right away the detectives had to grapple with a puzzle: since the castle had been searched from top to bottom, and everything had been taken away or locked up—how could this chariot of death be here?

They slowly retraced their steps, looking back every few seconds, as though they expected the vision to evaporate like a bad dream. But the chariot remained, reddened by the dying light, as if it were still freshly wet with the blood of massacres.

By now they'd reached the side door. Tom pushed against it, but then choked back an anguished cry: it was locked.

Before they could even discuss what to do, a strange sound rose in the great hall and was amplified by the enormous resonant space. The chariot had moved! It was moving! Horrified, the two men watched as the minaret oscillated slowly like a pendulum starting to swing, and then the spokes of the wheels glinted and the vehicle rolled forward a few feet.

Dickson and Tom drew back instinctively, though they were at the far end of the hall, well out of reach of the monstrous machine. They'd come to the great central double doors, and they threw their weight against them without much hope. The doors were locked, and their reinforced steel panels rang like an enormous gong.

The machine was still advancing slowly—but it was visibly accelerating. Now the engine inside it hummed smoothly.

"Let's attack it, Guv!" Tom drew his revolver.

But Dickson shook his head gravely. He'd just noticed that the sides of the chariot were smoother than porcelain and built of heavy steel plates.

The chariot was now following the walls. The great hall was circular, and the detectives could easily see that there was no corner in which to hide. The walls were as smooth as the machine itself—impossible to climb.

They'd already circled the hall twice, the chariot following on their heels but making no effort to overtake them. Now, suddenly, it sped up. The wheels began to turn faster, the minaret swayed harder, the sides of the mechanical monster occasionally scraped the stone walls. The detectives had to walk faster to stay ahead of it, and then gradually faster and faster. By now the chariot of Juggernaut was rolling so fast that they had to run ahead of it.

Even as he ran, Dickson kept his eye on the machine and calculated their chances of escaping it: maybe by crouching down and letting the high wheels pass over them? He bent low, but immediately straightened up with a cry of horror.

Four long scythe blades, attached to the underside of the chariot and turning at the same speed as the wheels, steadily sliced the air. Anyone who escaped being crushed by the wheels would be shredded by the terrible giant knives.

The chariot was now moving quickly and resolutely.

"To the middle of the room, my boy!" cried Dickson to his assistant without slowing down. "That satanic machine might be able to follow us, but it'll have to maneuver, and we'll gain some time."

Tom obeyed and ran to the center of the temple, but there he instantly leaped back with a cry of horror and pain: he'd just stepped on a vast iron disc that was slowly growing dark red. Through the soles of his shoes he could smell scorching.

Now they could see the fate that awaited them: either to be burned alive on the enormous disc, or to die crushed under the wheels or mangled by the scythes of the murderous vehicle. Because from now on they were forced to run in a circle—the same circle followed by the chariot of Juggernaut. And already that circular course was making their heads spin and their stomachs nauseous; sweat ran from every pore.

A terrible heat began to radiate from the glowing disc in the center, and the sickening smell of hot metal poisoned the air.

To run! To run forever in that circle of hell, until their strength gave out! And then would come death—and what a death!

Tom was visibly tiring; he began to stumble. Sometimes the chariot was only two revolutions of its wheels behind him. Dickson held him up, but he too could feel his strength failing.

"What an abominably creative piece of work!..."

Creativity! Ah, yes—now he understood! Mysteras was back! Mysteras, the criminal most enamored of creativity.

He let out a howl of hatred. "Mysteras!"

Inside the chariot someone began to laugh. But it was that laugh—that single laugh—that changed the course of events.

Dickson had heard where it came from: out of the minaret of the bloodstained vehicle. "Run ahead of me, Tom!" he directed.

Then he slowed down, knowing that the chariot would slow down too, to prolong their agony. And it did indeed slow down. At that moment it was crossing in front of the windows, which still showed some light, and the minaret was silhouetted against them.

"Fast! Run with all your might, my boy! Run!" shouted Dickson.

Tom leaped forward with a frenzy born of despair, because he could tell that his employer had just thought of some maneuver to save them. Inside the chariot a maneuver was needed as well, to match the speed of the runners.

Dickson saw the hesitation, and a shadow moved inside the minaret. Quick as a flash he raised his revolver and fired like a machine gun, with a sound of thunder.

A cry of pain and anger echoed from the machine, which swerved abruptly. The detectives had to flatten themselves against the wall to avoid the terrible massive machine, now suddenly directionless.

A window shattered, but at the same time the chariot barreled straight across the hall. A jet of flame rose as it crossed the hot iron disc, and like a tank it rammed the central doors, bursting them into pieces. A moment later with a hellish noise it crashed into the outer walls.

"Quick, my boy," panted Dickson as he dragged Tom away. "This old castle won't hold up under the impact."

Indeed, by the fading twilight they saw the walls gaping, the roofs sagging... But they were already running across the lawn, and they dove into a ditch, whose icy water struck them like a healing balm. The castle crumbled in a cloud of dust, followed by towering flames. By the time they got onto the road back to London, a great inferno lit the sky blood red behind them.

8. Fatal Water

Harry Dickson's mind was at peace: Mysteras was dead.

Granted, his remains hadn't been found, but the castle in Stoke Newington had burned to the ground. Everything had been reduced to ash—and even the terrible chariot of Juggernaut had left behind no more than a few shapeless lumps of melted steel. How then could the slightest trace of human ashes be identified?

But time passed, and the detective and his assistant found that other matters required their attention. That's when they got bad news about Mr. Hamilton. The old man's nerves had never fully recovered, and he went from one emotional crisis to another.

One day Dickson was visited by Dr. Dorgin. "I don't fear for my patient's life," said the doctor, "but for his sanity. His nightmare of the Tribunal of Terror has returned. Once again he finds himself arraigned before those awful judges in ermine hoods. My expertise is limited; I've consulted Dr. Garfield-Borinsky on his behalf, but he seems to feel scarcely more hope than I do. He finally agreed to take on his case personally, though he's a scientist who's not looking for patients. I've taken Mr. Hamilton to him, and he'll remain there for treatment.

"Dr. Garfield-Borinsky will try to abolish the effect of that old hypnosis, he says, but he makes no guarantees. He had me explain the business about the Tribunal of Terror from start to finish, and asked me to assist him in the work. And he hopes that you might help him locate the source of the hypnosis, without which all of our efforts will be in vain, he says."

Harry Dickson agreed, and visited Hamilton that same day.

Dr. Garfield-Borinsky lived in a modest house on a quiet back street near Covent Garden. He received the detective with a certain rough cordiality. He was an ill-dressed elderly man with a sad, absentminded demeanor, whose every gesture suggested a misanthrope.

"In my time I've written a fair number of books on hypnosis, and even on its use in crime," he said as he invited Dickson to have a seat in his old-fashioned office. "But I owe it to you to be candid: ultimately I'm powerless. Far from having given up its secrets, hypnotism remains almost completely a mystery."

"A few of whose veils you've lifted,' said Dickson politely, bowing to him.

The scientist shrugged impatiently: he disliked flattery. "Tell me about this Mysteras. I don't read the papers."

Dickson satisfied him, while striving to be as concise as possible.

"So Mysteras is dead," said the scientist when he was done. "Pity. He alone could've lifted the hypnotic spell that hangs over Hamilton. But I'll do what I can. Would you like to see the patient?"

A bright, comfortable room had been prepared for the old man, and a nurse had been specially assigned to him. Hamilton seemed to recognize no one—and he took fright at Dickson's entrance, asking him in a dull voice not to make him appear before the awful Tribunal of Terror anymore.

"Will the treatment take long, doctor?" asked Dickson just to say something, because he felt sad and discouraged.

The scientist raised his arms to heaven. "Months perhaps! Who can say? I'm not even sure I can cure him!"

They parted after those pessimistic words.

Dorgin, who was one of the few people Hamilton still recognized, was staying in London at his patient's request. The simple village doctor found himself ill at ease in the big city, and his only distraction, once he'd paid his futile daily call on his patient, was to come to Baker Street, where Dickson always gave him a warm welcome.

"Who could've predicted," he said one evening while drinking a cup of tea at the detective's fireside, "that I'd become attending physician to the great Garfield-Borinsky himself. Anyway it's a well-known fact that even the greatest doctors can't treat themselves. Poor Garfield suffers terribly, but eminent practitioner though he is, he absolutely refuses any surgical intervention."

"What's his complaint?" asked the detective politely.

"The beginnings of paralysis in his left leg," answered Dorgin, "which I believe is caused by a malignant tumor nestled in the thigh muscles. Sadly, I fear I can't count on him to cure my patient."

But Dorgin was mistaken: Hamilton regained his sanity and his health improved. But his innate intelligence seemed to have been compromised—instead of a quick-witted old man he was now no more than a hypochondriac, with a fearful manner, always seeing the worst in everything.

Dorgin—who'd rejoiced at the first signs of his patient's recovery—lost courage anew, and as usual came to Harry Dickson to complain about it. "Once again, he spends his life at the Tribunal of Terror," he confided to the detective.

Dickson gestured angrily. "Will this sinister business never come to an end?" he grumbled.

Dorgin looked embarrassed. "I don't like to speak ill of my fellow man, and especially not of a colleague, but I find that Dr. Garfield-Borinsky thinks of Hamilton more as a research subject than as a patient."

"Sadly, that's to be expected with men of his stature," said the detective. "And I fear we have no choice but to leave things in his hands, because he's the only man in all of England who can treat a case like ours."

"I'd like you to visit my patient."

"Would it do any good?"

"Yes," the village doctor replied simply, and a stubborn line furrowed his brow.

"All right," said the detective, a little taken aback by the good doctor's abruptness.

But Dorgin shook his head, apparently not yet satisfied by the promise. "Mr. Dickson," he said after a long hesitation, "have you ever had occasion to get into a house... hmm... clandestinely? Like a burglar, say?"

The detective observed the little man with curiosity. He was starting to appreciate his good country sense and especially his cheerful even temperament. "Of course, my good doctor. And Tom here can attest that I owe a lot to certain illegal entries of that type."

"Very good," said Dorgin. "Very good indeed, Mr. Dickson."

He shook the ashes out his pipe and bid them goodnight in his old familiar way.

Dickson remained pensive. Then he rose abruptly and called Tom, who was up on the library ladder looking through their books. "Pass me the medical directory, my boy, and the set of notebooks bound in blue that are shelved next to those volumes."

The detective studied the directory, then leafed through the notebooks more urgently than the younger man expected of his employer at such a time. He knew that the notebooks held a great many notations in Dickson's hand, as well as special police information.

Not all doctors in London share the same reputation. A few are a little too interested in toxicology, in ways that can be dangerous for some of their patients. Others deal secretly in narcotics. Others employ grave robbers, or when necessary the sinister imitators of the notorious Burke, who manufactured cadavers himself, in the terrible time of the "resurrection men."

Dickson turned pages, compared notes, opened volume after volume. And Tom watched his face grow darker and darker. Finally he asked his assistant to reshelve everything and to get his hat, his coat, and his revolvers.

"At what hotel is Dr. Dorgin staying?" he asked Tom.

"At first—based on your recommendation, I think, Guv—he chose a very comfortable guesthouse in Arundel Street. But two or three days ago he moved to the Arrowsmith, in Covent Garden, an old dump. I assume it's to be closer to his patient."

The detective's eyes glittered. "Tom, my boy, your employer's a great fool, did you know that?" he growled.

"How so?" said the young man in surprise.

"A thousand reasons, I tell you! To mention only one: for having forgotten that the Arrowsmith Hotel is where that eccentric Lady Missant, the most thoroughgoing old miser in the British Isles, was found dead six months ago—a woman who when she traveled took her entire fortune with her in cash in an enormous suitcase. For having forgotten that the Arrowsmith Hotel is where a certain Mr. Morros—who'd just cashed a check for ten thousand pounds at the Bank of England—died a few weeks ago. They both died of natural causes, but their money was gone; for lack of evidence, neither the hotelkeeper nor the staff were charged. And after all, they might well be innocent."

Dickson was still talking as he opened the front door and hailed a taxi. Calling out "Arrowsmith Hotel!" he asked the cabbie to step on it. The promise of a handsome tip did wonders, and they reached their destination shortly.

The Arrowsmith Hotel was a tall building with an unappealing look—in spite of placards touting its wine cellar, its menu, and the comforts of its rooms.

"Dr. Dorgin?" the detective asked the desk clerk.

"Room 36," he replied. "The doctor went up to his room only half an hour ago. If you'd like, I can ring him."

He unhooked the handset and dialed the number; a few minutes went by in silence... The clerk shook his head in surprise. "If the doctor weren't a guest who stays up very late, I'd say he's fast asleep," he said, trying to make a joke. "I'll ring again."

But there was no more answer than the first time.

"Perhaps he went out," offered Tom.

"Oh, indeed, no, sir," objected the desk clerk. "No so much as a fly could come and go here without my noticing! I know my job!"

"Then I'll go knock on his door," said Dickson firmly.

"To whom do I have the honor of speaking?" asked the clerk. "The hotel rules require me to ask visitors' names in a case like this."

The detective showed him his police credentials, and the man jumped.

"Ye gods—Mr. Dickson! I hope there's nothing wrong! The hotel has seen a couple of nasty doings recently..."

But Dickson didn't seem interested in listening to his complaints; followed by his assistant, he took the steep stairs four at a time. Room 36 was on the third floor and looked out on the garden—if you could call a garden that dismal courtyard, with nothing but a few limp laurel bushes in pots and some thin climbing lichwort.

"The key's in the lock on the inside, Guv," observed Tom. He rapped on the door: no answer.

"Let's waste no time. Pass me the thingamajigs, my boy," said Dickson.

They were a pair of long, thin needle-nose pliers, which he used to take hold of the head of the key in the lock and turn it with ease. One simple turn unlocked it, and the door opened.

Barely was the door ajar when Dickson rushed into the room and went to the bed. It was empty... but they didn't have to look far to find the occupant of the room: he lay on the floor, his left hand clutching at his heart—dead of an embolism.

"Hold on a minute!" said the detective, to keep his assistant from raising the alarm.

He bent over the body and examined the hands. The clenched hand exhibited two gray spots ringed with red, like burn marks.

Dickson growled like an animal. "Did it rain today, Tom?"

"Not at all, Guv. It was fine all day."

"Then in that case it seems to have rained only over Covent Garden, my boy," chuckled the detective. "Look: the open window, the sill, and even the wall outside are damp."

"As if they'd been watered from a distance with a hose, Guv. Look at the splash marks on the wall plaster."

"A gold star for that excellent observation, Tom. And now we know all we need to know to put an end to these crimes once and for all."

"Crimes, Guv?" cried Tom.

"Yes, my boy. Poor Dr. Dorgin died as a result of that water!"

"Poisoned?"

"Not at all, my boy! That water is as pure as what Mrs. Crown uses to make her tea. But it also has the property of being a good conductor of electricity. It was used to electrocute our unfortunate friend!"

"But then we ought to find an electrical wire, and..."

"As if one couldn't be pulled away in less time that it takes to tell. For example, if it had been stretched between this window and the house we can see beyond the garden wall."

"Who lives there, Guv?" asked Tom. "It looks awfully sad and silent."

"That's Dr. Garfield-Borinsky's place, my boy." Dickson folded his arms and stared out at the mysterious house.

9. The True Finale

At midnight an elite police team under the direction of Superintendent Goodfield and Tom Wills burst into the Arrowsmith Hotel and made all the occupants come out of their rooms. (Luckily there weren't many.) Guests and staff were kept under watch in a ground-floor room.

"No harm will come to you, ladies and gentlemen," Goodfield explained politely. "But it's my duty to warn you that any attempt to communicate with the outside while we're in charge here will be treated as complicity in a very serious matter."

"No—I'll go alone," Dickson had announced. And alone he'd climbed the back wall between the hotel garden and Dr. Garfield-Borinsky's house.

All was dark and silent there: not a sliver of light brought life to the gloomy windows hung with heavy curtains. The detective found a windowed door, skillfully cut out one pane, slid back the bolt, and got into the house.

He crossed a dusty hallway, onto which opened an unused kitchen. He ran the white beam of his flashlight around the kitchen, and saw that everything was coated with telltale dust. Yellowed mushrooms and large patches of mold were testimony of total neglect. He chuckled softly.

Before him were the stairs going up. Luckily the steps were thickly carpeted. Suddenly he stopped. A little light from the street came through a high transom, and in that dim glow something glittered. The detective saw that a wide strip of copper ran from side to side across one of the middle steps, with insulated wires at both edges.

"An expert in the field," murmured Dickson.

He drew a pair of rubber-handled pliers from his pocket, then changed his mind and went back down to the basement, where he soon found the electric meter. The little red pointer behind the isinglass dial cover was motionless: therefore no light was on in the house, no electrical device was running.

Dickson quickly pulled out all the fuses and flipped off the main circuit breaker. The house was without power. To be extra sure, he pulled down the drying line stretched across the laundry room and gripped the zinc wire in his rubber-handled pliers. Back at the stairs, he held it against the copper strip: no sparks.

"Onward. He relied too heavily on that defense—childish, really. The quality of the thinking is declining, I have to say."

When he reached the landing going up to the second floor, a powerful odor of paraffin struck his nostrils. "He's gotten out the old oil lamps," he said to himself.

Before him stood a door that threw a faint outline of light on the floor. Dickson recognized it: the doctor's office. For a few seconds he stood still in front of that door—a door he had to open, and one that would open onto the conclusion of a great drama.

With his revolver in his right hand, he took hold of the door handle, turned it gently, found that it offered no resistance—and with a sudden move threw open the door. The office lay before him, lit by a tall oil lamp whose round flame quickly bent in the airflow from the door.

Dr. Garfield-Borinsky sat pensively, his head in his hands, at a desk covered with papers. He raised his head and recognized his visitor. For a moment he blinked; but it must've been a fleeting emotion, because he remained perfectly calm.

"Good evening, Dickson. You've got a funny way of calling on people. I assume it comes with your profession."

"Mysteras!" said the detective quietly. "From now on I'll call you by no name but that horrible one."

The doctor shrugged. "I'm surprised you didn't figure it out long ago. I'm very tired, Dickson."

The detective nodded. "The beginnings of paralysis, right?"

The criminal smiled weakly. "You hit me with two bullets, Dickson. It's over for me."

He motioned to an armchair across from him. "Have a seat. I suppose we need to talk."

The detective sat down. Mysteras leaned back in his chair and eyed his adversary. Dickson could see how much the great criminal had aged, and how his gaze had dimmed and saddened.

False whiskers, carelessly pulled off, lay scattered on the table. The face the detective saw now was no longer that of Garfield-Borinsky but that of Mysteras, the criminal doctor.

The man understood his look. "Yes, I eliminated that patsy Garfield and took his place. It was easy to do, with his white whiskers and his myopia."

"And you're farsighted, doctor. You took a chance. Unfortunately I only picked up on it mentally a few hours ago, while going through some police notes on London doctors. I'll admit that slip on my part."

"Small cause, great effect," chuckled Mysteras. "Because here you are, Dickson!"

A silence fell between them; they studied each other, but without animosity.

As if toying idly, the doctor moved a heavy copper paperweight on the table, and Dickson saw his hands tremble.

"No use, Mysteras. I took care to switch off the mains. This electric chair I sat in so willingly is like any other perfectly harmless chair."

"All right." The doctor seemed unfazed.

"How's Hamilton doing?"

"The hypnosis I'm holding him under will wear off. I can't keep it going after my death, and I'll soon be dead. He'd made me his sole heir."

"Why did you kill Dorgin?"

A glitter of amusement appeared in the wretch's eye. "He found me out, Dickson—and I couldn't forgive him for that! That poor little country doctor was quicker than you. But his clear-sightedness cost him dearly."

"What was the point of that horrible business with the Hindu fanatics?"

Mysteras cackled. "The winning question, Dickson! I knew that sooner or later it would attract your attention. That's all I needed. And I wanted to sacrifice you to my one and only goddess: my creativity! Will that do as an explanation?"

"I believe you're in earnest," the great avenger said slowly. "And now I'll ask you to surrender without a struggle."

Mysteras's only answer was to spread open his dressing gown, revealing a weak, emaciated body dressed in sweat-drenched flannels, above two dreadfully thin legs. "Tomorrow, or at most the day after, they'd stop supporting me, Dickson. What struggle could I put up against you?" He looked at his adversary's hand, gripping the revolver. "The hangman will wait for me in vain. Pass me the gun!"

Dickson didn't move.

"My whole life I was a man of honor, and a scholar," said Mysteras in a low voice trembling with suppressed emotion.

The detective had set the revolver on his lap. He still kept silent, but his eyes shone with intense life.

"Considering all of that, Dickson, pass me your revolver," insisted Mysteras.

"Doctor," said Dickson calmly, "I don't know why I feel an odd pity for you. I guess in the end I still have some respect for all of your learning. You'll have to answer to God for terrible things. In His name, I ask you: will you use this weapon against yourself, the very moment I hand it to you?"

Mysteras's hands shook. "Yes," he said in a low voice.

Without another word, Dickson held out his Browning. The criminal seized it eagerly, examined it with an expert eye—and then with a savage cry he aimed it at the detective and fired three times. Three longs tongues of flame lit the darkness of the room.

Harry Dickson didn't move. He smiled scornfully. "A simple bit of sleight of hand," he said in an icy voice. "If you'd aimed at your own heart, I would immediately have given you this revolver, loaded with real bullets and not with blanks!" He showed his adversary a big automatic.

Mysteras roared like a wild beast. "All right, arrest me—but you don't have me yet! They can't hang me for six weeks at least, and in that time Mysteras can perform miracles!"

"Who's talking about six weeks, Mysteras?" The detective's voice was colder than ever. "Let's call it six minutes—barely that!"

"What do you mean, villain?" shrieked Mysteras.

"I mean that, indeed, six weeks would give you plenty of time to commit a few more crimes, even from inside a cell. And I feel you've committed enough already. Do you have a last wish? If it's in my power, I'll grant it."

The criminal's face had gone white as a sheet. "You're... going to... kill me... Dickson? But you have no right..."

"Your skills are demonic, Mysteras," said the detective, ignoring his enemy's question. "I even owe you a certain admiration. To think that you knew in advance that a case like Hamilton's would have to be referred to you, since only Garfield-Borinsky could treat it. You had it all figured out! As for me, I'll repeat what I said. I want to see Mysteras dead with my own eyes!"

"Murderer, assassin!" howled the criminal.

"You've got two minutes, not a second longer, to offer me something besides empty insults," said Dickson firmly. "Or to repent, if you're capable of it."

Mysteras closed his eyes. "I can't offer you money, can I, Dickson—not even a fortune?"

The detective didn't bother to answer. He kept his eyes on a pendulum clock that marked off the seconds metallically.

Mysteras still seemed to be thinking. "I was fading… I was fading… I was fading…" he murmured three times. Then he sat still, his chest open to his enemy.

The clock gears ground as it prepared to ring the late-night hour. But the silvery chimes went unheard, because a shot rang out, followed immediately by another.

Struck in the heart, the doctor slid to the floor and lay still.

An hour later, the body of Mysteras was on its way to the dissecting theater, to serve as a subject for criminologists.

A private car followed the hearse at a distance, then turned onto the Harwich road. It was taking Hamilton—freed forever from his Tribunal of Terror—toward Rose Grange and a complete recovery.

"Mr. Dickson," murmured the old man, "I owe you more than my life…"

But by his side the great detective, overcome by fatigue and catching a little rest, was fast asleep, already resting on his victor's bed of laurels.

Harry Dickson

LE SHERLOCK HOLMES
AMERICAIN

No. 106   Le Chemin des dieux.   Prix fr. 1.50

C'est lui ! murmura-t-on autour de Dickson, c'est lui, l'épouvantable mandarin !

THE PATH OF THE GODS

1. The Ridiculous Dinner

They were getting bored. Lord Denverton's receptions were never very entertaining, but this one beat all. Dinner dragged on, and had been mediocre besides: the soup had been served lukewarm, the pasta was half-cooked, the appetizers were dressed in too-sour mayonnaise, the fish wasn't fresh, and the poultry arrived with the wings burned and the meat limp and bloody. They'd been served grocery store wine and drugstore whisky. When the ice cream showed up it was half melted. That was the last the straw: the guests were on the verge of complaining.

Denverton, presiding at table, didn't seem bothered by the dreadful standard of the menu. He did nothing but look off into space, and his guests might well have thought he had something against them, to make them sit for hours in front of dishes of doubtful quality, badly prepared, in an atmosphere reeking of boredom and awkwardness. But Denverton was fabulously wealthy, Denverton was powerful, Denverton could afford to offend cabinet ministers and members of Parliament and other big shots. He declined the dish of gooey ice cream the headwaiter offered him, and absentmindedly peeled a very hard peach, which he left untouched on his plate.

Dinner was reaching its end, and the guests, knowing his lordship wouldn't keep them long past dessert, began to breathe more easily. Coffee and liqueurs were served. Then came a moment of watchful silence. Finally the headwaiter returned carrying a large tray on which lay a pile of yellow envelopes, one for each guest. He slowly made the rounds, each guest avidly taking the envelope meant for him. The headwaiter skipped only one guest, who shook his head. And yet that guest had already gotten a note, right at the beginning of dinner: *Don't eat! Stay here with me this evening!*

He reread the note, which it had cost him no regret or difficulty to obey, so bad had been the food. Then he went back to observing his twenty or so fellow guests seated around the table, all looking much happier now that they'd gotten their envelopes. They were mostly people of modest station: clerks and shopkeepers in the City. Their presence in this setting, the opulent dining room of the Dukes of Denverton, was a genuine shock.

Finally his lordship rose; that was the signal for a general withdrawal. A few of the guests bowed awkwardly to their host, who returned their politesse with the slightest, stiffest bend of his body. Most fled straight to the cloakroom; others tore open their envelopes and counted the banknotes that dropped out: "Fifty pounds! What are the odds!"

In the dining room now remained only the guest who'd received the note from Lord Denverton, and Denverton himself. They stood on opposite sides of the room and watched each other without drawing nearer. The host moved first. "Mr. Dickson," he said carefully, "how does it happen that you were among these guests chosen at random?"

Harry Dickson nodded slightly. "The invitation went to a man I arrested a few days ago for a string of crimes, each worse than the last. He gave it to me, saying, 'Well, friend Harry, go to Lord Denverton's in my place. I think you'll find it a couple of profitable hours.'"

Denverton blushed. "Is that all, Mr. Dickson?"

"Yes... But are you acquainted with the people who just left?"

"Not in the least!" cried Denverton.

A strange reply—and yet it didn't seem to faze the detective. "I thought as much. Let me tell you about them: Samuel Bird, hat maker in Battersea, three times a bankrupt. Lewis Stoneroad, seven convictions for forgery. Morris Lapland... hmm... a few morals charges that made him familiar with Dartmoor. Gustave Parant, one murder on his conscience, though there wasn't enough proof to hang him—but a nasty customer even so. I could go on like that, down to the twenti-eth man."

Denverton was in agonies. "I don't know whether it's God or the devil who sent you, Mr. Dickson, but allow me to invite you to share my personal dinner, and we can talk…"

Sensing a mystery, Dickson accepted with a simple nod.

They were served in a small room draped in magnificent silk and furnished with uncommon taste and discretion. The menu was exquisite: caviar, cold duck, foie gras, fine fruit. They ate in silence, or close to it, exchanging only small talk.

The detective plucked one perfect golden grape from its bunch. "Was it a wager?" he asked finally.

"No. I'd rather have lost."

"Quite right, I understand."

Silence fell again. A servant quietly brought champagne. Denverton swallowed two full glasses, one after the other. "A clause in my uncle Denverton's will," he said softly.

"Your whole fortune came from him?" asked Dickson casually.

"Yes, I'm the last of the Denvertons."

"How long have you been in possession?"

"Since his death, three years ago."

"So this was the third dinner of that kind you've given?"

"The third, indeed. And it'll go on…"

"Can you show me the clause?"

Denverton once again poured himself a generous glass of champagne. "Of course. It's not long, and I know it by heart:

Every year, on this date, twenty guests you do not know—and whom you must not know—will take their places around the formal dining table of the Denvertons and will be treated to dinner by you, my heir. At the end of the meal, at which you will preside, you will hand each of them the sum of fifty pounds."

"That's it?" asked Dickson in surprise.

"That's it!"

"What penalty did your uncle prescribe in case of non-compliance?"

"None clearly defined. Just this:

Beware not to disobey this order, or calamity will fall on you from all sides, and the fortune of the Denvertons will be lost to you."

"Is it the same guests each time?"

"Not at all! They're different every year. I've researched the process carefully. The invitations are sent out by an intermediary, a notary well respected in the City. He knows no more than I do. He gets the invitations, with my request to distribute them, and he collects a handsome fee for doing it."

Dickson let the champagne fizz and grow still. A hundred questions rose to his lips, but he suppressed them all. The late Stanton Denverton had been neither an eccentric nor a madman; just a man of good common sense whom all England had known as such. Finally he asked simply, "No other clause?"

"Um, not really... I can make no alterations to this old house. I'm especially forbidden to make changes to the formal dining room."

"The room where you receive your annual guests—whom by the way you treat rather shabbily!"

Denverton smiled. "My only revenge!" That moment of levity helped to drive away the atmosphere of gloom.

Dickson reflected aloud. "No one's harmed. No one complains. I came because I was driven by the curiosity that's natural to my trade. In fact, my role here should end now, without ever starting."

Denverton reddened slightly. "And what if I asked you to find out what's behind this whole peculiar business?"

The detective observed the nobleman's glum face for a long while. The man was so miserable, it wasn't surprising that he radiated misery all around him.

"Would you permit me a few questions?"

"Please!"

"Lord Denverton, you had no fortune at the time your uncle's death gave you possession of his title and his wealth?"

"Not only no fortune—I had debts. My name was only Wrenworth. From time to time my uncle had sent me subsidies. He kept his distance from me, and hardly ever left this vast mansion. In his youth he'd traveled a great deal."

"Is the staff here the same as in your late uncle's time?"

"No, there's been a complete turnover. The will set aside suitable bequests for all the old servants at Denverton House."

So now what? Dickson's initial curiosity was fading. He felt boredom rising toward him like a dark tide. Where could this investigation lead? To some senile whim of the deceased, some deep obsession nursed for years by the fantasy of a spoiled old rich man. Bah!

He thought again of the old crook on whom he'd found the letter of invitation, and who'd held it out to him, saying, "Why would a moneybags like that invite a rascal like me? The great Harry Dickson should go find out!"

Though he'd been skillfully questioned, the crook knew nothing about it himself—which had made it all the more enticing to the detective. His interest had held up through the entire ridiculous dinner, but now it was flagging...

An obsession! A folly that a mischievous old man, now dead, wanted to prolong beyond the grave by the simple trick of a clause in a will, perpetuating his senile wishes. With an irritated gesture Dickson cut the tip of the splendid Henry Clay his host had offered him, and slightly broke the leaf. He raised his eyes, looking for an ashtray in which to set the damaged cigar. Then he lowered his head again. He couldn't be sure what he'd just seen: at the far end of the room, some rapid and menacing movement—maybe a hand. He couldn't have said. Something had happened, but what?

Having set down the cigar, Dickson drew back his hand and rested it on the arm of his chair, where it encountered something hard and cold: the jade handle of a small dagger, sunk to the hilt in the club leather, a few inches from his heart. "So," he murmured, "someone was targeting me! Therefore I must be a nuisance to someone in this house. All right! That settles the last of my hesitations!"

He pulled out the little weapon and slipped it into his pocket. Denverton had seen nothing, and was yawning.

"Well, sir," said Dickson, rising, "purely for the entertainment, I'm happy to look into your late uncle's strange intentions. My blood's up, as they say—or it nearly was!"

Denverton shook his head without understanding. For him the important thing was that Dickson not abandon him to his misery, that the detective find a way to put an end to those awful obligatory dinners! "Have a little more whisky, Mr. Dickson, or some brandy."

Dickson declined; he needed to be alone to think. An obsequious butler showed him to the door. The street was foggy, and the newly lit globes of the street lamps were surrounded by the reddish halo that precedes the famous London fog.

Dickson went a few steps in search of a cruising taxi. Seeing a cab approaching with its flag up, he put out his arm—but another hand held his back.

"What kind of mess are you getting yourself into, friend?" murmured a voice in the fog.

The detective whirled around and found himself face to face with a little man, badly dressed and badly groomed. But Dickson's experienced eye could see through the makeup, and he recognized the voice. "By heavens, it's Bun..."

The other man cut him off. "No names, please! Even more than the walls, the fog has ears! I'll see you at your place in an hour!"

Dickson hailed another cab and had himself driven home to Baker Street. On the way, paying no attention to the dark streets that rolled by, he frowned and murmured, "Bunny Lipton! What kind of a crazy business is he going to drag me into now?"

2. In Which the Path of the Gods is Mentioned for the First Time

Bunny Lipton, head of the Oriental division of the secret police, and a man well acquainted with the most terrible secrets of China and India, had already been mixed up more than once in the adventures of the famous Harry Dickson. He was a small, clever, capable man. Like Dickson, he had courage, patience, a lawman's intuition, and trust in that mysterious luck of the avenger known as fate. He lacked the great man's genius, and he readily admitted it.

He seemed to be in a very bad mood that evening when he showed up at his famous colleague's house.

"I thought you were off somewhere in the boondocks of China, Bunny," said Dickson after shaking his hand warmly.

"I wish to God I was!" replied the policeman sadly. "I'd happily solve the most Chinese of puzzles in the heart of China—but not here, in London! Cases pick up a different flavor here, they get Europeanized, which is no help to me when I'm trying to solve them... You know, Dickson, on the one hand I'd rather see you a thousand miles away from that wasp's nest tonight—and on the other hand I'm delighted to find you by my side once again."

Dickson burst out laughing. "To tell you the truth, I don't have a clue what's going on. It was just curiosity that led me to Denverton House tonight. I'll tell you everything I know..."

When the detective was done, which didn't take long, Lipton remained silent for a moment. His eyes shone. "That's exactly it, Dickson! The dinner held for twenty good-for-nothings on the same date every year. By the way, did you notice anything particular at the table?"

"Yes: one seat remained unoccupied!"

"The twenty-first place! Right! All's for the best in this, the best of all possible worlds—unless it's the worst one, after all! Lord Denverton didn't attach any importance to that absence; he's not smart enough! But that's the key to the whole thing, Dickson: the no-show guest!"

"I'd be grateful if you'd shed a little more light for me, Bunny."

"Alas! I'm forced to tell you a Chinese story, one that's indeed a genuine chinoiserie! It's twenty years old."

"Reign of terror over Peking! Reign of terror over the European concessions! Communications had been cut. The native population was fleeing, and some of them were trying to take refuge inside the concessions. Fuh-Suh had come down from the mountains and was crossing the plains at the head of an army of pirates, Boxer rebels, and Taiping rebels recruited from all across the enormous land of China. He dreamed of driving the Europeans into the sea and drowning them—unless he could chop them to pieces first.

"He practiced every horror: villages burned and leveled, fields plowed under, inhabitants wiped out. The British flag was his particular target—Anglican missionaries who fell into his hands had suffered the vilest tortures.

"For years, Fuh-Suh had exercised his reign of terror over the distant plains. Now he'd become greedy: he wanted the capital, the Imperial City, the Forbidden City, and above all the European concessions. For days the scales of destiny truly seemed to be tipping his way—and then a terrible epidemic broke out among his troops, decimating them more effectively than the most powerful artillery in the world could have.

"That was when the allied powers hastily landed fresh troops, who went on the attack against the invader. Fuh-Suh's army was cut to pieces, but he himself didn't fall into the avengers' hands. He was believed to be dead—but then skilled informers managed to learn that he was far from it.

"Fuh-Suh continued to kill from the shadows. He'd evolved from a conqueror into an assassin. For lots of Chinese, he'd become God. Years went by. Fuh-Suh's crimes continued unabating. Suddenly there was a let-up. Then it was learned that a secret society had been formed—as if there weren't already enough in China!—a society that hosted an annual dinner for twenty bandits. I know the society's rules; they're not long:

"Every year, twenty crooks will be summoned to a meal. They will eat, and will be paid for coming. A year will come when the guest who is always absent will show up and take his place at the table. That will be Fuh-Suh, who will return to earth along the Path of the Gods.

"It might be tempting to see it as just another ritual, like so many others in the Orient; and essentially it's just a symbol of the final resurrection. Fuh-Suh, now dead, will return to take his place among the living—and of course he'll be delighted to find himself, at his first earthly dinner, surrounded by villains and reprobates. We had only a faint interest in it—when suddenly I was called back to London. I got here a week ago, and was taken to meet the Prime Minister's private secretary. For several months now the P.M. himself, Lord Dambridge, has been convalescing from a serious illness at a seaside resort on the Continent.

"'Lipton,' said the secretary, 'I brought you back to reprimand you.'

"'That's a fine way to welcome a fellow, sir,' said I.

"'Are we going to allow Chinese ways to take hold here?'

"'Certainly not, sir, because they can't always be recommended!'

"'Well, then! For months now I've been inundated with anonymous notes, all of them saying, more or less, *Annual Denverton dinner equals annual Fuh-Suh dinner. For solution ask Bunny Lipton.* Fuh-Suh's name brought back too many ugly memories for us to ignore that advice; so I treated myself to the extravagance of summoning you from Peking to London.'"

Here Lipton turned to Dickson. "Well, that damned secretary's no fool, Dickson. Without really knowing why, I felt there really was an odd similarity between those mysterious dinners, taking place so far apart."

"We have no evidence that the mystery is in any way criminal," objected the detective.

"Alas, Dickson, that's not the case. The evening I arrived I received a parcel at my hotel, which contained a freshly severed head—the head of an elderly Chinese man whom I haven't succeeded in identifying. But I'd stake my life that he was the author of those anonymous notes addressed to the Prime Minister or to his secretary; and some unknown master has punished him for high treason!"

"It seems to me that you might investigate why the late Lord Denverton included such a peculiar clause in his will."

"As if I hadn't already done that, Dickson! I've overturned half a dozen notary's offices and questioned half a hundred lawyers in the past few days. Oh, I went to a lot of trouble, but... goose egg!" moaned Lipton.

"As I recall, the late Stanton Denverton was a man of good common sense, a little misanthropic, not a bad fellow. He'd traveled a lot."

"Yes, but not outside Europe. He was satisfied with very long stays at spa towns in France, Germany, Switzerland, Austria... He didn't like England; the climate disagreed with him. That's all I learned about him. As for his heir, he's an utter imbecile, equally incapable of good or evil."

"I share your opinion, Bunny. What do you think about the staff at Denverton House?"

"Unremarkable. Not one of them is worth a moment of our attention in this investigation."

"What do you say to this?" Dickson held out the little jade-handled dagger.

Lipton stared in it in horror. "The key to the Path of the Gods!" he cried.

"If I understand you, the Path of the Gods means the path to death?"

"More or less, but with a nuance. It really means the terrible road traveled by Death's emissaries—or should I say the dead themselves who wish to return among the living. I can't put it more clearly. It's a matter on which I've only ever gotten the vaguest information."

"So why give that strange name to this little dagger?"

"Have you looked at it?"

"Not yet."

"That's a little deadly treasure you're holding there," said Lipton with a smile. "The blade is pure platinum. The jade of the handle is unusual too; it's of a very rare variety. Look at its translucent green: it's called 'corpse cheek,' and it really does suggest an unhappy cadaver. But that doesn't stop collectors from paying enormous sums for it... I assume the clumsy knife thrower who meant that charming dagger for you will make some effort to get it back."

A silence fell between the two men. Dickson set a glass of whisky in front of his friend, who drank from it, his thoughts elsewhere.

"Hell if I know where all this is headed," said Lipton. "Have you ever started down a trail as muddled as this one, Dickson?"

The detective smiled; certainly, it had happened to him more than once. Silence. Lipton took small sips of the warming liquor. Dickson smoked. They could hear Mrs. Crown, the housekeeper, back in the kitchen, moving dishes. The clock on the wall slowly counted off the quiet seconds: one, two, one, two...

With surprise, Lipton followed his friend's eyes to the large clock face. "Are you expecting someone, Dickson?"

"Yes and no... Someone who shouldn't have left."

"Your assistant, Tom Wills? Indeed, I'd have liked to shake his hand."

Dickson pressed a buzzer. "Where did Tom go?" he asked Mrs. Crown when she came in, wiping her hands on a dish towel.

"But... he never left, sir!" cried the good woman. "A little before you came back, Mr. Dickson, I heard him pacing in the library."

"Very good, Mrs. Crown, that'll be all. I believe you didn't hear Tom leave."

"Fine—why not just say I'm going deaf!" grumbled the housekeeper, and she slammed the door.

Dickson went slowly toward the library and put his hand on the doorknob. Why, at that moment, did he and Lipton hesitate equally? Why didn't they immediately open the door to that familiar room? They both felt that something vague and dreadful lurked there.

"Dickson," murmured Lipton with a sad sigh, "I'm not sure why I'm afraid, standing before this door—the door to the room where Tom was heard for the last time! I encountered this kind of thing many times in China. Be careful!"

Already the detective was breaking the spell. With an angry growl he threw the door wide open, reached out, and flipped the wall switch. Bright light filled the room. Dickson and Lipton leaped back, so unexpected was the scene that met their eyes.

A creature of repellent ugliness crouched on a chair; his excessively wide eyes blinked in the bright light. His mouth hung open with incredible pendulous lips; an inhuman grimace distorted his face and gave it a bestial coldness. He uttered a menacing croak as the two men approached.

"Look out!" cried Lipton. "Don't touch him. Right now he's as strong as ten men, and he'd kill you with a sweep of his hand. He doesn't recognize us... I know this foul witchcraft."

"Recognize us..." stammered Dickson, glimpsing an awful truth. And then he noticed the familiar clothes, shredded by fierce claws. "Tom!" he cried.

The creature growled savagely.

"What's happened to him?" the detective cried.

Lipton took his arm to hold him back. "It's Chinese devilry. He must've been injected with yun-yun, a kind of oil that in less than an hour can transform a reasoning person into a monster like that."

"Is it incurable?" cried Dickson.

"Luckily, no. It seems that after a while the effects wear off. There's an antidote—but damned if I know where to find any of it here! Let me think…"

Tom didn't move, but a wild animal's growl emerged from his throat, and drool ran from his lips. He gave every sign of absolute cretinism, though a savage and sometimes murderous light shone in his enlarged eyes.

After pondering, poor Lipton shook his head; he knew of nothing that could help his friend.

Suddenly Dickson opened the door and went behind Tom, and then with an effort he pushed him onto the stairs. With another animal growl, the young man hopped down the stairs and reached the street.

"Quick, Bunny, after him!" called Dickson. "We have to keep him from hurting someone, or from being hurt. I expect the bandits who played this trick on him will try to get near him."

It was a dark night, and the fog still hung in places. After a moment's hesitation, Tom had begun to run. The two detectives had trouble keeping up.

3. On Tom Wills's Trail

Tom moved along erratically; sometimes his hesitant steps looked from a distance like the stumbling of a drunk. He went the length of Goswell Street, turned sharply onto City Road, and began following it toward Old Street.

"My word, Dickson," said Lipton, catching his breath, "he's heading to the house you just left."

"Denverton House? After all…"

Dickson didn't finish his thought. His face hardened, and he matched his pace to Tom's. In the distance the young man's silhouette was already receding into the foggy night.

"So much has happened in just a few hours!" murmured Lipton. "Hell if I know what there can be at Denverton House."

"Look out!" cried Dickson. "He's approaching the house. Oh! That's a little much!"

The two detectives had just watched Tom vanish as if the ground had swallowed him.

"Ah," murmured Dickson as they ran forward, "I should've thought of that: the basement! Still, I was shaken for a moment."

Indeed, a basement window opened onto street level, and no doubt led to the cellars of Denverton House.

"Do you understand how he got here?" asked Dickson.

Lipton nodded. "In the state he's in, I'm not surprised. He's being led by the will of another, who's guiding him by some of kind of hypnosis. But it mustn't be at full power, I think, because they're drawing him here to complete the job. Well! We're going to shove a stick in their spokes!"

Without a word, Dickson slid through the open window and set foot in the cellar; Lipton followed him. For a moment the two detectives stood still: footsteps fading into the distance proved they were on the right track. In total darkness, Tom was advancing without the help of any light. Dickson and Lipton didn't dare switch on their flashlights; and they were forced to make their way blindly by following the sound of Tom's footsteps. Still, their eyes gradually adapted to the dark, and they were able to proceed without too much stumbling or tripping. Ahead of them they heard a door close, and the sound of footsteps ended.

"He's gone up to the main floor," murmured Dickson.

A few seconds later they bumped into a stone staircase leading up to an open door. A faint light shone at the end of a long corridor. Dickson recognized where they were. At the end of the corridor was a hall, onto which opened the dining room where the ridiculous dinner had taken place. They could hear the footsteps again, now reverberating in the hall.

"Let's hope no one intercepts him," murmured Lipton. "Can you imagine if they gun him down as a simple burglar?"

"I assume he's been drawn here for quite a different purpose," murmured Dickson.

Still, they hurried to keep up with Tom. They'd reached the hall, which was lit by a single Moorish lantern that threw a prismatic glow around it and left the rest of the room in darkness. The double doors to the dining room were open; that room was lit, not by its great chandelier, but by two standing lamps with pink shades placed in a corner. Tom stood—alone, unmoving—silhouetted in front of one of the lamps.

Then the two detectives started: from some unknown location, a strange voice rose and chanted in a harsh tone and a bizarre language.

"Ancient Chinese!" murmured Lipton.

"Can you understand it?"

"Fairly well... Let me listen."

Lipton pulled his friend behind one of the open double doors, and in a low voice he began to translate what the invisible voice was singing. "O traveler on the Path of the Gods: offering it up as a sacrifice to you, I have taken the soul of this young barbarian, to punish his master, so that he may turn his impious eyes away forever from the sacred road you follow."

Here, a silence fell. Tom remained still, outlined against the pink light of the standing lamp.

The voice went on in a tone of genuine sadness, "You do not answer, O traveler on the Path of the Gods, because the time has not yet come."

"But I'll answer you!" boomed another voice.

It was Dickson—and Lipton came awfully close to crying out in fear. "Fool!" he cringed.

But Dickson went on, "If the soul of this young man is not immediately restored, I, Harry Dickson, will blow up the formal dining room with the grenade I have in my pocket, which has a time delay that I can set to go off whenever I want. Answer me!"

A few seconds passed. Then the voice spoke again—but this time in perfect English: "I accept, Harry Dickson. Withdraw into the small white-draped room where you dined earlier this evening. In ten minutes your assistant will be restored to you, in full possession of his wits."

Lipton broke in, speaking in Chinese. "Do you swear it by the traveler on the Path of the Gods?"

After a few seconds came the low and somber reply, "I swear it. But will your friend return the jade dagger?"

"Yes," said Lipton right away.

"As he withdraws, let him set it down on the little table by the lamp. Now give me your word of honor as well, that you will not return to this room until ten minutes have passed."

"Agreed," said Lipton.

They withdrew into the small side room described before, where nothing had changed since Dickson left it. They switched on a wall sconce and were silent for a while, lost in their own thoughts.

"I wonder how Denverton's mixed up in all this," said Lipton.

"Ask me again tomorrow," said Dickson, "but I'm afraid my answer will still be what it is now—that the present Lord Denverton is nothing more than an utter imbecile."

They kept their eyes on Dickson's pocket watch, which he'd set under the lamp. From the other side of the door they heard not a sound.

"Nine minutes!" said Lipton. "Only one more... I'm afraid..."

Dickson threw him an unhappy look, and began to follow the second hand as it made its way in short pulses around the marked dial. Finally he rose and went to the door. "The ten minutes are up," he called in a loud voice.

No answer.

He threw the door wide open. The dining room was brightly lit by the great chandelier. In an armchair, fast asleep, sat Tom Wills—with his clothes still in shreds but with the familiar smile on his face.

Dickson rushed to him. "Tom, my boy! Wake up!"

The young man stretched, yawned, opened his eyes, and smiled at his employer. A moment later he looked around in surprise at the setting for his awakening—and then in surprise at the unfortunate state of his dress. "My good brown suit! What happened to it?" he wailed.

"We'll talk about that later," answered Dickson, squeezing his hands affectionately.

"I'd be very interested in examining this peacefully slumbering house," said Lipton. "But I feel that for the moment we've agreed on a truce with whoever it was who restored Tom to us. I suggest we don't break it till tomorrow."

"Agreed," said Dickson.

The mysterious voice spoke not a word.

It was very late by the time they got back to Baker Street; still, Tom was invited to tell them what had happened to him. The question seemed to surprise him. "It's rather I who should be questioning you two," he said. "I must've fallen asleep in the library, and I woke up in an unfamiliar house with my good brown suit in rags!"

"Make an effort, Tom," said Lipton. "Tell us if you can remember anything at all that happened before you fell asleep."

Tom frowned and tried to think. "I was the library, looking for a book... I can't remember what book... Yes, I can, a book by Jack London. I couldn't find it right away... I could hear Mrs. Crown rattling pots and pans in the kitchen. I could smell fried fillet of sole, and that made me happy—my God, this is all so banal, so commonplace!"

"Never mind, my boy," said Dickson. "Keep going."

"I remember nothing else, or almost nothing... But something, like a cloth, touched my face. Oh, yes!... Before that, a book fell off the top shelf. Dust flew up..."

"Shush!" said Dickson. "I think I've heard enough: a book that fell, dust, a cloth... from the top shelf... But when we found Tom, everything in the library was in its place, and I automatically locked the door when we left. Come!"

He tiptoed to the library door and flung it open, and quickly raising his revolver he sprayed the top shelves of the bookcase with bullets. A body fell heavily in the darkness.

"Lights," said the detective.

Lipton and Tom stood there, stunned. On the floor writhed a Chinese man in his final agonies.

Lipton came close, and his face expressed his horror. "A Taiping! Let him die, Dickson, and above all don't try to help him. He'd use his last strength for some nasty trick—I know the type!"

The man glared at the three of them with an awful look, burning with hatred. Then his eyes rolled back and he lay still.

"Two bullets in the head," said Lipton admiringly. "Now that's called relying on your lucky star when you shoot! I assume this bandit was instructed to get all three of us; faithful to his orders, he would've waited."

"And in the dining room at Denverton House, they were expecting all three of us—but not quite in the manner in which we showed up," said Dickson. "Now, Bunny, I'll throw back at you the question with which our encounter this evening began: What kind of wasp's nest have we gotten ourselves into?"

4. The Second Chinese

The next day Harry Dickson received a letter from Lord Denverton. It was brief and formal:

Mr. Dickson,

Yesterday, in a moment of whimsy or boredom, I asked you to look into a couple of mysteries, or what I thought were such. I believe I do not have the right to dig into my uncle's past, or to require that he give me some kind of posthumous explanation. Let his wishes remain sacred. I would therefore beg you to drop this matter. An hour after you left, I and all of my staff quit Denverton House, where I've been unhappy, to go to my castle in Yorkshire.

I will not return until a year from now, on the occasion of the next obligatory dinner. I enclose a check for two hundred pounds, which I beg you to accept as your fee.

—Denverton

"Well, my boy, that explains why Denverton House seemed abandoned," said Dickson when he'd looked over the letter, "and proves that the young lord is nothing but a weakling and a fool."

"Maybe someone put the fear in him, Guv," suggested Tom.

"Possibly."

"What do we do? Leave things as they are?"

"I don't believe I will," said the detective. "Still, I'll wait to hear what they tell that excellent Bunny Lipton at the Foreign Office, so we can match our actions to his."

Lipton wasn't long in coming; he hadn't breakfasted, and his ill humor showed it. Only the grilled toast, tea, and jam Mrs. Crown served him smoothed away his frown.

When he'd read Denverton's letter he set it down crossly. "You're your own boss, Dickson, and you can drop the case if you like, but I've just been given explicit orders: Solve it! Solve what, I wonder? When I think that I'll have to face this chinoiserie—that's the word for it—alone, it doesn't exactly leave me feeling rosy."

"And what if I stick with you?" proposed Dickson.

Lipton gave a joyful yelp. "Rosiness returns! Rosy as the dawn, rosy as a peach, rosy as... all that's good and great!" cried the little man, his eyes shining with delight.

Dickson had trouble suppressing a smile at such enthusiasm, though it touched him deeply. "We'll have to part ways for a while," he said. "I don't believe we've reached the heart of the matter yet. We have some dull research ahead of us. For my part, I'll go spend a few days on the Continent."

"At a spa town?" asked Lipton with a wink.

"Good guess," answered Dickson, shaking his hand.

Lipton stayed in London to keep an eye on Denverton House. Dickson and Tom packed their bags that same day and went to Charing Cross Station. They took the night train to Dover, and the ferry to Ostend. From Ostend the express carried them across peaceful, happy Belgium. They got off at Luxembourg and went to the Hotel Continental at the center of that lovely city.

A late-afternoon sun gilded the grand ducal city; the murmur of moving water rose from the lush, verdant lower town. Everything about the old gabled houses leaning over the river's edge breathed peace and love of life.

"I'd rather nothing here be mixed up in a crime, Guv," murmured Tom as they strolled through a solitary rose garden, where the first buds were opening. He happily watched the people making their way slowly, by switchback paths, toward the upper town.

"I hope we'll find no more than a corollary to a crime here, my boy," said Dickson. "I mean something that was the hidden consequence of the original crime. As I said to Bunny Lipton, old Lord Denverton traveled a great deal on the Continent, and—but let's not anticipate. I believe I've discovered a faint glimmer of light, thanks to a fairly mundane deduction for which I can't claim much glory. I remembered that Denverton didn't die in London, but here in Luxembourg, and his body was taken back to England."

Dickson fell silent, and then Tom heard him murmur, "Schneider... I imagine there must be plenty of people by that name around here!"

"Who was Schneider?" asked Tom.

"Denverton's business agent in certain spa towns. The person who arranged his stays. He received a fairly handsome bequest at the old man's death. He's another element in the mystery of the late Denverton's life."

The street they were following, the walls of whose houses were stuccoed in green and pink, led toward the dismal grand ducal prison, then turned at a right angle down toward the river and more pleasant spots. A large garden opened up before them, with hedges of spindle bush, and green spaces that were half lawn, half vegetable plots. At the rear stood walls of gray stone covered in vines. An old gardener was weeding with the careful wisdom of experience, and he rose stiffly when he saw visitors approaching.

"Monsieur Schneider?" asked Dickson.

"What do you want of him?" asked the old man.

"To see him and speak with him, if possible."

"Hmm. To see him is easy enough; he's not ill-humored. As for speaking with him, that's another matter," chattered the gardener. "Come along anyway…"

With a gesture he invited them to follow him, and went into the large gray house that stood before them. They went down a long flagstone corridor, as cool as a cellar, which opened into a bright room, partly converted into an aviary. A frantic chirping greeted their arrival.

"Well, then, old Balthazar, how are the canaries this morning?" asked the gardener, stopping in front of an armchair that held a shapeless form.

The answer was a grunt. From out of a heap of clothing, a trembling hand emerged and reached feebly toward a side table on which stood a glass of rosé. The glass was lifted and carried to an enormous mouth in the middle of a face as simple-witted as could be imagined.

"Monsieur Schneider," said the gardener, introducing him with a certain irony.

Dickson clenched his fists. A memory no more than a day old came back to him. "I assume he hasn't always been like this?"

"Oh, no!" said the gardener quickly. "He was a perfectly sound man before this happened."

"And when was that?" asked the detective.

"Hmm… At my age, memory isn't what it used to be, you know," said the old man, "but it was a few years ago, anyway… after he stopped traveling. That's when it took him. Some days he's bad-tempered, other days, like today, he's not—or less so."

After giving the gardener a generous tip, Dickson took his leave.

"Time wasted, Guv?" asked Tom, looking at him sidelong.

"Not at all, my boy! Consider that not so many hours ago you looked just like that poor Schneider we've just left!"

"Impossible!" cried Tom, horrified.

"The Chinese poison took effect quite a long time ago. Unfortunately I don't know the antidote, so I can't try it on that living ruin we just saw."

"Would there be some benefit for us?"

"No doubt, but I can get along without it, I suppose," said the detective playfully as they walked up the hill toward the new town.

"If they wanted to keep that man from troubling them, Guv, why didn't the poisoners just kill him outright, rather than putting him into slow motion?" asked Tom.

Dickson stopped and stared at the fine foliage of a distant grove of oaks.

"What do you see, Guv?"

"There? Nothing at all, my boy, but it's you who've allowed me to see something. God's blood! Why was that man put into slow motion rather than killed? Ah, Tom, have you put your finger on the solution to the mystery?"

"I just asked the question, Guv," admitted Tom.

"When the problem is presented correctly, you can envision its solution, my boy," said Dickson sententiously, "I believe that if we can find an answer to your question, part of the mystery of Denverton House will be a mystery no longer. And now, let's eat!"

The Grand Duchy of Luxembourg dines well. Dickson still had fond memories of the bushels of crayfish and exquisite fried trout he'd enjoyed on a previous visit—an adventure to be told another time.

A bus full of happy tourists was going by just then. "Still two seats available, gentlemen!" cried the jovial conductor. "We're headed for Echternach!"

"All right," said Dickson, "with pleasure. We plan to have dinner at Larochette."

"Excellent choice, sir—but the road that direction is under repair, and I'll have to make a slight detour. I'll have to drop you at the Binzel-Schleft, and you'll have two kilometers to do on foot."

"Just enough to give us an appetite, my boy," said Dickson approvingly, as he took his seat on the bus next to Tom.

The glorious landscape rolled by like a movie. The sun was setting, but the tops of the trees in the forest and the crest of the rocky ridges glowed like molten gold. The deep Schluchten valleys, already filling with blue shadows, looked as formidable as chasms. The woods themselves, with their dark depths, were full of adventure and mystery—though on every peak a joyful fire seemed to blaze. A roaring stream thundered by next to the road. The last birds still awake called to each other from the dark underbrush.

"This is the Binzel-Schleft, gentlemen!" said the driver as he stopped the bus. "Follow the road. It's a twenty-minute walk to Larochette, where I'd recommend the Hôtel de la Poste."

In a cloud of dust, the bus disappeared around the next bend in the road, leaving the two detectives alone. On their left yawned the great dark Binzel fissure; steps cut into the rock led up the mountain.

"I'd like an extra fifteen minutes to have a closer look at this rock, Guv," said Tom.

"Granted, my boy," said Dickson, falling into step behind him.

They climbed the granite steps, pulled themselves up between boulders, rising from ridge to ridge and overlooking greater and greater depths, until they finally reached the top of the Binzel-Schleft. In truth it wasn't such a bad climb: the rocky plateau rose over the road by only a couple of hundred feet, and simply gave them an enjoyable view of the area—a rather dark view, because the dusk that was already noticeable on the path up had become almost night in the woods.

"Say, there's a car stopping," said Tom at the sound of brakes rising up from the valley. "The Schleft will have visitors even later than us this evening."

In the darkness they could hear footsteps rising toward them. Dickson and Tom waited, curious, to see the other tourists… but the wait grew long. No one was climbing now, and the Binzel-Schleft fell silent. Tom felt a strange unease; he'd been standing at the very edge, and had been the first to hear—and then not hear—the footsteps. He retreated toward his employer, whom he found searching the darkness with his eyes.

"Heads up, Tom," murmured Dickson. "There's someone behind those trees. He climbed straight up the rock, without using the stairs. Now he's behind us. I can't pinpoint his location; so let's be on our guard, my boy."

Suddenly a voice rang out from the sky over their heads—a voice Dickson recognized as the one he and Lipton had heard at Denverton House. "Drop your revolvers, gentlemen! They'd do you no good, since you can't see me, whereas I could easily kill you in your tracks if I felt like it."

Pop! Pop! They couldn't tell exactly where the sound came from—but a foot from Dickson's face a rock shattered under the impact of a bullet fired from a gun with a silencer.

"You see, gentlemen, I'd only have to aim a little to the right to end your lives. But I won't do it—as long as you obey me. Kindly go back down and get into the car that's waiting at the foot of the stairs."

A Chevrolet sat on the road, with all its lights off and one rear door open; it was a left-hand-drive, and no one was at the wheel.

"Kindly get in, gentlemen," said the voice, now closer than ever.

"No choice, or we'll be on the receiving end of a well-aimed shot," muttered Dickson.

They settled into comfortable seats. Then—without their seeing anyone—the door was slammed shut.

"Tom," said Dickson quickly, "do you have the wax? Fast!"

Both men bent over and rubbed their hands across their faces. That allowed them to stuff small balls of soft wax into their nostrils, and to slip into their mouths a little device that Dickson had invented only a few months earlier. It was a tube four centimeters long, that they were to keep in their mouths, making sure to breathe only through it. It contained one of the most effective poison-gas filters yet devised, designed by a young industrial-arts student in London.

They'd barely finished their maneuver when Dickson heard a soft whistling; and in spite of their precautions the two prisoners could smell a thick miasma enveloping them. The detective nudged Tom, and a few seconds later they both sank back onto the seat cushions like men who were fast asleep.

Just then a slim figure leapt out from the side of the road, got behind the wheel, and drove off at high speed. No one had gotten in next to the driver; the prisoners therefore had only him to worry about. By the glow from the headlights Dickson had seen the cruel visage of a Chinese man, and he decided to take steps accordingly.

Shortly before the Mullerthal region, a sharp bend in the road required vehicles to slow down. Little by little Dickson's hand had crept toward his backup revolver, and now he held it aimed at the driver. "The end justifies…" he muttered.

As they reached the sharp bend he went into action—like a thunderclap: two pistol shots hit the driver in the nape of the neck; at the same moment Dickson hurled himself against the glass partition, which shattered into a thousand pieces. Reaching over the fallen body of the Chinese man, he seized the steering wheel—just in time, because the car was veering dangerously off course. But Tom quickly opened the front door, pushed out the driver's body, and stepped on the brakes.

"Whew!" said Dickson, breathing in the fresh night air. "Darkness, the forest, solitude: we have everything we need to settle this business privately."

The Chinese man had been killed instantly. The detectives learned nothing by searching his pockets, and Dickson spent a few silent minutes thinking.

"I'm not going to give up now," he muttered. "Let's see what else we can get out of this, since for the moment we're one step ahead of the enemy. Look out!"

That last was a shout of alarm, because a powerful car was approaching from a distance, and the white beams of its headlights could already be seen under the dark sky.

"Put on the driver's cap, Tom," he called, "and make sure they don't see your face. I'll take care of this fellow!"

Matching his actions to his words, Dickson heaved the body into the back seat, propped it up against him like a man asleep, and assumed the same pose himself. Tom was already accelerating when the other car roared up behind them. In a few minutes it had caught up with the Chevrolet.

"Hey, lemon head!" shouted a voice in German. "The orders are changed! Don't cross the border at Irrel, because there's a night patrol. Orders are, go back to the house!"

And with that, the powerful car pulled past them and vanished into the night, and the sound of its engine soon faded in the distance.

"Guv! Guv!" cried Tom. "Did you recognize him?"

"I was sleeping, my boy, remember?"

"Luckily I wasn't. It was the old gardener from Luxembourg! But, by all the saints, he seemed to be in better shape tonight."

"So, I deduce that the orders are to go back to Schneider's house," said Dickson. "U-turn, my boy. Let's see what's going on in that run-down house."

"And the Chinese fellow?"

"We can't be burdened with him. Throw him into the bushes, which are dense enough to hide him for a while."

Dickson took the wheel, turned around, and headed back toward Luxembourg. When they passed through Larochette it was fast asleep, and only the windows at the Hôtel de la Poste were still lit. Tom bid a silent sad farewell to the crayfish and

140

the trout. But the Chevrolet, with an excellent appetite, ate up the kilometers…

5. A Night of Adventures

A few hundred meters into the grand ducal city, Harry Dickson parked the car in a side alley, where no one would see it. Then he and Tom walked briskly toward the city center, taking care to stick to the back streets of the lower town.

The town was asleep in the peace of the evening, cradled by the great murmuring waters of its river, forever washing the pebbles on its bed as smooth as skulls. That wonderful evening silence of small towns, hardly broken by the silvery leap of a trout, by the whisper of a night bird's wings…

The detectives would've been happy to linger, to forget that in the midst of this tranquil beauty they were on the trail of a crime—but a bend in the road put them right across from Schneider's house. When gilded by afternoon sun it had looked inviting, with its spindle hedge, its planters, and its vegetable plots; now it loomed dreadful and hostile out of the darkness. All the windows were dark; those on the ground floor were protected by heavy oak shutters. Around that silent house the only sound was the wind rustling the trees and the ivy that grew on the walls.

Dickson examined the grounds at length before making a decision. The peacefulness of the house had to be an illusion, a trick.

Behind the house stood outbuildings and a garage. The garage door was wide open, and the detectives approached it. There were oil stains on the concrete floor of the garage, but no car.

"The car driven by the mysterious gardener didn't come straight back," began Tom—but Dickson put his hand over his assistant's mouth to silence him. A car was coming down the steep street, and Tom recognized it: the one that had passed them on the road to Echternach.

The detectives leaped behind the spindle hedge. They'd barely hidden before the car roared into the driveway crossing the garden and entered the garage. From where they were, Dickson and Tom could hear the gardener-chauffeur give a grunt of surprise and say to himself, "Well, well, the little jalopy isn't back yet. But it can make good time when it wants to."

Leaving the garage door open, the chauffeur walked toward the house. He was no longer the stooped old man of that afternoon, but a well-built and much younger man, though his face—covered in wrinkles and marked by senility—would've fooled anyone at first sight. He went inside by the servants' door, and the two detectives could hear him quickly climbing stairs.

Dickson knew it was time to roll the dice. "Tom, we need to part ways for an hour. The chauffeur is probably going to be told to go find the Chevrolet driven by the Chinese man. Run back to where we hid the car; park it on the side of the road like it's broken down. The chauffeur here will get out of his car to see what's wrong. Jump him—and above all take him alive. One shot of the drug we always have with us will do the job, if need be.

"Then drive like mad for the Belgian border; you can get to Arlon in a few minutes. On the Rue de la Montagne in Arlon you'll find the office and home of Anatole Lamy, shipping agent. Wake him up and tell him I sent you. Nothing will surprise him, and you can trust him completely. I don't know what's inside this house. If by dawn I haven't met you at Lamy's, ask him to take action. He'll understand what that means, and he knows his way around action. Now run, and God protect you!"

Dickson remained alone, hidden behind the hedge. The gardener-chauffeur hadn't returned, which pleased him, since he figured that would give Tom enough time to get back to where they'd left the Chevrolet. Finally the servants' door opened and the chauffeur emerged. He looked unhappy and afraid. The detective could hear him swearing under his breath as he started the car and then reversed it down the driveway to the street.

"He's going the right way," Dickson rejoiced as he saw the car head out the main road toward Echternach.

The kitchen door had been left unlocked. The detective crawled carefully toward it, making sure to stay under the cover of the shadows of the spindle hedge. He reached the door without trouble, and a few seconds later he was inside the dark, silent house.

Tom had barely parked the Chevrolet by the side of the road, with its running lights lit, when he heard the powerful engine of the other car. He plunged into the nearest bushes, paying no attention to the brambles and nettles that scratched him.

The Chevrolet looked like a car abandoned by the road while its owners had gone to get help nearby. The vehicle approaching was a big French car that Tom knew well. A few meters from his hiding place the car braked to a stop, and the chauffeur got out and walked calmly over to the Chevrolet.

"Hey, Su-Su!" he called quietly.

At that moment Tom leaped out of the bushes and struck the chauffeur so hard with a bludgeon that he dropped to the ground and lay still.

"Now for the shot," chuckled Tom, holding up a hypodermic, "and then hitting the road for Belgium! And to think that I've got my choice of wheels!" he said, comparing the two cars. "That's all right, I'll stick with that Chevrolet—it's brought me luck!"

He parked the big French car where the Chevrolet had been, up the side alley. Then, with his involuntary passenger fast asleep on the back seat, Tom sped toward the border.

"This sweet little car has certainly seen service as a mobile dormitory tonight!" he laughed to himself. He drove through the sleeping city of Luxembourg, wondering what his employer could be up to, then headed for the border. For the past few years that border had become purely nominal, since the Belgium-Luxembourg customs agreement did away with any border posts between those two friendly nations.

Down the road, a few distant pinpricks of light denoted the railroad signals at the Arlon station. Tom passed it on his left, and entered the small country town. An antique streetlight on one corner dimly lit a sign, and with satisfaction he read, in white letters on a blue background, *Rue de la Montagne*. A little further on, a fine copper nameplate announced to pass-ersby that this was the residence of *Anatole Lamy—Shipping Agent—Customs Agent*.

Lights were still on at the home of this solid Arlon citizen, because Tom could see bright lines between the slats of the sliding shutters. And indeed he didn't have to wait long: at his first ring of the bell, the door opened and a man in shirt-sleeves eyed him curiously.

"Monsieur Lamy?"

"Himself, my dear sir. How can I help you?" the man replied cordially.

"I come on behalf of Harry Dickson," murmured Tom.

Lamy didn't bat an eye, and answered in a peculiar way: "Of course, Monsieur Sellier! Delighted to be of service! I'll go open the garage door. Put your car in there, and come join me in the dining room. I'm a night owl, and not easily inconvenienced!" He'd spoken loudly enough for all the neighbors to hear, if by chance they weren't deep in their beauty sleep.

Lamy himself soon opened the double doors of the garage, and then closed them again behind the car. Tom gestured to point out the man asleep in the car, and Lamy replied with a barely perceptible nod.

"Mr. Dickson wants him alive," said Tom quietly. "If all goes well, he'll be here himself at dawn. If he's not, I'm supposed to ask you to accompany me back to Luxembourg, to the house of a Mr. Schneider."

Lamy didn't move, but Tom saw that he had his full attention.

"What shall we do with my prisoner?" asked the young man.

"We'll put him someplace where he can wake up when he wants, and even make as much noise as he wants," said Lamy, opening the car door and taking the man in his arms. Tom was astonished to see Lamy—a little bald man with muttonchops that made him look like a country notary—display such physical strength: he carried the chauffeur like a sleeping child being carried to bed.

But, though Lamy seemed like a man not easily taken by surprise, he exclaimed, "But—it's Arno!"

"You know him?"

"There must be a mistake," murmured Lamy. "There's been a mix-up! Why is Arno a prisoner? He's one of ours!"

Before Tom could answer, there was a knock in a distinctive pattern at the back door.

"Ah!" said Lamy, setting down his burden. "We'll find out right away what happened."

He unlocked a door at the rear and let in several men dressed in European clothes, but whose yellow faces made clear their Asian origins. Tom retreated, with vague fears of a trap. But those fears were soon cleared up: behind the three Orientals appeared a tall, thin figure, and Tom recognized the smiling face of Harry Dickson.

Dickson presented them to his assistant: "Messrs. Matsuko, Saito, and Timotu. Not Chinese, but Japanese, as their names suggest. As it happens, we followed the wrong trail, though these gentlemen will acknowledge that the honors of the day are ours."

"It's true, Mr. Dickson," said Matsuko, a stiff little Japanese with exquisite manners. "It's true! We thought Su-Su was one of ours. In fact, he was an accomplice of the headless Voice, and he proved it by helping him take you both prisoner. By shooting Su-Su on the road to Echternach, gentlemen, you executed a traitor."

Tom stared dumbfounded at his employer.

"I wonder if these gentlemen could explain matters to my assistant," said Dickson.

"Come into the parlor," said Lamy. "I believe there'll be much to say."

Once they were settled in comfortable armchairs, with cigars and hot tea in front of them, Dickson began, "It turns out that these gentlemen, private detectives in the service of His Imperial Majesty the Mikado—and incidentally accredited by all the European powers—have been pursuing the same investigation as I have: the Path of the Gods."

"Ah!" cried Tom. "So we're finally going to find out what that damned Path is?"

The Japanese shook their heads sadly. "That's what we don't know yet. As of now we can assert only that it will lead to unprecedented horrors that will drench China in blood and cause the death of thousands of European and Japanese expatriates."

"The return of Fuh-Suh the Terrible," said Dickson.

The three Japanese nodded as one.

"But what connection does all that have with that tidy little house in the suburbs of Luxembourg—the quietest town in the world?" cried Tom.

"Plenty," replied Matsuko. "Monsieur Lamy will agree: that's the house that always attracts the headless Voice."

"Huh? That's a hell of a name!" exclaimed the young man irreverently—earning him a disapproving glance from his employer.

"Well, you can always hear the voice, but you never see to whom it belongs," said Saito.

Dickson nodded in turn. "I've heard it myself, twice: once in London, once last night, when it almost got me. But for something that's only a voice, it's pretty handy with a revolver."

"Could that be Fuh-Suh?" asked Tom.

They all shook their heads no. "Not at all. Fuh-Suh was a dreadful being, acting with incredible mastery, a leader of men, a genius… The headless Voice must be some kind of familiar, a demon he domesticated. That fits the legends. In any case, for a servant his skills are still formidable."

"But Fuh-Suh disappeared," said Tom.

"He'll come back along the Path of the Gods," said Timotu with a grave face. "I promise you, that's already common knowledge in China."

Matsuko turned to Dickson. "I can't tell you how delighted we are to have you with us on this strange case, sir. Up to now we were unaware of Denverton House—whose role in all this is as unknown to us as it is to you. But we've had our eye on Schneider's house for four years. You found it in three days—that's impressive, you have to admit!"

"How did you learn that Schneider's house might also be involved in all this?" asked Dickson.

"Partly by chance," replied Matsuko. "Mr. Arno, a European detective in the service of His Majesty the Mikado, was vacationing in Europe. One day in the street he noticed Schneider on his doorstep and recognized his symptoms as those of a man under the influence of that mysterious Chinese drug—whose nature and antidote are both unknown to us. He sensed that something suspicious was going on, notified our agency, and was given orders to remain on the spot. Arno got himself hired as a gardener at Schneider's house—the management of which is entrusted to a Belgian notary, thanks to a referral by Monsieur Lamy, who's a friend of Japan as well as of England. Arno had a Chinese servant, Su-Su, whom he wanted to keep with him. He set him up in Luxembourg at a prosperous confectioner's shop. Every evening the boy would go to his master for orders. Did you notice Schneider's fine aviary? Well, that was a clever trick thought up by Arno. He knew that everywhere the headless Voice was heard, whether in China or abroad, birds were caught and eaten alive. Bizarre, isn't it? But it's a fact that we've confirmed, without being able to explain it. From time to time, indeed, birds disappeared from Schneider's aviary, and Arno found nothing but the bloody remains. And he heard the Voice itself, scolding someone in Chinese and issuing dire threats."

"Poor Arno!" said Tom repentantly.

"Oh, well! You did him a good turn by eliminating Su-Su—a traitor, who was probably getting ready to knock him off, as soon as the headless Voice directed him to."

"And now," asked Lamy, speaking for the first time, "can I arrange for you to get some sleep? I've put Arno to bed. Tomorrow he won't feel any the worse for what Mr. Wills did to him. If you'd like to go to bed yourselves, gentlemen, you know my house is as comfortable as it is roomy."

Dickson shook his head. "I'm afraid, gentlemen, I must inflict a sleepless night on you. Or should I say, at least on me and on my assistant, Tom."

"Allow us to join you," insisted Matsuko.

Dickson shook his head again. "Too many people could hinder my plans. By the way, Dr. Matsuko, those bird disappearances probably happened at night, no?"

"Indeed, Mr. Dickson."

"And the headless Voice, likewise, seemed to prefer to make itself heard at night?"

"Mostly, yes... What do you deduce from that?"

"Nothing for now. But, with a little luck, we should soon be able to tell you more about that extraordinary Voice."

6. The Disembodied Voice

"No, my boy, we won't be getting any sleep tonight! Too bad—we can rest later. We're headed back to Luxembourg, and even beyond: we're going to the Binzel-Schleft!"

"Such happy memories!" said Tom, getting into the car, to Dickson, who was already behind the wheel. "Tell me what happened to you at Schneider's house, Guv."

"Oh, the story won't take more than two minutes to tell, my boy. I'd barely gotten into the house when I heard voices nearby in the parlor. Voices speaking Japanese, not Chinese. In the darkness I could see bright light at a keyhole. I was curious and put my eye to it. I'll admit I was stunned when I recognized those Japanese detectives, with whom I'd already been in touch and whose integrity and trustworthiness were beyond doubt. Instead of being behind enemy lines, I was on friendly soil. Without hesitating, I burst in. Though it isn't easy to startle those good Japanese, I promise you I had a moment to enjoy their stunned faces. It didn't last; we soon explained ourselves, and learned that we'd been following different trails leading to the same mysterious goal."

"Say, Guv," said Tom, "Bunny Lipton must be having quite a time in London right now!"

"Good old Bunny can take it easy: nothing's going to disturb the London peace while the headless Voice is away."

"Sure, Guv, but you don't think it's a widespread conspiracy?"

"Not at all!" said Dickson simply. Then he fell silent and gave his attention to the road. Luxembourg was far away. The road wound through enormous dark woods. No lights shone in the few villages they passed through; barely even a watchdog barked from time to time.

High looming rocks stood silhouetted to the right of the road, and Dickson slowed down.

"Are we at Binzel?" asked Tom.

"No more than a kilometer away, but we'll do the rest on foot. Our best chance for success is not to be heard."

Tom shuddered as he saw his employer draw from his pocket a long dagger whose blade was blackened to avoid nighttime reflections off the steel. "Are you going to need that wicked thing?" he asked uneasily.

"Could be," answered the detective. "From now on, speak only if I say it's all right. Much depends on it."

Without exchanging a word, they walked for a long while, not on the paved road but on the thick moss along the shoulder, which muffled their footsteps as effectively as the best felt soles could have. Finally Dickson motioned to Tom to stop, and pointed to a dark fissure in the granite cliff: the Binzel-Schleft. Now that deep night surrounded it, how menacing and full of dangers seemed that dark opening in the rocks! As he followed on his employer's heels, Tom pictured himself climbing the steep steps of a castle turret some cursed midnight, at the mercy of the worst whims of the Beyond.

At last they reached the rocky plateau, and from there they plunged into the dense woods that covered the Binzel ridges. It was no longer pitch black, because the moon had risen; it was still low behind the trees, but its thin silver arrows already split the sylvan darkness. That feeble light was enough to allow Dickson to move forward without stumbling too much against trees and stumps, and he led Tom along behind him.

A sad, mournful howl rose from the depths of the woods: the cry of the wildcat on the hunt for its nocturnal prey. It came closer, drew away, came closer again, then fell silent among the distant trees.

By the faint moonlight filtering through the trees Tom could see that Dickson was crouching down and stretching out on the moss, with one hand reaching forward. A slight shadow extended beyond that hand—and Tom recognized it as the strange blackened blade that reflected no light.

Other creatures of the night called, shrieked, howled… and then in perfect unison they all fell silent.

Tac… taca… tac. The sound rang out in front of them— the only sound in the night, as if everything held still for it. And yet it was only a soft, crisp snap, like two small pieces of wood struck against each other rhythmically. Tom pictured a clumsy, fearful child playing the castanets as quietly as possible, so as not to disturb the sleep of some terrible adult.

Tac… taca… tac. What menace that dull sound conveyed to the young man! His feeling was followed by the proof— when he saw his employer retreating as cautiously as possible into the shadows of the massive oaks that surrounded their hiding place. Tom couldn't stand it any longer, and he crawled back quietly until he joined Dickson.

The sound began to fade as if it were moving away from them, deeper into the forest.

"What was that?" asked Tom in a voice barely above a whisper. "It gave me the creeps."

"A Chinese birdcall," replied Dickson just as quietly.

"What for?" asked Tom in astonishment.

"That's the sound Chinese poachers use to attract game birds at night. It seems to have the power to awaken birds like pheasants and partridges and to make them hurry toward the source of the sound. Silence—it's coming back... Anyway, it might very well do our job for us."

Tac... taca... tac. The sound became clearer, and this time seemed to be headed cautiously, hesitantly, straight toward them. Tom watched his employer tear a few twigs off a nearby shrub, twist them, then raise them to his mouth. They made a staccato sound, followed—to Tom's complete astonishment—by a *tac... taca... tac* almost identical to the sound from the forest.

The answer came immediately, and was repeated feverishly; and then it sounded very close by. Dickson set down his improvised birdcall and stood still, his nerves on edge, his hand stretched out on the grass.

"Look out, my boy," he murmured to his assistant. "Keep your revolver at the ready, but fire only if you see that things are going against me. Silence!"

Tac... taca... tac. Now it was very close, to their left, where the moonlight had begun to shine a little brighter. And then Tom saw it: a squat shape, barely bigger than a ten-year-old child, was advancing slowly from tree to tree—not crawling but upright on stubby, severely bowed legs. The massive torso suggested uncommon strength; the head, sunk between the shoulders, couldn't yet be distinguished.

The creature was now advancing only imperceptibly, while still making that peculiar sound: *tac... taca... tac.* Finally, fully lit by a moonbeam, it stood out against the darker bushes. Tom felt Dickson's hand on his arm, imposing calm and total silence.

It was a terrifying sight: tucked deep between great round shoulders, a revolting head cackled in the moonlight. Its muddy yellow complexion shaded to green around two enormous bulging eyes. It had almost no chin, but the lower half of its nightmare face was split by an immense mouth, out of which stuck two terrible white canines. Its eyes were as fixed and lidless as those of an octopus. In their murky depths could be seen an intelligent, desperate cruelty. The creature had stopped its birdcalls; now from time to time it growled quietly in anxious fury.

Sometimes it sniffed the air forcefully, and then it growled even more. Could it smell the presence of danger? Tom was inclined to think so, and he tightened his grip on the revolver in his fist. The monster stood still in a circle of moonlight, and now the detectives could see that it was dressed in a filthy black loincloth that left its legs and arms and hairy torso exposed. The completely bald head only added to its repulsive ugliness.

Tac... taca... tac. Tom almost cried out in fear, because Dickson had begun making his own birdcall again, though the horrible creature was now only ten paces away. But the idea of a trap didn't seem to occur to the monster: it crouched down, then crawled rapidly toward the two detectives' hiding place. They were completely in shadow, with a bush screening them from the advancing figure.

It came straight toward them, and as it left the circle of moonlight they could see only its dark, massive silhouette. That was for the best, because if Tom had seen that terrifying face approaching he wouldn't have been able to resist firing a couple of metal-jacketed bullets into it—whereas his employer had clearly said, "Intervene only if things are going against me."

The monster reached the bush and stretched out a simian paw to part the foliage. At that moment Dickson's hand lunged at the lower half of the creature's torso. Tom heard a muffled "Huh!" and got ready to fire, but the thing stood still, its talons stretched out toward the bush, its hideous face a little thrown back, its bulging eyes reflecting the moonlight. Then, with a long sigh, the creature slid to the ground and moved no more.

And now in turn Dickson sighed deeply. "Help me carry this thing to the car, Tom," he said, pointing to the body.

It was hard work. In spite of its short stature, the monster was very heavy, and Dickson urged his assistant to make no noise. The strange wild-animal smell the thing gave off almost made Tom nauseous.

"Easy, my boy, easy," said Dickson as they took the peculiar cadaver down the steps of the Binzel-Schleft.

"Why, Guv? Isn't the headless Voice dead? What can it do to us now?"

"Dead? I should say not! As for being dangerous, that all depends where it is right now. Remember the shots fired by that gun with a silencer!"

Tom shook his head; once again he'd given up trying to understand, and now wasn't the time for questions.

"Bring the car up, my boy," said Dickson. "Stop when you reach the foot of the Binzel, but don't turn the engine off. The moment I'm in, along with our passenger, take off in high gear. We're returning to Arlon by a back road."

"We're a regular taxi service tonight, Guv!" murmured Tom. "Or more like a hearse service! Fascinating work!"

He carried out his employer's instructions to the letter. When the car was once again speeding down the road back, Dickson sighed with relief. "Thank God, IT was deep in the woods. Otherwise that might've cost us dearly."

"IT, Guv? The headless Voice?"

"Indeed, my boy. Did you think, even for a minute, that this horrible sallow brute, that we've just slain like a rampaging beast, could possible speak in the civilized way the Voice does, or could make such learned use of the fearful poisons of the Middle Kingdom, or could handle a well-aimed revolver with such skill?"

In the back rolled the lifeless body of the strange Oriental, striking the doors and the seats with muffled thuds. The smell of musk and decomposition it gave off was so strong that by the time they reached Arlon both detectives felt truly ill.

The three Japanese and Monsieur Lamy were soon awakened, and they gathered around the awful remains.

"I believe it's an orangutan from Borneo," said Matsuko. "They're mysterious creatures, with a capacity for training and even a certain devotion to their masters. Are they human? Are they apes? I'd lean toward the first option, because they can be taught a few simple words. When they're angry they're terrifying. I know that a few Chinese mandarins keep them."

"But the Voice..." began Saito.

Dickson smiled. "It still lives, but not for long. I promise you: its death warrant is already signed. Monsieur Lamy, please ask the grand ducal government to close the Binzel woods to the public for a week. That's longer than we'll need."

Timotu, who'd been bent over the man of the jungles, stood up and showed them his smudged finger. "My word! This creature must've been wearing makeup and false whiskers!"

"I can easily believe it," said Dickson. "And indeed it's very likely. But now, gentlemen, I beg you to grant me—and my assistant—a few hours' sleep. Here comes the dawn, rising over the beautiful countryside of the Ardennes."

7. The Disembodied Voice (Cont'd)

Harry Dickson spent a day around Arlon, thinking. Lamy had come through handsomely, and the trout and the crayfish arrived by special delivery. The three Japanese did justice to the food as well, and by a sort of truce little was said about the mystery of the Path of the Gods. During the day Dickson had telephoned London and spoken with Bunny Lipton, who was deeply bored on the banks of the Thames.

"I'm sorry, Bunny," said Dickson. "But you'll have to suffer patiently. Denverton House will remain quiet, and I give you permission to spend your time drinking ale and reading the satirical papers."

Two days passed before Dickson suggested to his friends that they return to Luxembourg. They found Schneider's house in perfect order and perfectly quiet. Arno, who'd gone back there, reported that nothing had happened. Schneider himself continued in that vegetative state they'd already observed.

Arno very decently had no hard feelings toward Tom. "Those are the risks of the job," he said. "Maybe some fine day I'll return the favor, my dear boy, but for now let's have a glass of rosé and drink to our reconciliation and lasting friendship."

Dickson and the three Japanese joined heartily in that invitation, and they all spent a charming, cordial hour together.

"And now," said Dickson, "back to the Binzel."

Arno took the wheel of the big French car, while Tom drove his favorite, the Chevrolet. A representative of the grand ducal police joined them for the journey. Two kilometers in each direction from Binzel, a discreet watch had been posted, whose principal job was to keep strangers out of the woods. But since it was still early in the season, there were hardly any tourists to be turned away by the ban.

As they were all climbing the brown rock steps up the fissure, Dickson seemed to have doubts again. "I wonder whether two days will have been enough to overcome the last of his powers of resistance,' he murmured. "But you never know…"

Matsuko started with surprise, and he came close and whispered in Dickson's ear. The detective smiled. "Quite right, doctor!"

"Yes," said Matsuko, "I noticed those small cuts behind the orangutan's ears, but I hadn't thought of THAT. In fact, they say that in the terrible Fuh-Suh's entourage…"

He didn't finish: all of them stopped and stared at each other. From the depths of the forest emerged a harrowing roar that rose and fell with a strange, piercing tone, sounding like a cry of distress but also of despair and incredible anger.

"The headless Voice!" murmured Arno, turning pale. "My God, I've never heard anything so awful."

Dickson stood still, listening, with a serious expression. Matsuko turned to him. "You think that…"

"It's dying," said the detective.

"Dying of what, Guv?" asked Tom.

"Of hunger!" came the strange reply.

Saito spoke up. "I once witnessed the torture of a Chinese bandit, who was condemned to be buried alive in an ant-hill."

"Good Lord, it's awful," murmured Dickson. "And yet we'd be risking our lives if we went any closer."

"Is it a man, Guv?" asked Tom.

"Barely," said Dickson gruffly. He stood thinking, with his brow furrowed. "But it doesn't matter—I'd rather risk my hide than listen to that agony any longer. Mr. Saito, I hadn't considered fire ants. We have to put an end to the torture."

Clearly the detective's mind was made up: he was already giving them detailed instructions. He'd go on alone. Matsuko would follow him at a distance, so as not to lose sight of him and to able to intervene only in case of dire need.

The Voice was already getting quieter. It was only a moan, growing gradually weaker, broken from time to time by a long howl of rage and agony.

Dickson advanced toward it, slipping from tree to tree, followed at a distance by the Japanese detective. Then Dickson stopped: the Voice had begun again, but now it spoke in words of despair: "The Path of the Gods! Too late!"

Ahead of the detective the trees thinned out, and a small clearing lay in a slight hollow. The Voice arose from its center. When he'd reached the edge of the clearing, Dickson took cover behind a thick tree trunk and looked out intently.

Matsuko—contrary to orders—joined him. "Do you see something, Mr. Dickson?" he murmured.

The detective shook his head. He saw only moss and small thorn bushes, nothing that could conceal a human form.

The clearing was empty. And yet only a few seconds earlier the moaning had come from its center.

"Ants!" said the Japanese suddenly.

A patch of red rippled at the center of the clearing, moving around an object that was certainly no more than two feet high and that resembled a shapeless lump of soil. Suddenly that object howled, "The Path of the Gods—finished!"

"Heavens!" cried Matsuko. "That's what it is! How awful!"

Had the shapeless thing heard him? An arm gnawed to the bone rose above the swarming mass. The tip of that raw stump held an automatic revolver with a silencer attached. But two shots had already rung out from the edge of the clearing, and the small arm fell back among the voracious ants.

Dickson plucked up a handful of dry grass, lit it, and stuffed it into the anthill. The innumerable, infinitesimal army stampeded away, and a strange thing came into view: a human head, its flesh already half eaten away by ants. It was attached to a stunted body—indeed just half a torso—with only one tiny arm, the one that held the revolver in a hand no bigger than that of a small monkey.

Matsuko fell back in superstitious fear. "I thought that's what it was! But you figured it out first, Mr. Dickson! A living Buddha! A vampire Buddha! The orangutan was both his means of transport and his food source!"

Drawn by the sound of the shots, the other Japanese, Lamy, Tom, and the grand ducal official stared at the scene, stunned.

"Gentlemen," said Dickson, "the curtain has fallen! The lead actor has left the stage. But the mystery remains unsolved—and the solution lies in London."

"Off we go!" cried the Japanese with an enthusiasm quite incompatible with the composure typical of their nation.

"There's plenty of time, gentlemen," laughed Dickson. "We'll rendezvous at Denverton House in a year. No invitations will go out. We'll be the only guests at Lord Denverton's ridiculous dinner."

8. The Path of the Gods

Indeed, Lord Denverton had rather few guests to entertain. The lawyer who, for four years, had received the invitations to pass on, hadn't had to worry about it this year. Around the table in the formal dining room at Denverton House sat only the great Harry Dickson, the three Japanese detectives—Matsuko, Saito, and Timotu—Bunny Lipton, come back for the occasion, and Tom Wills. The young lord presided over the dinner. It wasn't ridiculous, as the previous years' dinners had been; and the menu had been planned with meticulous care.

"What exactly are we waiting for, Mr. Dickson?" asked Denverton.

The detective shook his head in perplexity. "I don't know myself, my lord. I'm certainly waiting for something, but..." With a look of intense thought, he pushed away his glass of fine Napoleon cognac. "The dinner takes place at a set hour on a set date," he murmured. "And nothing can be altered in the formal dining room. That's all I have as reference points to reach a solution."

He leaned back in his chair and gazed at the ceiling. Then he began to laugh. "It was too easy, after all." He drank down his cognac without tasting it, and his eyes shone. "Everything's set, gentlemen. We just have wait a while."

"A long time?" asked Denverton a little impatiently.

Dickson gazed up at the skylight in the ceiling. "Oh, let's say no more than twenty minutes!"

The three Japanese, as if transfixed in their seats, fastened their black eyes on the detective with a look that was both admiring and slightly envious.

"Ten minutes!" announced Lipton.

Dickson kept his eyes on the skylight. A ray of sunshine came through it and lit the top of the room in gold. The other guests could see that Dickson was breathing heavily and clasping his hands nervously. His eyes never left the ceiling.

Suddenly he leapt up and went to the wall across from him. "A cane, a stick, anything!" he cried. He pulled a sword off a display rack of weapons and hurled himself at the wall. He'd just heard a slight click at a place high up on the molding, where a small spot of sunlight had just appeared. With all his strength he struck the center of the bright disc.

Lord Denverton and his guests began to shout: part of the wall had vanished, revealing a white marble staircase ornamented with designs in gold and jade.

"Gentlemen," said Dickson with feeling, "would you care to follow me along the Path of the Gods?"

"Ah!" murmured Matsuko and Lipton together. "So that's what it was?"

They all climbed the staircase, which was cleverly concealed inside the massive walls of Denverton House. An ebony door encrusted in gold and ivory stood at the top of the stairs, on a tiny landing tiled in jade and onyx. Dickson seized the silver door handle. Bright light immediately flooded the staircase, and now they noticed small, exquisite electric sconces positioned alongside the steps.

After great hesitation, Dickson opened the door. They were struck by a heavy, piercing odor of musk, incense, and myrrh, plus some other indefinable scent. The open door revealed a room of modest size, furnished half in European and half in Oriental style. Out of magnificent Chinese vases grew enormous artificial chrysanthemums—looking entirely alive.

"A man!" cried one of the Japanese detectives.

Someone dressed a dark silk kimono was stretched out in an armchair at a desk covered in papers; he looked asleep.

Dickson bent over a yellow face with narrow eyes, and lightly touched a cold, leathery cheek. "Dead." He thought a moment, then said, as if to himself, "They say certain Chinese drugs can prevent decomposition for many years."

Then Matsuko cried out in fear. "Mr. Lipton! Don't you recognize this dead man?"

"Oh!" murmured Lipton. "This is too much! I only caught sight of him once—but it's him!"

"The mandarin Fuh-Suh! The terror of the world!"

Dickson approached, holding a handkerchief soaked in powerfully scented rubbing alcohol. "Gentlemen, let this remain forever our secret! Or at least let it be shielded from public scandal. Lord Denverton, take a close look at this."

He began to rub the leathery face. Slowly, a thick layer of yellow pigment rubbed off, and wrinkles became visible, and the slanting eyes changed shape.

"Dear God!" cried the young lord, terrified. "Dear God—it's my uncle, Lord Denverton!"

"Known to the rest of the world as Fuh-Suh the Terrible," Dickson added gravely.

When everyone was seated around a table again—not in the formal dining room but in the young lord's private rooms—Dickson addressed them. "According to official records, Lord Denverton traveled to China only once, in the flower of his youth. During that visit he must've decided to embark on one of the most extraordinary adventures ever conceived. Its beginnings are murky, and shouldn't overly preoccupy us: if someday an adventure novelist wants to write the astonishing life of Denverton-Fuh-Suh, it'll be up to him to do the research. At university Denverton had had a friend named Schneider, who resembled him somewhat, and whose only ambition was to live, as splendidly as possible, at the expense of his near-lookalike.

"Denverton took it as a sign from the gods: from now on he could live a double life. For years and years he sent Schneider to stay—under his name—at various Continental spa towns. On the rare occasions when Denverton himself came back to London, Schneider stayed quietly at home in his native Luxembourg. Meanwhile, Fuh-Suh was born: he became a mandarin, a rabble-rouser, and a warrior—the terror of the Middle Kingdom.

"But little by little Denverton grew into the role: he began to believe in his Asiatic mission. Under who knows what religious influence, he became convinced that he was the emissary of the Eastern gods. It matched an ancient legend, that a mandarin warrior named Fuh, after a certain interval of years spent in the kingdom of shadows, would return among the living and resume his role. A sort of Chinese Frederick Barbarossa, if you will. Believing himself to be that legendary mandarin, Denverton acted accordingly. The same legend claimed that the prophesied return, along the Path of the Gods, would take place at a dinner hosted for crooks chosen at random.

"Steeped in that millenarian superstition, Denverton made ready for his return among the living, once death had struck him down. He came back to London, built a special retreat inside his house, and made his will accordingly. Here again the legend contributed a detail: it was said that, at one of those dinners, the sun itself would open the Path of the Gods to the mandarin returning from the dead.

"Denverton gave the gods a little help: he installed a solar lock. When the sun shining through the skylight struck a certain spot high up on the molding, a trigger made from ultra-sensitive metals would release the lock. If that was indeed the moment for the resurrection, the newly awakened mandarin would only have to open the door and rejoin the world of the living. If it wasn't the right time, then the cooling of those same metals would relock the secret door, and everything would quietly wait another year.

"That's why you saw me hasten to strike the spot lit by the sun. You'll observe that the place was chosen so skillfully—I should say, so astronomically—that the sun could only hit it from a position it reached just once a year. Extraordinary calculations in celestial mechanics must've been required to produce that result. So all of this involves a mixture of superstition, fanatical belief, science, and trickery.

"Still, that wasn't enough: he needed servants ready to protect the secret. That job went to a living Buddha, malformed, almost totally paralyzed, but gifted with enormous intelligence. That monster made use of an orangutan to compensate for his own deformity, as we've seen. Denverton had only one other servant, the one we killed in the library at Baker Street. That was a terrible setback for the Buddha, because his own movements were always at risk of discovery. But—by disguising his orangutan as well as possible—he managed to get back to Luxembourg and take refuge in Schneider's house. Once there, he corrupted or won over Arno's Chinese servant, as we know.

"Why, you might ask, didn't he eliminate Schneider? Simple: he too believed in the resurrection of Denverton-Fuh-Suh, and he thought having Schneider around as a double would subsequently become necessary again. So he merely turned him into a vegetable, whose wits he could restore when the master had returned along the Path of the Gods. Oh, there's no doubt—that living Buddha, Fuh-Suh's right-hand man, was prepared to fight for his master's cause."

"Why didn't he kill us, Guv?" asked Tom. "He had plenty of chances."

Dickson turned to Bunny Lipton. "I assume we owe that to the reputation our friend Bunny enjoys in the Orient. Remember that the sinister midget tried to kill me by flinging his platinum dagger at me, when he heard young Lord Denverton asking me to investigate. But he wasn't as handy at knife throwing as he was with an automatic pistol. Then he must've figured that Tom and I would make excellent hostages in case Bunny Lipton solved the mystery of the Path of the Gods. So instead of using murder weapons he turned to the ancient Chinese arsenal of toxicology."

Tom looked around the table. "Can I ask, what's meant by the term 'living Buddhas'?"

"They're strange creatures," answered Lipton, "raised by Buddhist monks for the faithful masses to worship. They're often children. When those Buddhas reach the age of reason they're summoned to the great Buddha—meaning generally that the monks send them on their way using poison. But occasionally some of them have real ability, and then mandarins pay very well to acquire them. That's what happened to the deformed, intelligent creature Denverton made his slave. I have no doubt the monster believed in his terrible master's return as much as he himself did."

"And what about the rascals Lord Denverton invited to dinner?" asked Tom.

"That was a leftover of the Chinese ritual. Of course he had to choose English crooks—who aren't in short supply—to witness the master's awakening. I assume that if by some miracle it had really happened, the lives of those present wouldn't have been worth much. The invitations were sent out by the living Buddha servant."

"The vampire Buddha," murmured Matsuko.

"It's true," said Dickson. "The malformed being lacked normal digestive organs, so he fed on human blood—that of his own coolie, the orangutan. I expected we'd run across a creature of that kind once I heard about birds disappearing at night. When we killed him he was out hunting for sleeping partridges."

Lord Denverton ordered champagne served. It was already foaming in the glasses when one of the Japanese lifted his head and sniffed the air. "It smells a lot like fire."

He'd barely spoken when a burning wave seemed to envelop them. Through the open door they saw a silk wall hanging curl up, engulfed in flames. At that moment the servants cried out, "Fire! Fire!"

"It must be coming from the Path of the Gods!" muttered Dickson, leaping up. He was right: flames were pouring out of the secret door.

"Alas! Three times alas!" cried Lipton. "Fuh-Suh's room was full of documents!"

But they had time only to flee, as the fire gained on them from all sides. When they'd reached the street they were impotent witnesses to the total destruction of Denverton House.

"I assume that fire was planned," said Matsuko. "The entry of an intruder into the hidden room would set off some kind of secret clockwork that only initiates would know how to disarm. It's not that surprising. And we were wrong not to have thought of it in the joy of our triumph."

"Oh, well," said Dickson. "This destruction will help preserve the secret surrounding a distinguished name. Fuh-Suh is no more, and that's the main thing, isn't it, Bunny?"

Lipton winked in agreement.

Thus ended the strange case of the Path of the Gods. But there was one addendum: a few days after the fire at Denverton House, poor Schneider fell ill, and his condition quickly worsened. Arno urged Dickson to come. At the gates of death, Schneider gradually seemed to regain his sanity. There was little the detective still needed to know, but even so he tried to question the dying man at the last.

"Didn't Denverton die in Luxembourg, in fact right here in this house? Wasn't his body taken back to London?"

The more Schneider's suffering increased, the more Dickson noticed his extraordinary resemblance to Denverton-Fuh-Suh. Suddenly he motioned for Dickson to approach. As the detective did so, the dying man lifted his hand and struck him right in the heart. But his arm was too weak, and the weapon that would've ended Dickson's life fell to the floor. It was the little platinum dagger with the jade handle.

Dickson stared at the sick man, whose face was now filled with terrible hatred.

"Even so," he howled, "I came back, along the Path of the Gods!" Then he fell back on his pillow and died.

As he traveled back to London, Dickson was troubled by doubts. "Which of them was Fuh-Suh? Schneider or Denverton?"

The express train he was taking seemed to hammer out the two names on the wheels, between the bumpers of the cars, under the steel of the bogies: *Schneider... Denverton... Schneider... Denverton...* and the steam engine puffed out *Fuh... Suh... Fuh... Suh...*

"It doesn't matter," murmured Harry Dickson, letting himself relax and laying his head back against the seat cushions in the first-class compartment. He sensed that some small mystery still hovered around this business, which seemed to be coming to an unsatisfactory end, like a badly told fairy tale.

He fell asleep a little weary in spirits, a little less at peace than he usually felt after one of his fierce struggles against human crime.

Harry Dickson

LE SHERLOCK HOLMES
AMERICAIN

No. 147 ■ ■   Le Lit du Diable.   ■ ■   Prix fr. 1.50

John Grestock fut témoin d'une scène aussi terrifiante qu'incroyable.

THE DEVIL'S BED

By Way of a Prologue:
1. John Greystock's Strange Adventure

Early in the last century, on the northwestern slopes of the Grampian Mountains, a major landslide occurred, presumably caused by an earthquake. A nearby stream was diverted from its course into the resulting basin—which was small at first, but which the flowing water soon expanded into a lake that within twenty years covered an area of several square miles. Around that time an island formed at the center of the lake; it was almost perfectly oval, with its larger end pointing north.

Another twenty years went by, and dense vegetation now covered the island. Then came people, though only a few, in fact just one family: the Greystocks, minor gentry, penniless or close to it, originally from the big city. They bought the island for a song, and built a fine house there.

People wondered why the Greystocks had chosen to live on that small patch of land won from the turbulent waters of the new lake, and rumor had it they were treasure hunters. They couldn't have found much, though, because around 1850 they locked the doors and windows and, as poor as church mice, left to seek their fortune in Edinburgh or (so people said) even further away.

Before then the place had had no name, and eventually the locals had named it after the landowners: the island was Greystock Island and the lonely house was Greystock Castle.

One day in 1858 the family's eldest son, John Greystock, returned to the area and had himself rowed out to the island. He found the house locked and dark.

The ferryman who'd brought him out refused to accompany him beyond the shore, saying, "Ye'd be better off going back where ye came from, Master John. The living are living and the dead are dead, and the latter especially want to be left in peace."

Greystock didn't get a chance to ask him to explain his enigmatic words, because the man and his boat were already far away, disappearing in the twilight mist.

Threading a path through brambles and wild oats, the young man finally reached his family's house. There it stood, somber and sinister in the evening gloom, its shutters still closed, its bricks still free of ivy, its massive front door still solid. In the eight years since they'd left, neither John nor his parents had given the house a thought, and he was a little surprised to find it still standing and so little marked by time. He had the door key, and he wondered whether it would still turn in the lock, which must be rusty by now.

An ominous cry made him start and turn: a drab bird, perched on a stone post, watched him with large round eyes. It remained motionless for a few seconds, then flew off, repeating its dismal cry.

"A striped bittern," murmured Greystock. "People around here would take that as an evil omen."

A flock of sandpipers with dagger-like beaks flew past, shrieking bitterly at the intruder come to disturb their peace.

Greystock put the key in the lock, and was surprised to find it turn easily in his fingers.

He'd brought everything he needed for an extended stay in the old family home, and had even thought vaguely of having more luggage sent on. He took a candle from his travel bag and lit it. Now he could see the hall: the walls glittered with crystallized calcium, rainwater had leaked through the ceiling, the wainscoting had rotted.

"I should've known," he murmured, "and I'd have been wiser to spend the night in the village and come out to the island tomorrow. Of course, that rattletrap wagon posing as a stagecoach was hours late—a charming country!"

In one corner hung a lantern, its hinges only partly eaten away by rust. Greystock put his candle in it and moved on toward the dining room. But he'd gone only a few steps before he hastily beat a retreat: the floor was so rotten that the boards sagged under his weight, and at the same moment a chunk of plaster dropped from the ceiling and broke at his feet.

"Poor old house!" he said sadly. "But how could it be otherwise, after eight years of neglect in this land of perpetual rain and fog?"

The kitchen seemed so cold, so dark, that he gave up exploring in that direction and returned to the front hall.

"Let's see what's left of my own room."

His bedroom lay on the far side of the house, looking out onto the lake. Greystock fondly recalled the dreams that room had nurtured for twenty years, and the love with which he'd furnished and decorated it. The thought of finding it, too, in ruins made his heart ache.

He cut diagonally across the hall, followed a long corridor swept by bitter wind, and reached his room. The door opened smoothly without a squeak. The light from his lantern preceded him.

"Oh!" he cried. "It's unbelievable!" He stopped on the threshold, stunned.

The room looked handsome, comfortable; the wainscoting glowed. Curtains with a floral pattern hung at the windows, small attractive pictures accented the walls, pewter tableware stood on the shining oak side tables, and against the wall stood a magnificent four-poster bed with fleur-de-lis curtains.

Greystock's head spun. While the rest of the house was a total ruin, this room was inviting, well kept up, ready to receive a guest—as if that was its purpose every day. On a bent-leg table stood an empty candlestick, its copper freshly polished and free of verdigris.

The lantern Greystock was carrying didn't cast enough light to drive away the shadows dancing on the walls, so he got another candle out of his bag and put it in the candlestick.

Together the lantern and the candlestick gave enough light to be reassuring. Looking around his old quarters, so oddly rediscovered, he noticed that the bed was newly made up with fine fresh white sheets and a soft quilt of pale silk.

"To think that, in the old days, I had nothing but a narrow sailor's cot," he murmured. "And now in the same spot I find a bed worthy of a fairy-tale prince!"

Greystock was a steady young fellow, in control of his nerves. He'd studied geometry, and immersion in the hard sciences had made him a practical man, without much imagination. Right away he drew conclusions. "Since we left, someone has moved in, occupying only this room. Of course it's the nicest room in the house."

Then a moment later he added, "This bed is certainly a curious piece of furniture!"

It was indeed a splendid example of cabinetmaking, engraved with large coats of arms unknown to him. Though he didn't care much about antique furniture, some of the proportions of the bed drew his interest as a mathematician and geometer. "I've never seen a wider or longer bed—a giant could stretch out in it easily."

A sudden look of disgust crossed his face: on the metal-inlaid sides of the bed frame he noticed dark, flaking stains running down to join murky clots on the lower rails. "That looks like... blood," he murmured. He came closer and reached out to touch the suspicious clots.

Probably instinct save him. At that moment he felt something like a breath on his face, and it seemed like the whole house had shuddered. He jumped back so fast that he knocked over his lantern, which rolled into a corner. A muffled thump rang out. The canopy had just dropped with all its weight onto the bed—and it must've been a considerable weight, because the floor shook from the impact.

"A nasty business," Greystock growled angrily. "If I'd stayed leaning over the bed a moment longer—or by chance had lain down—I'd have been flattened like butter on bread."

He had no time to reflect any further: the house was filling with sounds. Looking up, he saw an open rectangle in the ceiling, through which hung a thick cable fastened to a ring at the peak of the bed canopy. Suddenly two legs dressed in fawn-colored leather slid down the cable, and Greystock found a long flintlock pistol pointed at his face.

At the same moment the door was thrown open by someone holding another pistol. The two men in sturdy mountaineering dress who'd just burst into the room stared at Greystock, their eyes shining menacingly.

Greystock quickly recovered his cool. "I assume you're not aware that this is my property, and that I have the right to demand an explanation of why you're here and what's going on in my house!"

The two strangers lowered their pistols but went on staring at him in silence. Greystock heard more noises overheard, and realized that other people were waiting and watching around the open hole in the ceiling.

"There certainly are plenty of you," he said, "and I'm curious to know what you're all looking for here on this island, where my family—the proprietors—managed only to grow poorer and poorer."

"Poorer and poorer!" echoed one of the men.

Greystock noticed that the stranger had trouble articulating, and his voice sounded odd. The young man had a positive and courageous temperament, and all of his fear had dissipated; he even managed to smile with a certain arrogance. He pointed to the strange bed, with its collapsed canopy.

"Who are you exactly? I would ask whether you're gentlemen, but what happened to this bed is proof enough that you're not. Clearly British justice would consider you bandits." He spoke calmly, as though he were conversing with any stranger in the most normal manner.

The man who'd already spoken now answered in the same strained voice that had already aroused Greystock's curiosity. "Not bandits!"

"All right," replied Greystock. "I'd be happy to believe you—but you'll have to explain a little more clearly."

The two armed men had moved closer together. Now that the light from the candle fell fully on their faces, Greystock could examine them more easily: thin, hard faces; dry, sunburned skin; blank, staring eyes; one man's hair light red, the other's as white as an albino's; clothes of heavy wool, well tailored in the mountaineering style. Greystock had the disorienting sensation that he was witnessing something impossible.

The two men went on staring at him in that dour, impassive way—which would've disconcerted anyone less steady than the geometer. "Well?" he said impatiently. "Is that all you have to say to me?"

His eyes fell on the pistols they carried, which he was surprised to see were elegant and well made, and of a style quite unknown to him.

Finally one of the strangers—still the same man—sighed and, turning toward the bed, uttered a kind of croak. Up in the hole in the ceiling an arm waved, and a third bandit slid down the cable with the ease of a monkey.

Greystock started: the new arrival was a dwarf, as ugly as possible, with a tiny head jammed onto a gorilla's powerful trunk. He wore a gray tunic with bright red trim, he had white hair, and his eyes—an albino's eyes—glowed garnet red. He hopped down to the floor, and his enormous arms began a throat-cutting gesture, but one of the men, who seemed to be in charge, grunted again.

In the blink of an eye the dwarf vanished, only to return carrying a long narrow leather sack that looked very heavy. The redheaded man took it from him and reached into it.

"I have to say," murmured Greystock, "you certainly are a curious set of bandits."

The stranger held out a fistful of thick gold coins with an antique look to them. The gold dropped back into the sack with a muted ring, and the man held out the sack to Greystock.

"What does this mean?"

"Going!" replied the man with an effort.

"Who? Me?"

"For always... never coming back... here... never..." Thinking seemed to cost him as much effort as speaking. "Never tell... word..."

"Word of honor?"

"Word of honor!"

"But if I agree," said Greystock, "it can only be on condition that I'm convinced you're not plotting anything criminal here."

The man seemed not to understand. "Going!" he repeated.

"Who are you?" cried Greystock.

The man's enigmatic face stretched as if from the enormous effort of thinking; then a glimmer of understanding seemed to come. "Servants!" he blurted.

Gradually the dwarf had crept closer to Greystock. Now he lunged abruptly, opening his mouth wide to reveal enormous horrible canines, and made as if to bite him. But the strange man stopped him with a vicious blow with the butt of his pistol, and the dwarf fled up the cable, climbing like a monkey.

But other thoughts rose confusedly in Greystock's mind: he was a poor man, and had returned to the island only in search of money. For years he'd dreamt of emigrating and seeking his fortune in America or Australia. That fortune was here before him now—all he had to do was put out his hand. "I accept," he said abruptly. "And you have my word!"

The other stranger, who up to now hadn't said a thing, motioned to him to pick up the leather sack and follow him. He led Greystock out of the house and to the northwest edge of the lake. A small rowboat was hidden in a clump of reeds; they got into it, and the man began to row vigorously. When he reached the other side he picked up the sack of gold and threw it onto the bank. Greystock had time only to jump ashore, and already the boat was disappearing into the darkness.

That night he stayed at the inn, and there he found the boatman who'd taken him out to the island. "I knew ye'd have your fill quick enough," said the man. "But how did ye manage to get back?"

Greystock lied boldly. "I found my old rowboat. It leaked badly, but it got me to shore—after which it sank, along with some of my luggage."

"One of these days the island will do the same thing," said the boatman. "The devil sent it, and it'll return to him—that's Fate. In a few places it's already sunk more than two feet."

The next day Greystock reached Leith and boarded a ship bound for America. There he lived and there he died. But when he felt his end approaching, he put his strange adventure down in writing. That must've been between 1900 and 1905.

It was only twenty years later, by chance, at a book auction, that the pages in which that document had been hidden fell into other hands: the hands of the famous detective Harry Dickson.

2. Mr. Servus

The MacTavish auction house was patronized only by elderly bibliophiles, none of them wealthy; they never cracked open more than a book or two before bidding on a complete set of old tomes. Only a feeble daylight came through the dusty windows, though outside the sun shone brightly on a fresh spring day.

Dressed in a faded frock coat, MacTavish presided absentmindedly, expecting little from the current sale. "An encyclopedia… missing two volumes."

"And the others are stained and mildewed," said a complaining voice.

"There are cleaning products to fix that," the auctioneer protested weakly, shrugging his tired shoulders.

"You know perfectly well that's not true."

MacTavish grew even more discouraged. "Going for six pounds…"

"Why not the Crown Jewels, while you're at it!"

"Going for five pounds…"

"I say five shillings, and not a farthing more."

The encyclopedia went at that price, and the auctioneer moved on to the next lot. "The library of John Greystock, Esquire, comprising…" A fairly detailed inventory followed, to which no one listened.

"I'll break up this lot," cried MacTavish. "Three volumes of *The Local Geography of Scotland*, with handwritten annotations. Going for one pound…"

A gentleman rose and accepted the bid. MacTavish was about to bring down his little boxwood gavel when a harsh voice called out, "One pound, five shillings!"

The auctioneer gave a start, but hastened to revalue his merchandise. "A unique work, gentlemen! Nobody will bid more? What a pity!"

"Two pounds!"

"Three!" cried the harsh voice.

There were only a couple of dozen people in the room, and most of them weren't there to buy anything. Everyone turned in astonishment to see who could be competing for such a dull item. They saw a tall man in travel dress and a little wizened fellow with an anxious, pushy expression.

"I said three pounds!" cried the latter. "That should be enough."

"Five!" said the other gentleman.

The little man collapsed on a bench and passed a hand across his damp brow. "Six!" he gargled with effort.

"Eight!"

"Eight and… five—no—three shillings!"

"Magnificent books!" cried MacTavish, carried away with delight. "I say, mag-ni-fi-cent!"

"Come on, ten pounds!" said the man in travel dress calmly, as he got a cigarette casually out of his case.

His rival turned to him red-faced. "It's old paper… worth nothing."

But the gavel had already come down with a sharp crack. Harry Dickson gathered up his purchase. He'd paid attention to only one thing, a name: Greystock. And he'd come to Scotland to clear up a matter in which that name had been mentioned in passing.

A geologist by the name of Marlwood, a fellow of a London scientific society, had been found dead in the Scottish Highlands. After a week of exploring in one of the most untamed parts of the Grampians, he hadn't returned to his inn. A search party went out after him, and found his body in a remote cave. He seemed to have been struck hard on the head by a falling rock, but he hadn't died instantly, and the nature of the wound suggested that he'd suffered for quite a while before dying a lingering death. On the smooth side of a rock within reach of his hand was scratched a name: Greystock.

The London scientific society, not satisfied by the local jury's verdict of accidental death, had dispatched Harry Dickson to the scene. But after a few days of inquiry he'd come back to Leith, planning to return to London—and then with time to kill he'd found himself in MacTavish's auction rooms.

When he'd put away his purchase he tried to find the man who'd been counterbidding, but he was gone. The auctioneer was getting ready to leave, and Dickson directed his unsatisfied curiosity toward him. "Do you know the gentleman who wanted those books as much as I did?"

MacTavish shook his head. "He's not a regular customer, though I've seen him once or twice before. But I don't remember him ever having bought anything at all. His name is Servus, if I'm not mistaken. Does that help?"

"Not much," replied Dickson with a smile. "But if I can I'd like to learn more about the little man."

"He's an elderly eccentric, who calls himself a curator. My God, what a curator! He lives somewhere in the Highlands, in an old ruin called Limmock Castle, though the castle exists in name only—because can you really qualify as a castle a dozen fallen walls and a main building still standing only by a miracle, where he has to keep his crust of bread away from the rats and the ravens?"

"And of what is he curator?"

"Of a room, practically open to the elements, that he pretentiously calls a museum, where he keeps a heap of scrap metal. He charges the rare tourists who stray into that uninviting spot a few pennies to see his old knickknacks."

Dickson grew thoughtful. Limmock was the name of the village nearest to where Marlwood had died. Dickson had passed through there, but had found nothing but a couple of dozen wretched hovels gathered around an inn for cart-drivers—which might've been a flourishing place in its day, before progress and modern transportation ruined its trade forever. Yet no one there had said a word about Limmock Castle or its curator.

MacTavish, cheered by the day's profits, invited him to have a drink, and the detective accepted. They went to a near-by pub, known for its old-fashioned frothy Scotch ale.

Parched by conversation, the auctioneer started by knocking back a pint, then grew talkative. "Do you know Limmock?"

"Um… not really," admitted Dickson cautiously.

"A long time ago it had a certain fame, but it was a hard place to get to. Seismic activity had caused a lake to form, and, in the middle of the lake, an island. The island sank around eighteen sixty or sixty-one, I don't know exactly. It could even have been later. A few years after that, the water level in the lake began to fall, and the basin dried up. Land-slides finished it off."

While he was listening, Dickson had been leafing through the books he'd just bought, and he stopped at a couple of inserted sheets of paper covered with thin, cramped hand-writing.

"I'll have to take my leave," said MacTavish. "I'm dining with friends."

Dickson went on reading, and by the time he reached the end of John Greystock's strange adventure his cheeks were flushed. "We're going back to Limmock," he said to himself, "no matter what my worthy assistant Tom Wills has to say about it. I'll admit it's not exactly a charming spot."

He was wrapping up his parcel of books again when a shadow fell across the table. Someone outside the pub window was blocking the sunlight. Dickson quickly looked up. A squat, misshapen silhouette was standing on tiptoes to see into the pub. Dickson caught a glimpse of hollow, grimy cheeks, and a pair of fiery green eyes staring at him with hatred; a hairy mitt pressed against the glass. But when Dickson moved, the hideous man suddenly backed away, and the detective could hear his footsteps rushing off. The barman had seen nothing, and when Dickson reached the street it was quiet and empty and bright in the fine May sunshine.

"Time to pack our bags," he said to himself.

As Dickson had expected, he found his assistant disinclined to return to the fruitless wastes of the Highlands; but he merely had to tell him briefly about the auction, and the desperate counterbidding by Servus—curator of a rat's nest in the Grampians—and the hideous figure at the pub window, to rouse not only Tom Wills's interest but his enthusiasm.

They rented a car to take them to the gates of Limmock, if such a place could be imagined as having gates. Though they'd spent several days there before, the innkeeper received them without much enthusiasm; they weren't used to strangers in those parts. But Harry Dickson knew how to make himself agreeable; he declared that there was nothing like the Limmock air to restore a frazzled city-dweller's nerves, and he insisted that since leaving the village he and his companion had suffered in the fetid atmosphere of the metropolis. That explained their return, and the innkeeper became more cordial.

But three days went by before Dickson managed to pry open the innkeeper's tight-shut lips a little. "Limmock Castle?"

MacGregor, the innkeeper, started in fear. "A dirty ruin, sir, and no doubt cursed by God, for there's no viler place in all of Scotland. Everyone avoids it."

"And yet," retorted the detective, "I was told in Leith that it's worthwhile spending a few hours there on account of the famous museum…"

"Famous!" The innkeeper snickered scornfully. "Ye can safely give it a miss, sir, and even more so the person who calls himself the curator."

"Ah, you must be referring to Mr. Servus. He was pointed out to me in Leith."

"That awful midget treated himself to a holiday away? Incredible!"

"You don't seem to like him much, MacGregor."

"Who would, in my place?" retorted the innkeeper angrily. "Are ye aware that he doesn't hesitate to takes potshots at poor hunters who stray onto the castle grounds? It seems he has the right to. Anyway, no one's going to dispute that right, because there's no game worth catching on that cursed land."

"All right," said Dickson. "If by chance in our wanderings we pass that way, we'll pay him a visit. If not, we'll get by without seeing his museum of curios."

The next day, Harry Dickson and Tom Wills went to have a look at the basin and the old lake bed; but they found nothing but a bare expanse of stones and fallen rock.

But a surprise greeted them on their return. They'd barely crossed the threshold of the inn when MacGregor ran to meet them, waving his arms. "Ye'll never guess, sir!" he cried. "Do ye know who was here while ye were out, asking for the gentleman from London, as he called ye?"

"Um… no," admitted Dickson.

"The man from Limmock Castle! He seemed very disappointed to have missed ye, and said he'd come back around lunchtime. Unless ye give me instructions to throw him out, sir," he added hopefully.

"By no means, my dear MacGregor," replied the detective quickly. "I've got nothing against the little man—on the contrary: he could educate me about local archaeology. I might even invite him to lunch if he's willing."

MacGregor bowed, partly satisfied: at least his guest's tab would go up, and he was above all a Scotsman and therefore a friend to cold hard cash.

An enormous leg of lamb had just been set on the table when the door opened and Mr. Servus walked in. Dickson recognized right away the little man who'd bid so fiercely for the late John Greystock's books.

Paying no attention to MacGregor's unwelcoming look, the curator of Limmock Castle came straight to the travelers and pointed a skinny finger at Dickson's chest. "I don't know who you really are," he said in greeting.

Dickson bowed. "Why wouldn't you know, sir? I don't believe I make any secret of my identity."

"But, like lots of important people, you'd rather travel incognito, isn't that so?" cackled the little man maliciously.

"Why wouldn't I?"

"The better to spy on people, no doubt," grumbled Servus. "Yours is not an admirable profession."

"Not everyone shares your opinion, sir," the detective answered politely.

"I'm warning you..." began the little man with a threatening air.

Harry Dickson pulled out a chair and invited him to have a seat. "Come, come," he said soothingly. "I see no reason for you to hold anything against me. Unless you consider our little bibliophile face-off the other day to be sufficient cause for rancor. But I'd assume that as a collector you'd have to get used to being a good sport. Look, I meant to invite you to have lunch with us."

Hungrily, Servus eyed the mighty slab of meat. "I can't be bought," he murmured.

"Nor do I suppose that you have anything to sell," replied the detective promptly.

The little man drew himself up to his full height. "That may be, but the same might not be true of you, Mr. Dickson.

I've come to offer you fifty pounds for those old books you picked up the other day at the MacTavish auction."

"So you found the money you needed?" asked the detective innocently.

"People like you think they have the right to insult everybody else!"

"If I've offended you, I apologize immediately. Listen: I have no intention of letting those books go, at any price, but neither do I mean to hide them away like buried treasure. I'd be happy to lend them to you."

"What?" Servus was stunned. "You'd do that?"

"Why not?"

The curator of Limmock Castle accepted the seat he was offered, and didn't object when his host set a plate and cutlery before him. A moment later, like a starving man, he was devouring everything they could provide him; he even accepted a nip of old brandy with dessert.

Suddenly he said in a low voice, "And... the manuscript... Could I read it?"

"Of course," said Dickson, feigning surprise. "It's quite peculiar, in fact, and I'd already decided to tell you about it at some point. I think the time has come. Tom, my boy, you'll find the book in question in my suitcase."

The little curator's fingers trembled as he held the pages covered in handwriting, and right away he began reading eagerly. Watching him carefully, Harry Dickson observed his guest's growing disappointment as he reached the end of the manuscript. When he was done he handed the book back to the detective with a deep sigh. "That's not much help," he murmured.

"What were you expecting—no, what were you hoping to find, Mr. Servus?"

The little man started, and looked at his host with alarm. "Nothing—oh, nothing—that is to say... But don't ask me anything, I have nothing to say to you, I can tell you nothing."

"Marlwood died about three miles from Limmock Castle," said the detective, "and that would give me the right to ask you some questions, sir."

"I wouldn't answer," said Servus angrily. "I know nothing about Marlwood, nor about his death. Nothing—nothing!"

"I don't claim otherwise, but now that you're here, I think I'll seize the opportunity to ask you to do me the favor of showing me your castle."

"What? You want to see the ruins?"

"That's exactly why I came here."

"There's nothing to see," whimpered Servus. He was almost weeping.

"Who knows?" answered the detective mischievously, enjoying the little man's sudden embarrassment.

"And I'm not going back to the castle today!"

"Well, that settles it. In that case, I'll regretfully have to do without your company, and go alone."

"No!" cried Servus.

"Good. I feel like you're going change your mind and be our guide," said the detective sarcastically.

The little man turned serious. "I've heard surprising things about you, Mr. Dickson. I asked around in Leith about the man who'd robbed me of the books of the late John Greystock—may the devil take him—and I learned he was the most famous detective of modern times. Is it true that you've managed to solve in a few days cases that have stumped others for years?"

Harry Dickson smiled. "My flatterers say so, and I'd add that sometimes luck smiles on me and reason helps out."

"But you succeed, that's all that matters! Well, I've been trying to solve this for thirty years, and getting nowhere— nowhere!"

"Solve what?"

"The mystery!"

"Of the castle?"

"No—of the land!"

"That's a little vague, and you'll have to be more specif-ic. But why shouldn't we work together, Mr. Servus? Because I've got a feeling that Marlwood's death has something to do with the mystery you're talking about."

Drops of sweat shone on the curator's temples, but he didn't refuse.

"How did you come to live at Limmock Castle?" asked Dickson.

Servus breathed noisily. "I could decline to answer you, but you'd investigate and find out—and we'd lose lots of time."

"Very logical reasoning."

"My name isn't Servus, it's Cheswick Vane. Doesn't that name mean anything to you? It's true, you'd have to go back almost forty years in your recollections as a criminologist."

"My God!" said Dickson in a low voice. "Are you the Dr. Cheswick Vane of the Portland Square case?"

"Yes," the little man replied solemnly, "the same. I was twenty-five then. I was poor and proud. On day someone mocked my poverty; I struck him—and he fell dead. It hap-pened in Portland Square. I was sentenced to five years of hard labor. At the end of my term I left that terrible Dartmoor Prison, vowing never to return to London, nor to the scene of my crime. I went to Scotland, and knew nothing but misery.

"I became a vagabond, a nomad, going from fair to fair as a tooth-puller and quack doctor. That's how, one night, I reached this place, when it was still relatively prosperous. I met a man here whose name I'll never know. He suggested that I live at Limmock Castle as a sort of custodian. I agreed, because I was on the brink of despair. He said he'd come back to settle the terms, but I never saw him again. I moved into the castle, and that same night—without my knowing how—next to my bed I found a purse containing five hundred pounds in gold.

"I could've left, and started a new life with that money, but I'd sworn an oath never again to stray from what honest people call the path of righteousness, and so I stayed. A week later an attorney in Leith sent me papers, all drawn up in good order, formally making me the proprietor of Limmock Castle and all its grounds, free of taxes and duties in perpetuity—but with a clause explicitly forbidding me ever to sell the property. I asked the attorney a few questions, but the gentleman didn't know much. The owner of the estate, one Leeme, lived abroad and dealt with him through an intermediary, a lawyer in London who knew no more than he did.

"I've lived in that dismal place ever since, all alone— terribly alone—but faithful to the duty I accepted, as to which no one's ever asked me for an accounting. I hadn't been there long when the landslide occurred that finished off the lake, whose origins were so peculiar. In those days that was the only attraction that brought tourists to the area. The lake vanished, Limmock lost its fame, and this area, soon forgotten, went back to being a desolate wilderness."

"Why did Greystock and his books interest you enough that you were willing to spend so much for them?" asked Dickson when Servus had fallen silent.

The curator's brow clouded. "Greystock had lived in the house in the lake," he said evasively. Then he quickly changed the subject. "I had only nine pounds with me on the day of the auction, and I had only fifty more at the castle, out of the five hundred I received long ago."

"But about Greystock…" insisted the detective.

The little doctor gave a gesture of despair. "Yes, all right, Greystock… I knew he'd come back to this area, and had left again immediately, without drawing any profit from his abandoned property, though he was as poor as Job on his dung heap! I had a feeling that on his deathbed he would've wanted to reveal something. It seems I was right, though in fact his manuscript tells me nothing."

"On the contrary," replied Dickson softly. "It tells me why you call yourself Servus!"

"Ah!" Dr. Vane grew pale.

"When Greystock asked who the people in his house were, the only answer he got was a single word, 'servants.' And in Latin the word for 'servant' is '*servus*.'"

"And…" murmured the curator.

"The man you saw only once gave you that name!"

"Oh," whimpered the little man, "you've figured it out!"

"I wonder whose 'servant' you are!"

Dr. Cheswick Vane seemed to get smaller still; he curled up on his chair, pale and beaten. "I don't know… but I assume it's someone awful!"

"What's the mystery, doctor?" asked Dickson abruptly.

"I'll tell you… Yes, I'll tell you, because you're the only man who can shed a little light on the frightful shadows in which I've lived for thirty years and more! We'll leave tonight; I only want to travel by night. I'll see you soon, but…" He hesitated visibly. "What if something happens to me before then? You never know! My heart fails me sometimes. So why not tell you now what little I know? The mystery? You haven't guessed it yet, mister clairvoyant? The bed! The devil's bed! Greystock mentioned it! I thought he would, but he didn't know much—he was just an ignoramus looking for money. That bed is at the castle… Well! There are nights when someone sleeps in it!"

"Who?" cried Dickson.

"The devil, I'm telling you! Who else could it be? I'll see you this evening!" He left, almost running.

Harry Dickson waited for him all afternoon. When twilight fell, he and Tom Wills got ready to go.

Finally the door opened. It was MacGregor. "Are ye expecting the curator of Limmock Castle?" he asked. "Well, gentlemen, ye'll wait a long time!"

"Why? Did he go on alone?"

"Indeed, ye could put it that way. But as for coming back… He's just been found, out in the middle of the village commons, dead as a doornail!"

"What!" cried Dickson. "Did the poor man have a heart attack?"

185

The innkeeper answered scornfully, "An attack, no doubt, but by whom? We're all decent folk around here. Someone smashed in his skull with big rocks. Aye... there's not much left of it!"

3. Miss Rheina and Her Traveling Companion

We must now leave Harry Dickson and Tom Wills at the Limmock inn, which in any case they'd soon depart to head off into the Grampians on the steep path leading them to Limmock Castle. We'll pick up our story in Leith, the port city of Scotland's capital, in one of its most dismal neighborhoods.

This sinister area was wedged between two old cargo wharves, into which would drift an occasional trawler, salt-blistered right up to its funnel. The district got its name—The Seven Sweethearts—from a notorious old tavern, plenty of whose patrons had wound up in the hands of the Edinburgh hangman. The squalid tavern had been gone for almost a century, but the neighborhood kept the name.

You needed a strong stomach to make your way through its foul alleyways without feeling nauseous. A whole miserable world was born, lived, and died there, with a bare minimum of air and light: Jewish salt peddlers, loan sharks, fencers of stolen goods, harbor barflies, ex-cons, fallen women—the place teemed with them, deprived even of that picturesqueness so often found among the wretched of the earth.

On one of those nameless dead-end back streets stood a low house with many gables, whose only window opened almost at ground level. Six steps of worn stone led steeply down to a room that was partly a cellar, partly a shop, and that was lit from dawn to dusk by a noxious iron lamp burning soybean oil. A varnished wood sign informed passersby that here Jeremy Buzemeyer practiced the trade of taxidermy.

A stranger wandering into this lair for the first time would first be struck by its indescribable smell, which would eventually resolve itself into formalin, camphor, paste of iodine, and rotting flesh—because the rear of the room also served as the workshop of the macabre craftsman who owned the place. On a long black table lay spread out his glistening tools: pliers, brain scoops, little wooden mallets, drills, awls. Lined up next to them, ceramic bowls held strange treasures: glass eyes—yellow, green, black, blue, garnet—to replace the dead eyes of the seabirds destined to be stuffed.

The fairly large space was crowded with chairs and stools—but still the visitor would find nowhere to sit down, because stuffed birds occupied every seat. All the winged fauna of the North Sea islands was represented: blue-footed Flemish gulls, oyster-catchers with black and white bodies and scarlet feet, dark skuas, powerful gannets, graceful pink mergansers, big pochard ducks, shining grebes, snowy petrels, insolent red godwits, sturdy sheldrakes…

A man pushed open the door and asked curtly, "Mr. Jeremy Buzemeyer?"

"What's your business with him?" asked someone from the shadows.

"It's about this bird!"

"Then give it here."

"You're not Jeremy Buzemeyer."

"That doesn't concern you. Give me the bird."

The man stared at the person who emerged from the deep shadows of the room. It was a tall young woman with very black hair and a statuesque figure; a long gray smock covered her from neck to ankles. She barely glanced at the customer as she took the bleeding bundle he held.

She was silent a moment; then her lips trembled. "A crested grebe," she murmured as she examined the bird by the smoky light of the oil lamp.

"With a black and gold neck," the customer pointed out.

"Where did you get it?" she said slowly, fixing her dark eyes on the man for the first time.

"I shot it in the mountains."

"You're lying!"

"Hey!" cried the man angrily. "Keep out of it! After all, it's none of your business."

"These birds are never found in the mountains, you should know that." She went back to examining the bird. "It's blind."

"Oh, really? I don't care in the least."

"I assume you'd like to sell it?"

The man stifled a laugh. "That depends on how much you offer for it."

"The normal rate for something stolen."

"Are you mad? I shot it myself!"

"No doubt, but where?"

"That too is none of your business!"

The young woman didn't take offense, but she lowered her eyes, no doubt to keep the stranger from seeing the flash of anger in them. "Five pounds."

The customer was startled by the offer. "I beg your pardon, ma'am," he said in a strikingly milder tone. "I didn't know this little creature could be worth that much." He hesitated visibly, then added softly, "And if I brought you others?"

"What kind?" she asked coldly.

"Strange creatures: blind, yes, completely blind, like this grebe, but... here's the odd part: they have no feathers..."

"What, then?"

"A kind of tanned skin, like very soft leather. They're too plump to fly, but they're terrific swimmers."

"I could have a look," she answered. "Here's your money... now begone."

"It'll take me five or six days to come back with... one of the creatures I'm talking about."

"Begone," she said. "I could have a look—if you come back."

The man was too busy counting the fistful of silver coins she'd given him to notice the threat implied in the young woman's words. Bowing awkwardly, he turned and went back out to the street.

The girl followed him with her eyes, and when he turned the corner her features unfroze into an expression of great fear.

Turning toward a corner of the shop, where a low door led into a sort of dark basement kitchen, she gave a guttural call.

"Hanh!" replied a hoarse and very unpleasant voice.

"Someone's been there!"

"Hanh!" A vague form covered in rags emerged from the basement kitchen.

"I assume you saw him."

"Hanh!"

"Then be quick!"

The girl took the crested grebe, stretched it out on the polished table, and quickly cut it to pieces with a scalpel. When it was nothing but a heap of bleeding flesh and feathers, she took it with both hands and flung it into the coal stove that filled the room with stifling heat. There was a brief sizzling, followed by a horrible smell, and that was all.

An hour later, the ragged figure returned.

"Done?" she asked.

"Hanh!"

"The shop will be closed for a week or ten days."

"Hanh!"

She'd gone back to work. With her long, graceful—truly magnificent—fingers, she cut open a barred heron, cracking apart the breastbones and shaking in a desiccating powder. By dusk she'd mounted the long skin, covered in gray feathers, on a wooden framework. When that was done she took off the gray smock and disappeared for quite a while into the dark kitchen at the back.

When night had fallen, a very beautiful young woman dressed in elegant traveling clothes, wearing fine yellow leather boots, and carrying a game bag and a hunting rifle in a case, came down the little back street and headed toward the waterfront. From there she soon reached the ferry terminal, where the Highland express was docked. With great care, she took her seat in a first-class compartment and wrapped a tartan over her legs, because it was a cold night. Then, being alone in her compartment, she went to sleep with her head buried in the beige wool cushions.

The train stopped at a junction where, after a short wait, the Highlands branch line takes on passengers who've come from other parts of the country and are heading to the mountains. Through the fog-coated compartment windows, by the harsh light of tall stanchions along the platform, half-asleep passengers could be seen hurrying toward the wagons.

The sleeping woman had awoken; absentmindedly she wiped the window to gaze idly out. Suddenly she looked surprised and vexed. With a nervous gesture she threw herself back against the cushions, as if trying to hide from someone on the platform. But she must've failed, because a cry rang out—a cry of delighted surprise, presumably—and the compartment door was opened immediately.

"Rheina! Can it really be?" A tall, well-built young man bounded up the high steps and stood before her. "Rheina!" he repeated, his face full of joy. "You're back in Scotland, and you never told me!"

She held out her fine white hand. "And why would I have, Teddy—I beg your pardon, Sir Edward Haigh?"

"What? To you, Rheina, I'm Teddy, understood?"

The girl's beautiful eyes clouded with discontent. "I owe you nothing, Sir Edward. I've never allowed you to hope for a thing. And I wonder why you think I ought to have kept you informed as to my movements."

"Oh, Rheina!" said the young man sadly. "Can you have forgotten? Remember our holiday last year at Limmock."

Rheina's brow darkened. "Teddy, you know I live a life of hard study, and that my holiday was meant only to prepare me for the next exams. I had a momentary weakness for you, I'll admit, but a gentleman shouldn't remind me of that. I mean to live for my studies, and to do that I cannot burden my existence with either a fiancé or a husband."

"So you came back from Amsterdam only to work on a new doctorate in who knows what?" he asked tartly.

"Amsterdam or somewhere else, it doesn't matter, but indeed it's to take another degree."

"Zoology, biology?" asked Teddy mockingly. "I assume this time it's not geology, since you wouldn't go hunting rocks with a double-barreled shotgun."

"It's still science," she replied gently. "But enough about me; why don't we talk about you, sir?"

Teddy shrugged his shoulders. "My concerns, or rather the reason for my journey, will seem petty to a grande dame of science like you. You must remember Limmock Castle, which we visited together."

"Very well." She fixed her black eyes on the blue eyes of her companion. "But if you're trying to remind me that you were bold enough to dare to kiss me there, let me tell you, sir, that I remember nothing!"

"Alas!" cried Teddy piteously. "But it's not about that. Day before yesterday I was summoned by an attorney in Edinburgh, who told me something odd: 'I've just been notified,' he said, 'that a certain Mr. Servus, proprietor of Limmock Castle, recently met a violent death. The deceased was deeded the property by a certain Leeme, and the deed was transacted years ago by this firm—or to be exact, by a London colleague, who habitually sends me his Scottish business. One clause in that deed specified that at Servus's death the property would pass, cost free, to the heirs of a certain Greystock family. The Greystocks are dead, the family is extinct, but you're related to them, however distantly, through your mother. Please take possession of your new property!'"

Teddy fell back against the cushions, laughing. "I care nothing for that old rat's nest. I've got another, and much more comfortable, castle in the Highlands. Still, I'm going to make a proprietor's survey of my new estate."

"But I too am going to Limmock," said Rheina.

"God is good!" cried Teddy in transports of joy. "Here's to our new holidays! Oh, Rheina, do you know the Haigh motto? 'Never despair, never question!'"

She laughed prettily. "You're a young fool, Teddy, and you'll remain one. But since Limmock is small, I wouldn't begrudge your company—which you'd impose on me anyway."

"You read my mind, Rheina!" cried Teddy with adolescent enthusiasm. "What a pity you won't also read my heart!"

She smiled at him, and all of her earlier rancor seemed to melt away.

The train, pretentiously called an express, was really just a local that, since it ran overnight, skipped every third stop, earning the name of "the rapid." In any case, the tourist season—which would make the train push the pace a little—hadn't yet begun. So dawn was already gilding the rounded summits and the lower foothills of the Grampian Mountains when Rheina and Teddy reached the station serving Limmock—a remote enough service indeed, since it was still a dozen kilometers from there to the wretched village. The platform was deserted, and not a soul appeared, not even the solitary crewman-lamplighter-ticket-taker who was also the station master.

Teddy looked disapprovingly all around in search of some means of conveyance, but his companion seemed to guess his thoughts; she began to laugh with delight, in that low contralto laugh that made the sentimental Teddy Haigh shiver amorously.

"We'll have to walk, Teddy," she announced, with her dazzling, irresistible gaze fixed on him. "Twenty-five kilometers is a fine stretch to cover before noon, but I feel strong enough and in the mood to do it."

"But it's only twelve from here to Limmock!" protested Teddy.

"Who said anything about Limmock?" she replied mockingly. "Aren't you the laird of Limmock Castle? And do you think I want to stay at the village inn when I could be a guest of the lord of the manor?"

"What? You want to stay in those awful ruins?" cried Teddy, utterly stunned.

"Teddy," she answered solemnly, "Do me the favor of showing some romantic sensibility at least one week a year."

She was no longer the stern, cross companion she'd been at first, and Teddy Haigh's heart sang gratefully. "I'd reel off fifty kilometers with you!" he cried. "What am I saying? I'd walk around the world like this!" He began to sing at the top of his lungs. "I'd go to the ends of the earth with you—into hell if I had to!"

She gave him a long, odd, sidelong look. "What a child you are, Teddy Haigh!"

The larks were rising and greeting the day over the yellow moors, and a grouse took off from a pond, its dangling feet leaving a short silver wake on the still water. That's how Teddy and Rheina arrived in the Limmock district, without a welcome and without being seen by even a lowly station master.

4. The Terrors of Limmock Castle

Teddy knew nothing about Rheina, except that she came from Holland and was devoted to the natural sciences. He'd met her on holiday the previous year, at Limmock. He name was Miss Rheina Schooten; that was enough for the ebullient young man, since he was in love. Let us not cast the first stone: many another lover would've done just the same—that is, cared not at all about either the past or the means of his beloved. When they parted at the end of the holidays, she'd refused to give him her address, and hadn't promised to be in touch. But she'd come back: that was what mattered.

The day (or rather the night) they'd met again, both on their way to Limmock, was five days after Harry Dickson and Tom Wills first went to Limmock Castle—five days of sickening anxiety. The detectives had found an old medieval ruin, in which only the two rooms occupied by the late Mr. Servus were inhabitable. Asking no more, the two men had settled in. Tom had managed to rent a bicycle from the village innkeeper, which he used to make an occasional run for provisions. A bleak stay!

Unlike other castles in the Highlands, this one stood not on a height but in a dark, dank valley that resembled a stony gorge. A mountain brook roared through its crumbled moat. Facing the gloomy building rose rocky cliffs and dull slopes dotted with sparse and sickly vegetation.

An exploration of the castle revealed no secrets. The detectives wandered through great halls open to the elements: a nursery for pale lichens and home to colonies of barn owls and ravens. The "museum," as it was pretentiously called, occupied an enormous long and narrow hall, still in good condition, but filled with things of neither interest nor value.

The day after they arrived, Dickson found the little black room. A rack displaying ancient weapons skillfully concealed its entrance; moving aside the rack, he found a tiny oak door that opened into that strange, windowless chamber. It was a perfect cube, tiled in mosaics, handsome if somewhat faded with age, and paneled in splendid polished oak.

Shining his flashlight around, Dickson cried out, "Finally, my boy, we've found it!" It was the famous bed they'd been seeking since the day before.

He examined it carefully. It was certainly the one Greystock had described vaguely. But the sheets and covers were gone, and had been replaced by magnificent furs: red and black fox furs, carefully stitched together and worthy of a royal bed. The canopy had been removed, and the bed curtains, now of fine red silk, hung directly from the ceiling.

"Curious... curious..." murmured the detective.

Tom Wills had heard him. "Bah! It doesn't look like much to me, Guv!"

"My boy, the greatest archaeologist would have trouble identifying the style," replied Dickson. He shone his light at length around the extraordinary piece of furniture. "Still, it reminds me of something," he murmured. "I vaguely recognize an extremely ancient workmanship. Let's see... That same archaeologist would laugh at me, no doubt, but it seems like something... Babylonian."

Examining the bed frame, Tom cried, "Guv! It isn't wood!" He'd just scratched one of the lower rails with the blade of his pocketknife, revealing a thin line of greenish white. "It's gold!" he cried at the top of his lungs.

"It's much too hard for that, my boy."

With great difficulty, and after dulling more than one knife, Dickson managed to scrape off a flake of the metal, which he carried back to their rooms. Directing Tom to fetch a few vials and test tubes from their luggage, the detective set immediately to work.

Several times the younger man saw his employer shake his head thoughtfully. "No reaction to aqua regia, nor to mercury," he murmured in vexation. "So it's not gold... In fact it's no metal known..."

The detective lit his pipe and sat in the only armchair. Suddenly a single word fell from his lips: "Orichalcum!"

"Huh?" cried Tom.

"An unknown metal, my boy, considered mythical," Dickson explained. "The ancient people of Atlantis—of questionable existence—knew of it; the Assyrians did too; and no doubt a privileged few in great, vanished Babylon. Mr. Servus was the guardian of a priceless treasure."

He fell into a long and troubled reverie. "I'd give a lot to spend a few hours in the library of the British Museum," he said suddenly. "In the meantime I'll just have to rely on memory."

Tom learned little more that day. Anyway, he'd found a good hunting rifle and ammunition in Servus's room, and he'd spotted red-legged partridge on the nearest mountain. Aiming to spice up their meager fare, he went off hunting for delicious game birds.

When he returned at nightfall, triumphantly bearing a brace of bleeding partridges, he found his employer pale and anxious.

"Something's happened while I was gone, Guv!" cried Tom.

Dickson silenced him with a gesture. "Something's happened," he agreed softly.

Silently Tom mimed a question.

"The little door to the black room no longer opens!"

"Is it stuck?"

"No, my boy, it's locked from the inside!"

"Well, what's keeping you from breaking it down?"

"The heavy metal plating that's cleverly hidden under a facing of oak. I'd have to use dynamite, and even then!"

"So there's someone inside, Guv?"

"And someone who's not trying to hide! Come see."

They crossed the long museum hall and stopped a few feet from the little door. Tom could barely contain a start of fright. Heavy, regular, imposing footsteps rang out in the sealed room. They went back and forth, coming close to the door, then turning away, and then repeating their continual round.

"Who is it, Guv?" stammered Tom. "An elephant would tread more lightly."

As if to confirm his words, the floor shook from the tremendous steady pacing.

In the dim twilight coming through the high ogival windows of the hall, Tom could see his employer's tense, rigid features, and his haunted eyes staring desperately at the closed door.

"Danger, Guv?" whispered Tom.

Dickson nodded slowly. "My boy, it's lucky MacGregor's bicycle is an old tandem," he said through clenched teeth.

"We're leaving?"

"But we'll be back. Tonight we'll sleep at the inn, because we're not up to spending a whole night under the same roof as whoever is pacing around in the black room."

Tom set about getting his tandem bike ready, and attaching an improvised second seat. When he returned, he found the detective thumbing through a railway timetable.

"Are we going by train instead of bicycle, Guv?" he joked.

"Shh! Listen instead of laughing, my boy."

"Oh…" whimpered Tom—who could say no more, so frightened was he by the muffled sounds that reached them. Some kind of barbaric hymn, sung—it seemed—by an intoxicated mob, rose from so far away that it might be coming from the very bowels of the earth.

"Our luggage, Tom," the detective ordered quickly. "I don't intend to spend the night at Limmock Castle, though it's not my nature to run from danger. But no one can do the impossible. If that's what I think it is, we'd be no more than straws in a hurricane… if it came."

"Are we going back to Leith, Guv?" asked Tom.

"To London… What little light I can shed on this mystery of mysteries, that's where I might find it. I assume you're not afraid of doing twenty-five kilometers across the mountains on that rattletrap bike, my boy?"

Shortly after that they climbed on the bike, their luggage strapped to their backs, and began pedaling hard, taking advantage of the last light of day. Luckily the moon was rising over the mountains. Still, the ride was difficult, and in spite of their efforts their progress was slow and cautious, and they reached the train station only just before midnight. But they were in time to catch the night train to Edinburgh.

"Not a word to anyone, my boy," urged Dickson, "unless you want a ticket straight to Bedlam. Even people who are open to the impossible would think me raving mad if I told them my theory about the mystery of Limmock Castle."

The next day, Teddy Haigh and Rheina Schooten arrived at the ruined castle. Once the young man, playing his part as proprietor, had formally welcomed his guest to the manor, he became serious and even anxious. "What a dump!" he groaned. "In all decency I can't offer you hospitality here! Let's leave, Rheina!"

She burst into delighted laughter. "I wouldn't dream of it! On the contrary, I find the place charming, and I accept your invitation to stay with all my heart."

"If it's for a dieting camp, maybe," replied Teddy. "Because I have no idea what I could possibly set out to eat."

"You poor dear boy! Here's a fine gun and a sackful of cartridges, and I bet the mountains are teeming with furry and feathered beasts. And you can see at a glance the blue trout and even the salmon leaping in that brook beneath our feet."

"Have you considered the proprieties, Rheina?" Teddy asked awkwardly.

"Firstly, I've long since struck that word from my vocabulary," she retorted. "Secondly, my dear Teddy, you're a gentleman. And thirdly, perhaps..."

"Perhaps?" the young man murmured, blushing with hope.

"There's nothing like a stay alone—alone together, I mean—for getting to know one another. Perhaps by the end of the week you'll have turned my head, and I'll be madly in love with you!"

"Rheina!" cried the young man, giddy with joy. "I understand. There'll be no more delightful destination on earth than Limmock Castle this marvelous week!"

For better or worse, they settled in. Rheina took Mr. Servus's room, and Teddy Haigh got the other livable room. He set off with the rifle and the game bag, while she explored the surroundings for edibles, for what they had begun to call their "Robinsonade."

Rheina found excellent mushrooms and, in a hollow in a rock, a wild beehive whose comb was thick with honey. Teddy shot a big gray goose, as plump as could be. Dinner was splendid: the mushrooms were excellent fried in goose fat, and though the bird's meat was a little tough, the makeshift lord and lady of the manor chewed it happily. And the honey was pronounced superior to all the honey of Mount Hymettus.

When the table was cleared and the leftovers had been put away for the next day, and Teddy had gotten permission to light his pipe, he said, "Rheina, when I went up the mountain earlier, following that gray goose, I had a look around at the countryside. You can see a long way, a very long way, all the way to the roofs of Limmock. But I was brought up short in surprise: not far from the village I saw the glistening of a body of water that I don't recall having seen the last time. People say there used to be a lake around here, that appeared suddenly and later disappeared. I wouldn't be surprised if it's had the urge to show up again."

"Really?" Rheina stifled a yawn. "I do feel like I heard people mention it before. It's a curiosity—but not enough of one to make me leave Limmock Castle at the moment."

"Darling!" cried Teddy.

"Oh, Teddy, what a fortunate man you are! Look at that orange moon rising over the mountain, listen to the velvety wings of the wonderful night birds, and the wild song of the brook in the darkness."

"You know all this is yours, Rheina—you have only to say the word to become the lady of Limmock Castle! I'll send for an army of laborers from Edinburgh, and they'll work till these ruins have become a castle truly worthy of you, my beloved."

He began to make plans: already he envisioned creating a garden, a park, an ornamental pond. He'd put a motor road through the mountains, to reach the renovated castle by car. He'd put in tennis courts, golf links, carports...

Rheina listened in silence, her head tipped back slightly, her eyes half closed, her cheeks rosy in the wavering light of the single candle.

Teddy Haigh could see only the shadow of her long lashes on her cheeks, and not the gaze that filtered through the narrow gap of her eyelids, otherwise...

Otherwise, forgetting all his hopes for the future, he would've fled across the mountains through the night without glancing back at Limmock Castle or Rheina; unfathomable terror would've lent him wings to flee this place forever—the place on which he was building all his hopes for future happiness.

Night... Far away in the village the cracked bell in the small clock tower over the village hall was about to ring out the harsh peal of midnight. Clouds had covered the sky and hidden the moon. Owls hooted long and slow, sleepless ravens complained, bats whistled in the shadows.

"Hanh!"

Teddy Haigh slept, worn out by the hard work of the day but still able to dream the most wonderful dreams. Dreaming, he saw the long hall of the museum transformed into a luxurious library, with deep armchairs covered in soft leather, and a high baronial chimney next to which it would feel good to sit on winter evenings and talk of love with Lady Rheina Haigh.

In truth, that hall looked grimmer than ever—grimmer than it would've looked in the midst of the worst of nightmares.

Thump! Thump! Thump! Thump!

The sound of an awful tread arose—not from the museum, but from the small black room next to it, though the door remained shut.

Three steps from that door stood Rheina.

No light could've guided her there through the profound darkness—but to see her was to know she had no need of light: her eyes glowed, as green as a tiger's, and to her the night must be as bright as day.

"Hanh!"

A shape writhed at Rheina's feet.

"Death to all who draw near!" she croaked in a terrible voice. "The earth cracks open, the earth is in peril."

"Hanh!"

Something made a grinding sound behind the door.

The writhing creature flattened itself on the floor with a terrified whimper. Rheina herself staggered, turned terribly pale, and fell to her knees.

The door opened partway, only to reveal a blackness blacker than the surrounding night. Rheina's nyctalopic eyes could certainly have seen in there, but they were fixed on the floor, and no power could make her lift them toward the open door, so great was the terror that possessed her.

Then a harrowing faraway hymn arose, and, still prostrate, Rheina responded. Her throat gave out the same terrible unknown sounds that seemed to erupt from the abyss.

"Hanh!"

"Go!" commanded Rheina.

Teddy Haigh felt himself suddenly being seized around the middle. A great force raised him up between sky and earth. He awoke, he cried out, but he was carried at incredible speed across the museum hall and into the black room, whose door closed behind him.

At that same moment in the middle of the night, in London, Harry Dickson came running out of the British Museum, where he'd spent long hours hunched over books and parchments. His face was white and drenched in sweat, his teeth chattered, his limbs trembled, his blood froze.

Who would've recognized in this creature, petrified by inhuman terror, the great Harry Dickson, the man who faced the greatest dangers with a smile on his lips?

5. Master Culley

The inhabitants of Limmock witnessed the event in shock: the old lake had reclaimed its rights to its former bed. The water rose slowly at first, then faster, and the glistening expanse of the old days again took the place of the little rock-strewn wasteland. Greystock Island, however, had not returned.

MacGregor couldn't hide his joy as he presided over the village council that had quickly been summoned in the circumstances. "The tourists will come back, not to mention scientists and connoisseurs of mysteries!"

"Business will pick up, that's for sure," said the grocer, "and I believe I'd do well to add a line of photographic equipment to my stock."

"We'll charge a special fee to visit the lake, and we'll sell souvenirs, the proceeds to go to the community chest," suggested Culley, the tailor—who, due to his education, also served as village clerk and deputy mayor of Limmock.

"It's a great pity Mr. Servus is no longer with us," said MacGregor. "Not that I liked the old hoot owl, but his castle ruins would've added another attraction for the outsiders who are sure to come running."

"Why shouldn't the community itself manage the museum?" cried Culley, who took the municipal interest to heart as if it were his own.

"Hmm..." MacGregor hesitated. "Would that be legal?"

"The community is the community, and it's legal," decided the tailor.

"If Culley says so..."

Yes, that's what everyone thought: once Culley had spoken, there was nothing for it but to agree.

"Someone will have to go out to the castle to have a look at how we might best manage that museum—without breaking any laws," said MacGregor finally.

It was clear who that someone would be: Culley.

He raised no objections, and decided to do it that very day. The weather was fine, though a cold wind blew from the mountains. He put on sturdy boots and went back to his shop in search of clothing that would give him the look of a tourist. Then, armed with a good steel-tipped walking stick, he set off, equipped with a rucksack stuffed with provisions and bringing along a flask of Scotch whisky—an unprecedented gift from MacGregor.

"I'll reconnoiter the premises," Culley announced self-importantly. "And I probably won't be back till tomorrow."

Culley was no longer a young man, but he was hardy, in spite of shoulders hunched by his work; at one time he'd been a fine mountaineer, and after an hour he'd recovered a little of his former pace. But the Grampian trails were no longer as familiar to him, and—without exactly getting lost—he took a few wrong turns, which brought him out onto a small bare plateau that ended abruptly at the edge of a deep, narrow, rocky gorge.

"This isn't the right path," he muttered, eyeing the depths unhappily.

A steep path ran down into the gorge—more a goat track than a trail made by men—and Culley hesitated awhile before committing himself.

"A wooden cross," he murmured. "It's true, I remember now—this is where that poor scientist from London, Marlwood, met his death."

The accident hadn't made much of a stir in Limmock, since it wasn't the first time some careless soul had lost his life out on the dangerous Grampian hills. Culley himself had been on the jury that ruled Marlwood's death accidental.

"I'm not going to take my chances on that slope," he said after thinking it over. "One loose rock is all it would take to finish a fellow off. Might as well retrace my steps."

And yet he didn't turn around. He hesitated, his attention suddenly drawn: ten yards from the black wood cross, he could see small objects moving among the fallen rocks. Culley had sharp eyes, but he didn't rely on them; in his rucksack he had a pair of old but excellent binoculars. He aimed them at the objects and watched for a long while.

When he lowered the binoculars he whistled softly and crouched down behind a boulder to reflect more comfortably. "The ducks of Hell!" he murmured.

The moving objects were indeed strange web-footed birds, appearing and disappearing as they threaded their way awkwardly from rock to rock. Their heads were large and powerful; their pale ivory beaks were flat and broad; their misshapen wings were nothing but ridiculous stumps; a thin dark down covered their backs, but they were otherwise featherless; their odd, jerky, uncertain gait confirmed what Culley already knew—these birds were blind.

What he didn't know is that similar creatures are fairly common in places with large subterranean lakes, such as the Carniola region of Slovenia. They were originally ducks like any other, but once they'd strayed into the underground world they adapted. Their tactile senses had taken the place of their useless eyes, and their pointless plumage had given way to a leathery skin as tough as a shield.

In his youth the Limmock tailor had hiked these mountains in every direction, and he'd heard many a tale about those birds—terrifying legends that featured devils and other horrible denizens of the underworld. In those days Highlanders claimed plain and simple that the entrance to Hell was located in one of the gorges in the Grampians; for proof they offered the occasional rare sighting of those hideous birds, which now and again came to visit the world of mortals.

All those old wives' tales now coming back to mind made a strong impression on Culley. He wasn't exactly pleased to find himself alone in such company. On the other hand he felt the stirring of the Scotsman's natural greed and nose for a good deal. "What a reward I'd get from the Edinburgh scientific society if I found the nest of these disgusting creatures!"

The profit motive won out in the end. Firmly gripping his steel-tipped walking stick, he began to follow the path down; after forty-five minutes of straining and slipping and stumbling he reached the wooden cross. He bowed his head respectfully and muttered a prayer.

The ducks, though blind, were not at all deaf, and they'd vanished at the first sound of the pebbles knocked aside by his feet. But Culley had spotted where they'd gone, and it didn't take him long to find a narrow fissure in the rock, inside which some sort of natural staircase descended.

"Natural?" the tailor asked himself—and the answer he got was far from reassuring.

The enormous steps, though crudely aligned, seemed to have been hewn with an intelligent purpose; their regularity certainly provided food for thought. Still, the fear of devils and their familiars no longer held much sway over Culley. From his rucksack he took a little square-sided lantern, put a lit candle in it, and started down the stairs.

Each step was as broad as a landing, and he had to jump down from one to the next—but it was still easier going than the steep path had been earlier. Soon the daylight behind him had shrunk to a thin milky stripe, then to nothing but a reflection, which the next bend in the stairs extinguished.

The walls of the cave caught the candlelight, and what the tailor could see certainly encouraged him to pursue his underground exploration: magnificent crystals with blue and yellow tints glistened like fantastical gems.

Culley rejoiced—Limmock would finally have almost inexhaustible wealth. At the next village elections the deputy would have no trouble sending MacGregor back to his innkeeper's bar, and taking the noble title of mayor for himself.

Down he went, full of bold dreams for the future.

An automobile of strange design left the outskirts of Leith at dawn and seemed to be doing its best to stay off busy roads. It was an uncommon kind of vehicle, of the type used by the army in the mountains, and therefore seen only during maneuvers: heavy yet handling nimbly, it looked a little like a tank, though it ran on wheels rather than treads. It could climb the steepest slopes and go downhill at angles that would give pause to a veteran alpinist.

The car made a long detour to avoid the village of Limmock, and—running along the edge of one precipice after another—it reached the vicinity of Limmock Castle and stopped almost within sight of the ruins. The driver parked it between two great boulders that concealed it perfectly. That done, Harry Dickson hopped out, pale and drawn like a man after a string of sleepless nights. But his eyes shone feverishly. Next to him, looking a little fresher, stood Tom Wills.

They'd still been in London the night before. By special order, the night mail plane from London to Edinburgh had been held long enough for them to climb aboard.

When he came out of the British Museum, Dickson had literally run straight to the Prime Minister, Lord Dambridge, to alert him of his departure that night. They'd spoken for almost an hour, and when the interview was over the Prime Minister was as pale as the detective.

"If anyone but Dickson had told me that story," said Lord Dambridge, "I'd have had him committed on the spot."

"Remember the Knights of the Moon, my lord, remember the Iron Temple, and other adventures of that kind in which you yourself were involved; and remember also an image that was dear to me once: the mountains of Britain are like Swiss cheese, with a thousand subterranean holes."

"But this beats all for improbability!"

"Truth is stranger than fiction!"

"My dear Dickson, if a thing like this gets out—even if your frightening plan succeeds—half the country will go stark raving mad!"

"That's why I want to do this myself. Tom Wills's help is all I'll need. And I'll have to have a few supplies that the Edinburgh arsenal can furnish me."

"I'll phone the commander myself."

"Either I'll succeed, or you can strike Harry Dickson's name from the roll of the living!"

And now here the detectives were, in the middle of a lonely wilderness, both of them oddly equipped, in truth: they were dressed in supple leather and carried peculiar rucksacks, each holding three large connected cylinders. An expert would've recognized, with surprise and concern, that the triple apparatus combined the oxygen tank of a flamethrower with reservoirs of poison gas. The expert's fears would mount at the sight of Dickson and Tom filling a large leather bag with long hand grenades and with a few heavy cylinders armed with fuses.

"It's enough to bring down a fortress, Guv," groaned Tom, staggering under the weight.

"I hope so, my boy," murmured Dickson. "But what a fortress!"

They crossed the rocky saddle and followed a diagonal path that brought them out on a small pebble-strewn heath no more than a hundred yards from the castle. Dickson took out a long pistol of impressive caliber, and Tom followed his example.

"Fire without warning at anyone you see," said Dickson. "We have no choice!"

But they had no need to use their weapons: the door to the castle stood wide open, and the castle itself was empty.

"Ah," said Tom, "someone's been here while we were away, Guv!"

"Someone who smoked Navy cut tobacco in a fine briar pipe!"

"And ate roast wild goose!"

"Strange!"

"What?" asked Tom. "The dinner leftovers?"

"No, this feminine accessory." From under the table Dickson picked up a small rhinestone hair clip.

"It doesn't seem all that frightening, Guv."

"Who knows, my boy?"

Tom heard his employer whistle in the characteristic way he knew so well. The detective was holding a sheet of paper, browned but not consumed, that he'd retrieved from the ashes in the fireplace.

"What is it, Guv?" asked Tom. "Oh, an invoice! *Jeremy Buzemeyer, taxidermist*."

Dickson shook his head and pointed to a few lines scrawled on the back of the paper. "It's a map, Tom, and a pretty accurate one, showing exactly the tapering shape of the old Limmock Lake."

"But that's not all, Guv!"

"No, my boy," growled Dickson, "that's not all. Look at these parallel lines: don't they look like canals? I don't see what else they could be. Ah, Tom, THEY must have some engineers, and some first-class experts in hydraulics! Mark my words: Limmock Lake could easily return, if it hasn't already done so, and in that case…"

"In that case?…"

"We'd have no time to lose."

Dickson put the paper in his pocket and motioned to his assistant to follow him into the museum hall. Tom watched as he cautiously approached the little door leading to the black room. It was no longer locked, and it opened with a turn of the doorknob.

Tim switched on his flashlight. "Everything's still here. The bed…—ah!"

He stood frozen in horror: the bed was soaked with dripping blood, which hadn't yet even had time to dry.

"Understood!" muttered Dickson. "THEY've begun. The victim must've been sacrificed this very night. I've come too late for him, but—let's hope—not for others! The problem is to figure out how to reach THEM."

"Listen, Guv!"

Strange muffled sounds could be heard, followed by a dismal metallic grinding.

"Look out!" shouted Tom, jumping back. "The bed, Guv—look at the bed!"

A peculiar wave seemed to lift the entire bed, and soon with a sort of roar it rose almost to the ceiling, exposing beneath it a large, dark, square opening.

"Fire!" screamed Tom, as a hand gripped the edge of the hole and a head emerged from the shadows.

"No, don't shoot me!" cried a terrified voice. "Shoot the creature that's been chasing me like something possessed!"

A lit lantern emerged from the hole and rolled across the floor, while a man in tattered clothes fell at Dickson's feet.

"My name is Culley and I'm the deputy mayor of Limmock," the man wept. "But the one who's after me is the Devil incarnate!"

He had no sooner spoken than a wild croaking could be heard, and a pair of enormous hands burst out of the darkness. "Hanh!"

Some kind of oddly dressed gorilla, with a face as savage as it was hideous, leapt out of the hole and threw itself at them. A volley of shots rang out. With an unearthly wail the horrible creature collapsed. The exploding bullets with which the detectives had loaded their pistols had torn off half its skull and left a gaping hole in its torso.

"The ape-man that Greystock mentioned," said Dickson calmly. "We're on the right track. I thank you, Master Culley. But where have you just come from?"

"Who knows? A strange land, certainly. It's in the bowels of the earth, and yet sometimes ye can see just fine. At times it looks like a horrible cave, at other times like a magnificent palace. I think it's pyramids."

"Why pyramids?"

"It's full of those dried-up black things… Ah, I've got it—mummies!"

"They don't move?"

"Of course not," said Culley in surprise. "Why would mummies move? The only thing moving was this demon ye just killed—and crikey, was he ever moving! He started chasing me, but going lots slower, and all the time making those cries: Hanh! Hanh! I spotted a high staircase and I reckoned it would take me back to the surface. Right at the top of the stairs I found myself facing a wall; oddly, hanging from it I saw something like a bell pull. Without knowing quite why, I pulled it. Lucky for me, since the trapdoor opened immediately, and here I am!"

"Master Culley," said Dickson, "you strike me as a sturdy and stouthearted fellow. You'll be a help to us." He turned to Tom. "Run to the car with Culley, my boy, and bring back the two big steel spindles with straps attached. Master Culley, I assume you're not afraid to carry a sixty-pound load."

"Not at all," replied the master tailor proudly.

A few minutes later Tom and Culley were back. The tailor pointed to the two long spindles attached to his back. "What exactly are these things?"

"Dangerous neighbors, my friend," laughed Dickson. "Airplane bombs…"

6. Beauty and the Beast

Master Culley was right: without the detectives knowing quite when or how, they no longer needed either flashlights or lanterns to see their way through the subterranean caverns. Tom Wills was the first to notice it, and Harry Dickson could offer no more than a scientific conjecture.

"Clearly it's an electrical phenomenon. Cold blue light. Unfortunately we don't have the equipment we'd need to analyze it. Is it natural? Possibly, though I doubt it."

"In that case, Guv, the rats who live in these caves are no fools."

"My boy, I fear the only safe way for us to deal with THEM will result in the destruction of many secrets and discoveries," murmured his employer. "But we have no choice: we'll be up against such inhuman forces!"

The cavern they were walking through was certainly strange, and could be called a cavern only because it would've been hard to say what other name to give it. It was shaped like a half-cylinder, with smooth black walls. The pale, slightly iridescent light came from thin trails of vapor that moved slowly along the apex of the high vault in total silence.

"Look," said Culley. "Here's where that vile ape almost caught me. He was coming out of that hole, to your right, while I was coming down the stairs whose bottom steps ye can see to your left."

"Let's follow the ape's trail," said Tom cheerfully. "I hope it won't lead us up a tree!"

"Where did you see those mummies, Master Culley?" asked Dickson.

"Ah!..." said the tailor. "That's odd: they're not here anymore. And yet when I was running it seemed like they were all along the walls of the passage we've just left. They were all quite well behaved—by which I mean completely still."

"Well, they must not have stayed well behaved!" said Tom.

But the joke died on his lips: the rocky tunnel they'd been following ended abruptly, and they found themselves facing an enormous plaza bathed in milky light. They stood on the rim of a high ledge overlooking a deep, broad valley.

"A city, Guv!" cried Tom.

"A city... Yes, my boy, a city—but a city out of a nightmare!"

Colossal buildings lined stupendous avenues, and the public squares were of gargantuan dimensions.

After a moment to leave his companions to their astonishment, Dickson said softly, "This is an optical illusion, my friends. We're experiencing a phenomenon of refracted light, poorly studied as yet, but known occasionally in underground spaces. What we're seeing is just a trick with mirrors, and the mirrors are two small subterranean lakes that reflect shapes and—due to a difference in atmospheric density down here— multiply and enlarge those shapes almost to infinity."

"So the city isn't really that big, Guv?" asked Tom.

"No, since two spindle bombs will be more than enough to blow it all to kingdom come, which is exactly where it belongs," answered Dickson gravely.

"But what are we seeing down there?" asked Culley. "Is it really a city?"

"Yes. It's Babylon."

Tom's eyes widened. "Ba... by... lon?"

"I'll explain later, but I fear you'll be just as puzzled by my explanation as you are by the strange facts themselves."

"Is it uninhabited, Guv?"

"No—see for yourselves!"

Then Tom and Culley noticed larval shapes moving awkwardly among the rocks.

"The mummies!" cried the tailor.

"Yes... That's all they are for now—and thank heavens! Because otherwise we'd have no chance of ever again seeing beautiful blue sky."

Tom shook his head and gave up trying to understand. Culley, however, concluded that the Devil was mixed up in it, and that the Prince of Darkness had the power to build subterranean cities just as he pleased.

Dickson spent a long while observing the strange world below them, and he took a number of photos with a fast camera he'd brought. "That's all we'll be able to take away from here."

"Why nothing else, Guv?"

"I'll explain that later, Tom, like lots of other things. But for now you should know that it would truly be dangerous."

Suddenly he fell silent, and his companions saw him stagger and turn pale. "Back," he muttered. "Hide! Quick—behind this boulder, or all is lost!"

His companions obeyed without question, and a moment later all three of them were squeezed together in a narrow cavity in the rock, from which they could still see part of the landscape.

"Oh," murmured Tom, who, since he was nearest the opening, could see down into the extraordinary valley, "Men!"

He'd just spotted two men on a high ledge walking slowly together, dressed like mountaineers.

Dickson saw them too. "The men from Greystock House!" he said simply.

"Really, Guv? Then they should be over a hundred years old, and they don't look more than thirty."

"You're right, my boy. But for now, keep quiet and watch!"

The mummies had begun to move again, so slowly that they seemed to be struggling against some enormous invisible weight. And then that hymn—mentioned once before—rose again, wild and terrible... But it was not just the sound of that fanatical choir that caught the anxious attention of the three men: now heavy, unearthly footsteps slammed the ground and made the entire cliff shake.

"The footsteps from the black room," stammered Tom, seized by boundless fear.

"Stay calm, both of you," said Dickson. "This mind-boggling performance, out of the wildest nightmare, is reaching its end. But no matter what you see—don't move, don't cry out."

No sooner had he said the words than he himself needed a supreme effort to stifle a horrified cry.

Without anyone knowing exactly where it had come from, the THING was hoisting itself up onto the ledge by its arms—two misshapen stumps ending in sharp claws. Soon a monstrous snout appeared, like the grossly enlarged mouth of a scorpion. The eyes were barely visible, buried as they were in the creases of a black, oily skin. But an extraordinary maw split what must've been the creature's head. A few moments later, with an agility surprising in so ungainly a shape, the creature hopped up onto the rocky path, making the ground shake under its weight. In truth, it evoked no other thoughts but blackness, heaviness, and ugliness.

Tom and Culley had shrunk back against the cliff without daring to move—but they saw Dickson strike a triumphant pose. "Pass me the grenades, Tom!"

The young man automatically passed him the two long cylinders. Dickson clenched his teeth, then pulled out the pins and threw the powerful bombs at the monster. They exploded on impact.

Tom and Culley had pulled protective masks over their faces. They watched as smoke curled around the creature, which stood stock still, as if in surprise—but it didn't last. With a loud trumpeting cry the creature spun, tripped, and fell dumbfounded off the rocky cliff into the depths of the city.

"Hurrah!" cried Dickson. "That's the best thing that could've happened! Ah, my friends, we've had smooth sailing! And now let's wrap up the job."

A strange uproar was now rising from the abyss. Tom could see the two men he'd spotted before, now running back and forth in distress. Dickson took the spindle bombs and carefully pulled out the plungers. He did the same with the gas cylinders.

"What mysteries we're going to destroy," he murmured. "But it has to be! There's no place on earth for such creatures. Let them return to the night they should never have left!"

The bombs went over the edge of the cliff.

"Quickly now!" said Dickson. "Because it's possible the effect will be greater than we anticipated."

Indeed, almost immediately an incredible sheet of flame shot up from the depths.

"There—just as I said!" he cried in alarm. "We must've hit some munitions storage or who knows what!"

An immense rumbling rose in reply. The three of them sprinted up the corridor, where the air was already fiery and hard to breathe.

"The stairs!" cried Culley.

"Thank God!"

They emerged into the black room, but a hot wind followed right behind them.

"Even the Devil's bed will keep its secrets," murmured Dickson, with one last look at the strange frame of orichalcum. "No doubt it's for the best. Everything here must be cast into oblivion!"

By the time they reached the car, the first flames were already bursting out of Limmock Castle.

But the detective's job wasn't over, and what remained to be done was by no means the least peculiar part. After he'd spoken with Master Culley—who'd sworn on his honor to say not a word about all he'd seen—Harry Dickson returned to Leith in great haste. We'll follow him there, alongside Tom Wills, through the back streets of the old port, to the alley that led to Jeremy Buzemeyer's shop.

Night was falling. It was drizzling, and the meager streetlights in this sinister neighborhood were coming on. Dickson was nervous—as if he dreaded this encounter more than that terrible power in the abyss. Tom followed him automatically, resigned to living through unbelievable experiences without understanding them.

Through the greasy windows of the taxidermy shop shone a single small lamp. Dickson shivered; finishing the job sickened him oddly. But it had to be done…

"My boy, if it should happen that my hand isn't steady…" he murmured in his assistant's ear with feeling.

"Yes, Guv, I know…"

They reached the door, which was only latched. The long shadows of mounted seabirds and marsh birds stretched toward the detectives as they entered.

A tall young woman in a black smock set down the scalpel she was using to cut open the heavy body of a large pochard duck. "Can I help you, gentlemen?"

Her voice was melodious; her beautiful, calm face conveyed intelligence. Dickson hesitated. His heart stood still. And yet he knew the terrible price of hesitation.

But the young woman also seemed to understand. Her eyes opened wide, grew enormous, awful, terrifying. Harry Dickson was beaten. That hellish gaze would defeat even his great strength.

No… Tom Wills was there—and by chance he'd been looking at the redheaded bird, and he hadn't met the gaze of Rheina Schooten. While Dickson staggered, as if in the grip of an unknown power, two tongues of flame burst from over his shoulder. The young woman, hit right in the forehead, collapsed.

"Tom, my boy…" moaned the detective. "You've saved my life… You've saved the world."

He went to Rheina's lifeless body, and Tom heard him murmur in distress, "My God, what if it isn't?…"

But almost immediately he leapt back with a cry of horror and disgust. "Look, look!—It's beginning!"

Rheina's beautiful features had begun to melt, the outlines vanished, black patches spread across her cheeks, which sank into hollows and then were nothing but holes.

"What's going on, Guv?" asked Tom, shivering.

Dickson's reply was enigmatic. "Rhâna, high priestess of the demiurge Baal. Here's all that's left of her… mummy."

7. The Incredible Explanation

Harry Dickson never talked about that adventure later; only among a few close friends was he willing to lift the heavy veil cloaking the mystery. "Macrobiotics…" he began.

Right away his listeners protested, "What an awful word!"

"But what a marvelous one," he replied solemnly, "since it represents the art of prolonging life almost indefinitely! Back in the mists of time it was a science; in more recent centuries it became a haphazard, undirected search for the elixir of long life sought by Raymond Lulle and other alchemists and necromancers. The science seems to have been nurtured by the Egyptian priests: haven't you heard the bold hypothesis that the Egyptian mummies were actually a latent form of life, and could be reanimated in some predetermined future age?

"In Babylon, almost a thousand years before Christ, the greatest practitioners of that science were found among the priests serving the god—or rather the demon—Baal. But it was a hermetic science, meaning that it was confined to a small circle of initiates. During the reign of Nabonassar—the one who destroyed all the monuments and records proving the existence of his predecessors, so that he could claim to be the first king—those priestly adepts attracted his hostile attention, and had to go into exile.

"Exile where? I had to hunt through the rare documents that speak of them, but those references were clear enough to give me the key to this frightening mystery—though even then it took the form of a legend: Fleeing the king's anger, the priestly caste left the country and went to some volcanic region, which I still haven't identified. They descended into an extinct volcano and arrived at a vast subterranean world. That should come as no surprise to us: modern science now posits that all the volcanoes in the world, active or extinct, are interconnected. How did they live? Don't forget, highly adapted fauna and flora flourish deep underground. No doubt many of the exiles died; but some survived, and they devoted themselves to the arcana of the mysterious science of macrobiotics.

"They must've made enormous strides! Yes—don't stare at me like that. The subject has been covered, with a modicum of fiction but also plenty of truth, in a modern book that I highly recommend you read.

"So... those eccentric, unnerving exiles managed to push back the limits of life beyond our wildest imaginings. Meanwhile they continued to explore their underground world, until they reached the great region of caves underlying the Grampians. They liked the place, and they stayed. But, though their science had advanced—I assume all those nomads of the underworld were scientists—they still remained faithful to their ancient cult of the demiurge Baal. And their Baal was some antediluvian creature, some monstrous toad whose horrible life they'd prolonged. He's the one we killed with our grenades!

"I'm coming now to John Greystock's adventure. Evidence suggests that at some point the people underground had to get help from the aboveground world: maybe it was because of the lack of ventilation in the caverns—they were weakening, degenerating, and their demon Baal showed signs of senility. They had to have fresh air; nothing else would do. Their hydraulic engineers had no trouble creating Limmock Lake and the island—but unluckily for them it was immediately occupied. Of course, they could've killed the island's inhabitants, but they'd learned that over time the surface world had gained power. They waited for the Greystocks to leave, and then they installed their god in his famous sacrificial bed: yes, that horrifying demiurge both ate and slept in that bed. His victims were knocked unconscious by the fall of that immense canopy."

"Why didn't they kill John Greystock?" asked his listeners.

"Here I have only conjectures, and I admit they're weak. Remember the two men dressed like surface dwellers. The people of the abyss must've thought it wise to send out scouts into the fresh air. Two of their leaders must've blended into our world. Slowly they picked up our language and our ways—and in the process they may have acquired some of our morals, because they behaved toward Greystock not just like men, but like gentlemen!

"But a third emissary, this time a woman, was sent out into the foreign world: the high priestess of Baal, Rhâna, whose name and description I found in those old books I mentioned. She submitted to a meager, secretive life, though she had the help of a kind of monstrous servant, whom both John Greystock and Master Culley met. Rhâna certainly picked up none of our morals—but let's not anticipate.

"Greystock's visit left the two scouts afraid. They caused the island and the lake to disappear, and after that, when they saw that the demon Baal needed fresh air, they made use of Limmock Castle."

"And what about Servus?" the listeners cried.

Harry Dickson bowed his head. "I assume he met the two 'gentlemen' of the underworld, and in some way became their ally—without learning anything of their secret. When he heard about the auction of John Greystock's books, he must've feared the mystery would be exposed. That caused him to wrestle internally over whom to betray: his friends underground or his fellow-men aboveground. Rhâna—or rather her monstrous apelike servant—cut short his hesitation by killing him, just as Marlwood and some bird hunter were killed, because by chance they'd wandered into one of their 'air vents.' As for poor Teddy Haigh, the priestess offered him up as a sacrifice to her terrifying lord."

"How do you explain Rhâna's posthumous disintegration, Guv?" asked Tom Wills.

"I can't explain it, my boy, I can only report what I read in those books. It seems that when the macrobes die—which usually happens only by violence—they're quickly reduced to dust, as if they were nothing more than ordinary mummies brought to life by demonic powers."

"Ah!" someone sighed. "Why did you have to destroy that world?"

"And stop the human stampede toward the miraculous powers of macrobiotics? A wave of madness would've swept across the world, and God only knows if it would've led—among the ignorant masses and even among the rest—to some horrible revival of the worship of bloodthirsty demons!"

And then Harry Dickson concluded, "My friends, I'd much rather have dreamt all this—and not lived it!"

Bonus Story [3]

Atom Mudman Bezecny: *Harry's Homecoming*

New York City, 1933

When Harry Dickson got off the plane, the gears in his head were already turning at full speed. Had young Tom Wills been there, he would have seen the gleam in his mentor's eye, and grown excited despite the fact that it was a regular sight for him. Tom couldn't disguise his excitement any more than Dickson could hide when he was deep in thought. Keeping his mind on the various ideas he was mentally amalgamating, the detective sometimes worried that he kept Tom around specifically to fan his ego, which critics accused him of having—after all, there was a reason why he had taken up quarters in Baker Street. And Tom was indeed his most ardent "fan." But that thought merely made him miss 221B, and Tom's presence, especially since there was important business to take care of in town.

He had received an invitation to a conference of detectives and adventurers from the Americas—someone named Donald Carrick had signed it. Dickson had never heard of Carrick before, and most of the names on the guest list were just as obscure. He had hoped to see his friend Ardan mentioned, but no such luck. Still, the event might prove to have some value. Tom had had other engagements—he'd received a letter of his own from someone answering to the name of Tinker, who was hosting a parallel conference for the assistants and biographers of many European sleuths. Dickson couldn't help

---

[3] Originally published in *Tales of the Shadowmen 13: Sang Froid* (2016).

but be proud. The boy had great talents, and he really did want to make him into a respectable investigator of his own caliber. Now that he was gone, Dickson had no one to talk to—and so he was simply tumbling the same facts through his head.

The front page article of the paper he'd gotten on the plane had talked about an attempt on the life of Dr. Alfred Carroll, an outspoken critic of narcotics—chiefly marijuana. This had taken place after the doctor had publicly linked the local Grisson Gang to the semi-famous Burma Roberts case. Apparently, the Roberts girl had been given marijuana at a party sponsored by the Gang, and when the drug began to affect her health and push her into a life of crime, they had assisted her in the kidnapping of her own niece.

Dickson still had the paper tucked under his arm, just above his single suitcase. Already, he could see the shining towers of his once native home. He'd been meaning to return for some time now, to live up to his sobriquet as the "American Sherlock Holmes." The 1930s were proving to be a wild time in the United States, and he had to admit he wanted in on this wildness. Still, he still had many obligations in Europe, which had been wild since forever. For Harry Dickson, as for many others, New York represented adventure. He couldn't wait to start.

He was nearly outside the airport when someone bumped into him.

When the detective whirled to confront the guilty party, he was shocked to discover the age of the interloper. He was an old man, though it was clear he'd once been stocky. He still looked strong as a bull, but now shriveled with age. His clothes were too big for him, and there were atrophy marks on his exposed arms. His face was beardless, and he barely had any hair left at all. Dickson was able to tell he was probably nearly ninety—if not a hundred, or over.

"Pardon me, monsieur," the old man said, grinning. "I just wanted to know if I could borrow that paper. I've been keeping up on the Grisson Gang story."

Dickson wanted to keep the story for himself, so he silently waited as the elderly fellow skimmed the article. Despite a meager appearance—his clothes looked as old as their wearer—the old man was a quick reader. Not thirty seconds had passed before the paper was handed back to Dickson.

"*Merci beaucoup.*"

"There is an unusual accent to your voice, my friend," Dickson said then. "Obviously French, yet with some outside influence. Perhaps you have some Basque in you?" After a brief second the investigator grinned. "No, your expression says I'm wrong. I think you must have spent a number of years in Flanders, but come from a small French village like, say, Litan. Also, I have only heard that particular Flemish trace in your voice once before—and it does meld so intriguingly with the bumpkin-French—and that was when I was passing through a small town by the name of Quiquendone a few years ago, doing research on a forty-odd year old case involving a scientist who could make plants grow to titanic size, and drive men and women out of their minds. His name was Doctor Ox. That's your name, isn't it?"

"I am impressed. Few these have heard of Litan, my place of birth, but perhaps fewer still have heard of Quiquendone. You are Harry Dickson, the so-called 'American Sherlock Holmes.' I certainly hope that wasn't a title you chose for yourself."

"I believe it was assigned by the media of some country or another," the detective replied.

"Well, if you can live to even a quarter-portion of Holmes' name, monsieur Dickson, perhaps I will have to borrow a moment of your time. You see, my interest in the Grisson Gang is a professional matter. One of tremendous and absolute urgency, at that. I..."

The detective cut him off. "I'm here on business of my own, Doctor. While encountering a man of your reputation is a rare privilege, I must admit I'm not interested in taking a case from a man whose legend is that of an impressive criminal record."

"My most recent crime occurred in 1881, when I exposed the son of the famed Captain Hatteras to a hallucinogenic gas of my own devising. I created and tested it to prove my ultimate theory: that humanity is not special in the universe, being only a composite of various chemicals. Over the last fifty years, I have seen that science has rallied to my side. In any case, the statute of limitations has long expired."

"I can only take your word, doctor, and I don't trust it."

"Age has neutered me. I never meant to hurt anyone, and now, truly, I can't. In any case, Monsieur Dickson, I have learned that, at my age, one can master the skills that you detectives boast about. I can see from your face that the business that draws you here is not of immediate concern. You would have a few days, or even a week, during which you could assist me with my misadventure."

Dickson was silent. He had to admit that his thoughts about Tom had moved to the realization that his absence meant boredom. In truth, he arrived early with the hopes of picking up something to write home about...

Doctor Ox's persistence had convinced him. He could take a leap of faith—such leaps were the fuel of his career.

"When do we start?" he asked.

"Immediately, Monsieur Dickson!"

Doctor Ox had a car parked nearby, and he proved to be a skilled driver. Considering his age and ambition, Dickson realized the old man relished the idea of an automobile. Like many scientists, and indeed, many *mad* scientists, he doubtlessly lived in the future, and craved the technology from eras yet to come. To live for so long in the 19th century only to be given one of these vehicles would be like manna from Heaven.

Dickson wondered if Doctor Ox had ever met his old nemesis, Professor Flax—such a possibility seemed likely. He harbored the belief that the criminal tendencies of such men canceled any progressive traits they night have had, but he accepted that some of them probably contributed *some* good things to the world.

Doctor Ox was wasting no time in presenting the details of his case, knowing that a detective thrived off of them. Dickson sat with his arms folded across his chest, wearing his best neutral, professional face. However, he felt as if he was letting off some faint excitement, and he suspected that the uncanny doctor was able to feel that he was not as detached as he had initially seemed.

"Today's article is the last piece of the puzzle," Doctor Ox elucidated. "The Grisson Gang is planning on using my greatest invention commercially."

"That's a statement that requires more context, doctor," the detective replied. "Your greatest product appears to have been a growth hormone combined with a psychosis-inducing drug."

"Those were just some youthful experiments—I had no idea what I was doing. You know how it is when you're forty." And he snickered. "The plant expansion probably had to do with some herakleophorbia I casually mixed in. Of course, it wasn't called herakleophorbia then, and when it was 'invented,' I wasn't given any of the credit..."

"While I do thrive on details, doctor, I sense you are derailing yourself."

"Too right. Well, throughout my life, I've been curious about the potential of a drug that induces madness. I wondered if perhaps I could make the derangement I put upon Quiquendone a pleasurable experience. I knew of opium, of course, and hashish as well. But I wanted to create whimsical fantasies beyond either of them, via a substance as undetectable as the gas I used in Flanders. I became something of an expert in the drug world, and Georges Hatteras was my first test subject. With the aid of a catalyst potion, I gave him a wonderful dream, where he met Lindenbrock and Nemo alike, all through my hypnotic direction. But I still wasn't satisfied.

"My studies took me to Africa, where I learned of the miraculous *taduki*. It's supposed to induce visions of one's previous incarnations, but in my experience, that is merely superstitious nonsense. I spent three years of my life fighting an addiction to *taduki*, which I gained after just two experiments with it. Eventually, however, I found that I could synthesize the active diethylamide within *taduki*, the active substance that creates hallucinations. In a drink, pill, or gas, I could create a drug that unhinged the mind, but in a pleasurable way.

"Have you heard of the Assassins, Dickson? Of course you have. They are said these days to be, or have been, servants of the Si-Fan. In some of the old stories, anyway, the Assassins took their name from the word *hashishin*, etymologically related to the word hashish. The leader of the Assassins would use hashish, as well as romantic company, to bend the minds of his servants to his will. If I became the master of the ultimate pleasure-drug, I could create an army of criminals that would lay down their lives to me...of a size rivaling those of Moriarty...or even Quartz!"

Dickson raised a skeptical—and confused—eyebrow.

"So I'm assisting a criminal enterprise, then?"

"Ha! I said I *could* create such an army, Dickson—but only if I was interested in such a thing."

"You mean to say you're not?"

"It would only be criminal if possession of it became criminal. In my old age, I have decided to serve a noble goal, albeit a hedonistic one. I want to spread pleasure to the world."

"You would become a common drug-dealer, then, doctor?"

Doctor Ox spat. "During my *taduki* years, I was virtually enslaved by a wicked dealer named Malaglou. I curse him and his whole family. I do not peddle dope, monsieur. I offer freedom."

"Something that can also be used as a weapon does not open the path to freedom."

"Are you some sort of sage, now, Dickson? Do you fancy yourself a philosopher? Let us cease talking now. I still have a standing in the chemistry field, even if it's mostly through infamy—and that gave me a contact at a certain Chicago dessert corporation whose executive, named Pelton or something similar, employed some contacts in the criminal underworld. We're meeting one of them here in this alley. He is a Chinese-American called Ichabod Chang."

Dickson again raised an eyebrow. He never thought he'd hear a name like that. Doctor Ox parked on the street, and already Dickson's eyes could make out a hunched figure standing in the dingy darkness.

The doctor ambled quickly towards this man. Chang's face was rough and serious—to some people who had paranoid suspicions about non-whites, it might be intimidating, but Dickson knew better. Chang had faced the pain of that paranoia his entire life, and that was what had hardened him. Ultimately, the detective did not want to speculate further on this man's life, as that, in his mind, would be to make him a spectacle. Too often, the Chinese people of America had been made into such by the nation's white—made into things to gape at, rather than human beings.

For now, Doctor Ox was talking.

"Good evening, Chang. Thank you for meeting with me this evening."

"Well, we are all brothers, doctor, and you are in need. And it says in Deuteronomy 15:11: 'You shall open wide your hand to your brother, to the needy and the poor, in your land.'"

"Er, yes." The doctor turned back to face Dickson. "Chang is something of a Bible scholar."

"Of course," Dickson said simply.

"Not merely a scholar—a library," said Chang. "I have memorized the Gospel. In any case, I know that you seek insight into tracking something of value to you, doctor, but I am here only to pass you on to the one who has the answer. There is an associate of mine, one of my favorite celebrities whom I also correspond with. Her name is O. Ming Lee. Visit the circus in town, and you will find her."

Doctor Ox turned to face Dickson. "That circus is at Central Park, and today is its final day! It will be simplicity itself to locate this Lee girl, and from there, we will recover my formula!"

The detective saw a look in the doctor's eyes that he had seen before—the sort of desperation that wracks an addict. He wondered if this was the hunger of *taduki*. He had been in Africa before, and heard stories of those who languished under the addiction of the legendary drug, and he had no reason to doubt Ox's own story of falling under its power. Evidently, the doctor had not been able to work out the addictive properties of his creation, and so there was another dimension to his desire to reclaim it.

"Then drive on, doctor," the detective replied. He had the sensation of being on thin ice.

They got back in the car, and soon they were on their way to the circus. Already, night was falling upon them, and the spotlights were coming up under the distant big top.

Harry Dickson rarely used the expression "pick your jaw up off the floor," either verbally or in his head. However, both he and Doctor Ox needed to pick their jaws up at this point. Even though their discussion with O. Ming Lee had been going on now for several minutes, the woman herself was a source of constant surprise. She had been quick to introduce herself under her stage name: "Legga, the Spider-Woman." She had obtained this moniker because she had no less than six arms and four legs. Calling her a spider was a simplification—because she had ten limbs, she was more like a squid. She was clad in a red dress featuring a pattern derived from the Western conception of the Asian aesthetic—the only modification that had been made to it was that there were four extra holes on the torso, to accommodate her arms.

"Chang is a correspondent of mine, it's true," Lee was saying. "He is not the first of my friends to get mixed up in criminal business. He serves the executive Pelton because the man was a friend of his father's." She paused then. "I'm not sure I want to talk about my *second* friend, who was pulled to the underworld. If I can call still him a friend."

"This second man... he was your lover, Ms. Lee?" Dickson asked gently. His face was relaxed, his eyebrows faintly tilted upward.

"Yes. Don Maxwell was his name. He was Ichabod's half-brother—Ichabod's father was named Dong Chang, and he had an affair with a New Yorker with the surname Maxwell before he settled down and married. Ms. Maxwell gave birth to a boy named Don, a corruption of Dong."

"I see."

"I'm surprised that Don Maxwell's name doesn't strike a bell in you, Detective Dickson. To me, you seem like someone who might have once had an interest in vaudeville."

"Not worth my time, Ms. Lee—though I do enjoy the theater now and then."

"I would imagine. In any case, Maxwell always said such great things," Lee said bitterly. "He said he'd deserved to be on the same bill as Rice, and he would bring vaudeville back with his impressions. I tried to tell him that a traveling circus is no way to bring vaudeville back, but he insisted. His idea was that after he resurrected his type of theater, he could leave the circus behind and be a star. But he kept jumping at those assistant jobs with scientists. Thorkel, and someone named Vornoff, were some of the names. Got to pay the bills somehow—that dough isn't going to come from a carny wage."

"Those scientists—what was the...?"

"The last one, the one he saw before he disappeared? His name is Doctor Meirschultz, and it's him who has found his way into the leadership of the Grisson Gang."

Once again, the woman with ten limbs had stunned the two men.

"Don started working for Meirschultz later last year, and unlike his past jobs, he stuck with it for awhile. He always explained it to me that he liked to milk a few months' pay from his employers before quickly getting out. That's because a lot of the men he worked with would end up using him for experiments. The last thing he ever said to me—in a letter, because Meirschultz refused to let him leave—was that, yes,

Meirschultz was behind the gangs. That letter came over six months ago, and I feel like his nightmare about experimentation finally came true."

"Thank you for yielding that information so easily, Ms. Lee," Dickson said. "Where is Meirschultz's lab? We'll depart at once, and see if we can learn what happened to Don."

"You should take me with you," Lee said suddenly. "I can help you get inside. Sometimes, Meirschultz keeps his quarters protected. He took on some guards when I kept trying to contact Don."

Doctor Ox grunted. "I have no objections," he said then. He had a weird grin and wild eyes as he spoke. "But you must let me study your anatomy at some point! You are a marvel of the potential of the human body."

Lee didn't seem to see a scientific intent in the doctor, and slapped him across the face with just two of her arms.

Soon they stood outside of a worn-down building that was apparently the home of Doctor Meirschultz. On the way, Dickson asked O. Ming Lee: "What did Meirschultz study, exactly?"

"According to Don, he had an interest in raising the dead," the Chinese girl replied simply.

"Ah!" Doctor Ox declared then, with enthusiasm. "A time-honored tradition."

"If you want to call it that," the so-called Spider-Woman said. "Meirschultz seems to believe that bringing all the world's dead back to life would somehow improve things."

Dickson observed that Doctor Ox seemed to take bemusement in the prospect of a fellow scientist bringing the dead out of their graves. Having just recently met none other than the supposed "Heir of Dracula" himself, he was not amused. Lord, were they all as mad as Flax? Indeed, he really was starting to see that bit of his old foe's soul in Doctor Ox— hopefully not literally.

"Like I said, Meirschultz has security," Lee said. "Some-day soon, he probably won't be able to afford their services.

But I have a plan for dealing with them. Doctor Ox, your professional credentials will help. The main push behind this trick, though, is going to involve people being scared of a lady like myself."

"I understand," Dickson said. Doctor Ox remained in the dark, not having the patience for deduction that Dickson did, but he figured he would know what was going on soon enough.

They exited the car, and Dickson lead the scientist forward. The doctor observed that Lee stayed behind. As they approached the door, Dickson recognized the guards as the typical American pinstripe-and-fedora gangsters—no doubt they were part of the Grisson Gang.

Dickson halted and waited for Doctor Ox to catch up to him, then whispered in the old man's ear: "Say to them exactly what I tell you to say."

The formerly-stout scientist approached the guards.

"Stop! Put 'em up!" barked one of the thugs.

"I am Doctor Ox. Doctor Meirschultz invited me to come here."

"Doctor. Meirschultz wouldn't invite no one. Man's a damn shut-in."

"No, you don't understand," Dickson said then. "Didn't he tell you we were sent to stop the, er, monster, that he created from escaping?"

"Th' *what* now?"

If he hadn't gotten prior warning, even a hardened man like Dickson would have to run in panic from the sight of the Human Spider. Evidently her act incorporated the deed of charging at crowds screaming monstrously, as she was good at it. The detective knew his setup had definitely helped produce the reaction he'd wanted in the guards, and he couldn't hide a proud grin as, shrieking in terror, the men stopping them immediately bolted into the dead of night. They were so fast that he couldn't tell exactly where they'd run off to—it didn't matter, at least for now.

"Cowards," hissed Doctor Ox. "I hear their leader, Slim Grisson himself, is what you Americans would call a momma's boy. His mother is the true master of the Gang."

Dickson said nothing. He noticed that O. Ming Lee was crying. He had become aware that she must have held some degree of shame for her appearance, and so their tactic was at her expense. He stepped towards her, and gently set his hand on her red-garbed shoulder—a shoulder from which three arms emerged. He figured that would be enough.

At once, she stopped crying, and turned to face Dickson. Without fear she set one on her hands on his shoulder in turn. "Thank you, Mr. Dickson."

"It's no trouble. Thank you for the assistance. Will you be joining us in ending this? Your company would make bearable the disappointment I'm about to get over the simplicity of this case."

"I can't. I have my act in the morning. In any case, I really shouldn't see Don, no matter what state he's in. I'm afraid that I've moved on with my life, and whatever he and I had is over."

Dickson nodded, and she began to move back to the road. "I'll catch a cab," she said over her shoulder.

He was pleased to see that in that glance, she was smiling.

"Marvelous," he mused, once she was out of sight.

"You are perhaps smitten, detective?" Doctor Ox said.

"In a purely aromantic and asexual way, doctor. I am fascinated, as you were, in her appearance, but I saw the person within as well. It's amazing how the human spirit always stays the same, no matter what the body looks like."

"Enough poems, Dickson. Let's get inside and get Meirschultz's hands off my work."

Doctor Ox pushed his frail frame against the lab's door, and summoned the heavy strength of his youth and namesake. To Dickson's surprise, the door yielded, breaking off its hinges—he caught it, to prevent it from smashing to the ground and giving away their presence.

Inside the building, there was only silence, and darkness. It didn't look like anyone was home.

Past an entrance parlor was simply a large chamber that represented, presumably, Doctor Meirschultz's lab proper. To Dickson, it seemed almost like the stereotype of a lab, with beakers, test tubes, and flasks scattered almost absentmindedly atop endless seas of incomprehensible papers. In his eyes these were all clues, or pieces of evidence that could send Meirschultz to jail before he *did* find the secret of bringing corpses back to life.

Already Doctor Ox was standing near one of the counters, inspecting a syringe.

"'Super-adrenaline,'" the scientist read off the needle's label. "A euphemistic name if ever I heard one." He squinted, and Dickson observed with him that the formula for this substance was written below.

"Good God," the doctor gasped. "This is my drug! My psychosis-formula! He did steal it, that plagiarist basta—"

"Quiet, doctor," Dickson whispered. "We really shouldn't be caught here. Especially if Meirschultz is insistent on experimenting with human subjects..."

"Human subjects indeed!" a boisterous voice called out.

Suddenly, the lights were on in the lab, and Harry Dickson realized that even his dedication to observation had not quite taken in just how many dark corners the room had had. In one of these corners, their enemies had been waiting. The man who had bellowed at them, who crept from the darkness, had to have been Meirschultz. In a lot of ways, he was a match for the old photographs Dickson had seen of Doctor Ox. He was broad and strong-looking, but unlike Ox, he had an enormous Santa Claus-like beard, and thick circle-lens spectacles.

"You can vell imagine I vill use human subjects," the loud man said. "You have finally caught up with me, Ox. You are old and past your prime. Your vork, as primitive as it is, will be the token vith vhich I buy my way into greatness. It has already served me vell—in exchange for keeping my lab safe and obtaining chemicals for me, the Grisson Gang has applied a diluted version of your formula to their street product, their marijuana, to increase its potency. That was my promise to them: they would take the formula to become rich financially, so that I may become rich scientifically!"

Doctor Ox snorted. "What a tawdry use, but I expect nothing less from a group of imbecile mobsters. In any case, you're mad, Meirschultz, and that means something coming from the 'Terror of Quiquendone.' Even I can't rationalize why giving a hallucinogen to street criminals will help you resurrect the dead!"

"You have not paid attention to my vording, Ox. I will use your vork to *buy* the secret of life from someone who has better contacts than I."

Harry Dickson observed that Meirschultz was not alone. Hunched behind him was a thin pale man whose eyes and hair were even wilder than the scientist's. This must have been the ill-fated Don Maxwell. He looked like he had seen some of the worst atrocities imaginable. Ignoring Maxwell, Dickson said: "Who's this partner, then, Meirschultz? Who wants to use Ox's formula in exchange for the secret?"

"There is no point, Harry Dickson, in disguising my presence." There was a new voice in the room now, but the speaker didn't emerge from any shadow. He was just suddenly and simply there. "I am an emissary of Doctor Meirschultz's 'seller.'"

Dressed in a business suit was a stout Chinese man—his face was naturally round, made even rounder by a faint chubbiness. He had prominent eyebrows, and Dickson couldn't determine his age. He had a hateful look to him which was different from the hardness of Ichabod Chang. It was a willful hardness, rooted entirely in the glee of destroying human life.

"I am Li Shoon," the burly man said simply.

"Li Shoon?" Dickson murmured then. "I've heard of a Li Shoon Yen, a name which provokes a weird fear in the criminals who speak it."

"You are mistaken, and you suffer from a confusion of the ranks," Li Shoon interrupted. "The name is Li *Chang* Yen.

It is a crime in itself to compare someone like me to him—he is the Master, and I am meant to die for him."

"And who is Li Chang Yen, then?"

"I will not yield that information easily, but perhaps the good Doctor Ox will know of him in one of his many, many names, his numberless faces. Consider a case from the Paris news bulletins of the hunchbacked crime-lord from a few decades back... Dickson, you'd be too young to remember."

Doctor Ox seemed to pale at Shoon's reference, but Dickson remained unimpressed.

"If you won't name your employer, then perhaps you'll identify yourself," the detective said.

"Sixteen years ago, I fought a minor investigator of some note, a 'gentlemen adventurer' named Donald Carrick. He called himself the Human Hound, and he killed my good servant, Weng-yu," Shoon explained. "Even you, Ox, would consider him arrogant, and Dickson resembles the Great Detective himself next to Carrick's foolhardiness. I allowed Carrick to think he'd killed me, but this was only a ruse so that I could wipe him from the world."

"So you sent the invitation that called me to America," Dickson said. "Carrick is dead, because you caught him off-guard by faking your death. And you used his name to forge a lure for me."

"But of course, Mr. Dickson. That I may obtain Ox's psychedelic and kill one of the men on Li Chang Yen's list of potential threats in one fell swoop is too good an offer to pass up. All I have to do is tell Dr. Meirschultz where to find a man named Legendre..."

"Again," Doctor Ox cried. "What use is there in you and your Master using and abusing my formula?"

"It's just possible, Doctor Ox, that your creation can be used to control the minds of those who imbibe it. Thus far, the Master has had many substances that can bind a man's will to his, like the Black Lotus, but he is always interested in obtaining more. It is a wise criminal who has diversity in his arsenal, and there are none wiser than my Master."

235

"There's more desperation than wisdom in that, you realize," Dickson said. "Or, at least, there's greed, which is rooted in desperation. And he's especially desperate if he is forced to resort to sending secret-leaking agents like you out. It's an unwise criminal who reveals the identity of his employer."

"How dare you?" There was no change in the enemy agent's face—he was perpetually filled with wrath. Doctor Ox was staring at Meirschultz, who was cringing just as Maxwell was, giant beads of sweat pouring down his aged face.

"I dare pretty easily, Li Shoon," Dickson shot back. "You realize that once I get out of this, I can begin tracking down your master!"

"You will not get away, though even if you did, you would not stop the Master. Greater men than you have tried for more than twenty years, and they have all failed to date. Now, if you excuse me, I would like to try to demonstrate, for the benefit the scientists in the room, a chemical marvel of my own—I call it the Lachesis venom, named of course for the Greek Fate. It's most efficient at cutting one's thread of life, and it is beyond even the Master's own toxins..."

Meirschultz cringed, and Dickson theorized that Li Shoon had taken pains to demonstrate his poison's effects before the burly scientist's eyes. The detective turned to look at what his foe's manner of dispensing his hidden weapon. But he never did see if it was a powder, a fluid, or a gas—to his regret. An ability to recognize that poison, he realized later, would have been a good skill to have. But suddenly his vision began to become clouded, as if his eyes had grown rheumy. Light blurred and attained a weird glow. It took him a little time to notice that Li Shoon seemed to be having the same issues with his vision. At once, Dickson's mind was flooded with a confusion akin to and yet searingly stronger than alcohol intoxication. The logic centers of his mind were still active—perhaps overly so. His brain was quickly flooded with weird fantasies and theories. And now the blurred light was breaking, and turning into shapes...

"Tom?"

The young man was standing there. But hadn't he gone with—with Sexton Blake's helper?

"Tom, how are you here? I thought you were in England... m-meeting with..."

"Monsieur Dickson, you are raving without reason," Doctor Ox said then. Immediately, to Dickson, the vision of Tom vanished, and he shook his head in genuine bewilderment. "You'll recall that, when I experimented on Quiquendone, my drug, rudimentary as it was at the time, could be dispersed without odor, color, or taste. Five minutes ago, I crushed a vial of it in my fist."

Dickson exhaled sharply, an act that shook him to his bones. "O-of course, doctor." It was hard for him to believe that this was not the sensation of death—that Li Shoon hadn't managed to unleash his toxin.

The remaining events were a blur to Harry Dickson when he later tried to recollect them.

Li Shoon was reeling, seemingly having had a poorer response to the drug than anyone else. Dickson didn't remember what Meirschultz and Maxwell were up to... though he had the lasting impression that Maxwell was screaming. Doctor Ox's words were turning into mush once they passed through his ears. Before he could do anything, the scientist was at Li Shoon's side, having smashed a flask. He drove the twinkling shards of glass into his belly, and crimson flowers poured from the wound, and danced wildly in the air.

As he died, Li Shoon spoke...

"Li Chang Yen—no matter what name he takes—always gets revenge. He will already know what has transpired here, and who was involved..."

Dickson remembered that *verbatim*. It was hard not to, especially because of what that statement triggered.

He passed out, having no choice in the matter. He had been the closest to Ox when the doctor had broken his vial, after all. But his mind started the act of unraveling the details behind Li Shoon's scheme—and he thought of his Master. The name he mentioned hadn't made sense at the time, but Ox's drug was making the sum of Dickson's memory merge into a single concentrated moment. He remembered now the hunchback called Hanoi Shan—and that name, "Shan," stretched and twisted like verbal putty until it became "Satan." And that name, in its ballet, turned around so it was backwards, instead being "Natas"...

And then, Maxwell's scream was gone. The lab was gone, along with everyone in it. A quick turn of the head revealed he was on the lab's lawn. He was now staring up into the night sky, which he realized was bizarrely clear for New York.

He stood up, then, the grass feeling disturbingly wet in his fingers. Without looking back, he dashed down to the road. Doctor Ox's car was gone, confirming his suspicion that the scientist had reclaimed his drug and fled back to the underworld. That left the detective without transportation, but he could stand the walk back. The exercise would help him clear his mind.

The next day, he returned to London.

There was no point in doing otherwise. Donald Carrick's invitation was a fake, and so there was no conference here. Dickson was glad to see New York again, but he had now spent so much of his life in Europe. He would have to make another homecoming soon—but Baker Street beckoned him, and he could never resist.

It was only when he sat alone in 221B that he remembered that *He* was supposed to live in London. He wouldn't be worthy of living here, though, if he wasn't willing to put his life on the line. He couldn't buckle to fear of Li Chang Yen, even though he now had a guess at what varieties of death the owner of that name could supply.

It wasn't long before Tom Wills came back home.

"Tom!" Dickson was glad he could greet his apprentice in the flesh, and overjoyed that he wasn't just a shade made by drugs.

"Good to see you, Guv!" Tom replied. And the elder detective stood so they could shake hands.

They exchanged pleasantries—Tom couldn't hold back the experiences he'd had with his host. It was better that way. The young man had had a much more cheerful experience than he, and Dickson didn't feel like overshadowing that with the implications of his adventure.

Tom was wrapping things up. "...and so that's what I found out about albinism. But before I took off, Guv..." And Dickson's ears perked up. "Tinker got a little obsessed with a story he read in the paper. I couldn't make heads or tails of it, Guv. It was about the murder of some circus freak or another..."

"Freak? What do you mean, Tom?"

"Some sort of spider-lady, Guv," Tom said then. "A Chinese bird named O. Ming Lee."

Harry Dickson felt a chill run through his entire body. He was suddenly struck with a deep sadness at Lee's death—while also feeling revulsion at the evil they'd come close to, which had caught up with her. He knew for sure not all of them would escape that presence, and he wondered if the world would ever hear from Doctor Ox again.

"O. Ming Lee was a wonderful person, Tom," he sighed.

"You knew her?!"

"Yes, I... I'll get to it." He was having rare difficulty with his speech. "I doubt the world will ever again see a Spider-Woman."

"God willing, Guv!"

Dickson forgave him for saying that. He hadn't met her.

And he hadn't seen her cry.

Harry Dickson

THE AMERICAN SHERLOCK HOLMES
THE HEIR OF DRACULA

adapted by
Jean-Marc & Randy LOFFICIER

Harry Dickson

THE AMERICAN SHERLOCK HOLMES

Vs. THE SPIDER

adapted by
Jean-Marc & Randy LOFFICIER